THE
GLOVEMAKER

Ann Weisgarber was born and raised in Kettering, Ohio. She has lived in Boston, Massachusetts, and Des Moines, Iowa, but now splits her time between Sugar Land, Texas, and Galveston, Texas. Her first novel *The Personal History of Rachel DuPree* was longlisted for the Orange Prize and shortlisted for the Orange Prize for New Writers. Her follow-up book, *The Promise*, was a finalist in the Western Writers of America Best Historical Fiction Awards. *The Glovemaker* is her third novel.

THE
GLOVEMAKER

—◆—

ANN WEISGARBER

PICADOR

First published 2019 by Mantle

This paperback edition first published 2020 by Picador
an imprint of Pan Macmillan
The Smithson, 6 Briset Street, London EC1M 5NR
Associated companies throughout the world
www.panmacmillan.com

ISBN 978-0-2307-4578-0

1 3 5 7 9 8 6 4 2

A CIP catalogue record for this book is available from the British Library.

Typeset in New Caledonia by Jouve (UK), Milton Keynes
Printed and bound by CPI Group (UK) Ltd, Croydon, CR0 4YY

MIX
Paper from
responsible sources
FSC® C116313

Visit **www.panmacmillan.com** to read more about all our books
and to buy them. You will also find features, author interviews and
news of any author events, and you can sign up for e-newsletters
so that you're always first to hear about our new releases.

For Cynthia Rogers

1849–1927

Faith is things which are hoped for and not seen.

Book of Mormon, Ether 12:6

It is a love of liberty which inspires my Soul, civil and religious liberty to the whole of the human race, love of liberty was diffused into my Soul by my grandfathers.

Joseph Smith – Prophet, Founder,
and First President of The Church of
Jesus Christ of Latter-day Saints

Be it enacted by the Senate and House of Representatives of the United States of America in Congress assembled, That . . . 'Every person who has a husband or wife living who, in a Territory or other place over which the United States have exclusive jurisdiction, hereafter marries another, whether married or single, and any man who hereafter simultaneously, or on the same day, marries more than one woman in a Territory . . . is guilty of polygamy.'

Edmunds Act 1882

That the marshal of said Territory of Utah, and his deputies, all of Utah, shall possess and may exercise all the powers in executing the laws of the United States or of said Territory, possessed and exercised by sheriffs, constables, and their deputies as peace officers; and each of them shall cause all offenders against the law, in his view, to enter into recognizance to keep the peace and to appear at the next term of the court having jurisdiction of the case, and to commit to jail in case of failure to give such recognizance. They shall quell and suppress assaults and batteries, riots, routs, affrays, and insurrections.

Edmunds-Tucker Act 1887

— —

NELS – THE RAVINE

December 15, 1887

Samuel Tyler was fourteen days past due.

He always came home when he said he would. Trouble of some sort, I figured, had gotten in his way. His wagon might have broken down. One of his mules could have taken sick. Or maybe one went lame.

I'd known Samuel since I was eleven and he was twelve. I was forty now. Him and me were stepbrothers. If he were in some kind of trouble, he'd expect me to look for him. Like I'd expect him to do for me.

Me and a neighbor, Carson Miller, packed our saddlebags and bedrolls, and went looking for Samuel. Carson and I were the only men in Junction, Utah Territory, who didn't have wives and children. It wouldn't much matter if we weren't home for Christmas.

We rode through the Wastelands, then pointed our horses south, the direction Samuel would be coming from. We rode hunched in our coats against the cold. Climbing up into the mountains, we read the trail for signs of Samuel's wagon and mules.

Nothing. The second day on the trail, the air thinned. Carson and I were high in the mountains a good ways from our home in Utah's deep canyon country. Snow four or five inches deep covered the trail. I was glad for Carson's company. He was a dark-haired man not yet twenty. His eyesight was sharp, and young as he was, he kept his thoughts mostly to himself. From time to time, we got off our horses, brushed the snow aside with our hands, and looked for tracks.

Still nothing.

We were three days out from Junction when we rounded a bend. We held up our horses quick. Up ahead, a rockslide had taken out the trail.

The slide was at a tight spot on the side of a cliff. Carson and I sat on our horses and looked at the mound of broken rocks. A boulder the size of a barn teetered on the edge of the mound. A spill of rocks, dirt, and spindly trees went over the side and into the ravine far below. Above us, three ravens, their black wings spread wide, dipped and soared on streams of air.

The rockslide gave me a bad feeling. They always did. I took them as a reminder from God that everything, even boulders, could find themselves in places they hadn't expected.

Looking at the rockslide, Carson said, 'Bet it made a ruckus when it all came down.'

'Likely,' I said. 'A man would hear it a good ways off.'

'There's snow between some of the broken rocks. But the sky's been clear the past week.'

'No telling when the slide happened. Not exactly. Or when it last snowed here.'

'That's so.'

I got off my horse, Bob, and walked closer to the rockslide. A man might hear this mighty pile of rocks come down but it could be too late to do anything about it. Especially a man driving a wagon. Like Samuel would be.

Samuel was a wheelwright, and carried his tools and supplies in a wagon. In a tight place like this, if a man got caught in the start of a rockslide, his mules would panic. If a man got caught, he couldn't get himself turned around.

I said, 'It's fair to say that Samuel might have been here maybe some seventeen, eighteen days ago. The chances of him being here at the exact moment of the slide are narrow.'

Carson grunted his agreement.

The ravine was maybe a quarter of a mile deep. Carson got off his horse and stood beside me. The cliff on the other side was fifty yards across, give or take. Both sides were steep and sheer.

I looked into the ravine. The spill had plowed up more trees and rocks as it crashed to the bottom. Midway down, a boulder, nearly as big as my cabin, was lodged into place. On the narrow floor, piles of snow were in the shadows but not in the parts where the sun reached. I squinted, studying the rubble.

Plenty could go bad in the canyon country even for a man who knew what he was doing. He could camp in the wrong place. He wouldn't know it was the wrong place until a rumble woke him in the middle of the night, rocks raining on him and the soil giving way.

'You see anything down there?' I said. My eyes weren't as sharp as they had been.

Carson got down on his hands and knees in the snow. He leaned forward a little to see better without going over the side. I did the same some twenty feet from him.

I didn't see anything other than rocks, patches of snow, and shadows.

Carson, still on his hands and knees, looked toward me and said, 'Brother Nels.'

His tone carried a warning. He saw something down there.

The bad feeling I had about the slide deepened. I left where I was and got down beside him.

Carson leaned forward more. I took hold of his coat to keep him from going over the side. 'What is it?' I said.

He didn't say anything. He kept staring into the ravine.

'You see something?' I said.

Carson blinked hard. He started to say something, then gave his head a slow shake. Finally, he sat back on his heels. 'No. Thought I had but I didn't. Just rocks.'

'What'd you think you saw?'

'Glints. The kind that comes off metal when the light is right. Glints making the shape of an arc.'

'You saw metal down there?'

'Thought I did. At first. But it's crystals, or something like them.'

The notion of metal in the ravine shook me. It might be some man's tool. 'Hold onto me,' I said. I crawled closer to the edge to take a look. Carson had me by my coat.

I looked until my eyes ached. I inched away from the edge. Carson let go of me. I said, 'I didn't see any glints. You sure you did?'

'Yep. Crystals, most probably.'

Gypsum, I thought but didn't say. Samuel, a man who admired rocks, would speak up and tell us the crystals were gypsum. If he were here.

I tilted the brim of my hat and looked up. The ravens were gone. For reasons I couldn't explain, I took that to be a good sign. I stood and walked close to where the trail was blocked by the pile of rocks. Carson came and studied it with me. The slide had taken out maybe some twenty feet of the trail. Samuel would have been coming from the opposite side. Even if he were on foot, he wouldn't be foolish enough to try to climb over the rubble. It was unsteady. The rocks would give way.

I said, 'Likely Samuel had some strong words when he came across this slide.'

'Yep,' Carson said.

'He wouldn't be any too pleased about having to turn around.' I paused. 'It's reasonable to figure he's backtracked south, circled to the west, turned north and is coming through the Fish Lakes. It'd add another five, six weeks to his getting-home time.'

'Those Fish Lakes are mighty high.' Carson got himself away from the edge of the drop-off and stood. He brushed the snow from his knees and then his gloves. He said, 'Those mountains take some doing to get through. Especially this time of year, what with the snow deep in the passes.'

Carson didn't know Samuel like I did. Samuel had been traveling Utah Territory's back country since he was eighteen. He studied the land like it was a living, breathing thing. He read the layers of color in the rocky sides of mountains. He knew what rocks were made of. He could tell how wind, rain, and snow had shaped them. Samuel knew which ones had been raised up out of the earth. He found passes through mountains when other men couldn't. The Fish Lakes wouldn't stop him from getting home.

I said, 'Samuel knows what he's doing.'

———

Three days later we got back to Junction. It was a town on the floor of a canyon with only one easy way in and out. Red cliffs hemmed us in from all sides. Samuel's cabin was the first one a person came across. It was dusk and like I figured there'd be, a lamplight was in the east window. Deborah, Samuel's wife, was waiting for us to get home.

Just before getting to Junction, Carson and I decided he'd take the job of telling five of the families about the trail being torn up. It'd be up to me to tell Deborah's sister and brother-in-law who lived on the other side of Deborah's plum orchard. Before doing that, though, I'd tell Deborah about the slide and how Samuel had to turn around. It was only right this fell to me. Samuel was my stepbrother. I'd known Deborah since the day she and Samuel married.

At Junction, Carson and I tipped our hats to each other. He went on and followed Sulphur Creek. I directed Bob, my horse, toward Samuel's cabin. I worked out in my mind how best to explain matters to Deborah. I'd tell her that Samuel was probably coming through the Fish Lake Mountains. He could be up to six weeks late. That would put him home by the second week in January at the latest. There was no need to look for him sooner. There was no need to worry.

Halfway to Samuel and Deborah's, my brown long-haired dog, Sally, came running. I'd left her with Deborah while I was gone. Sally yapped her hello, bounding in great leaps as she circled Bob.

Up ahead and holding a lantern, Deborah stood waiting in the doorway of her cabin.

—·—

CHAPTER ONE

DEBORAH – TROUBLE

January 11, 1888

Bare knuckles pounded hard on my cabin door, someone wanting to be let in. My nerves leaped.

Samuel. My husband. He was home. Safe. Finally.

No. Not Samuel. He'd call to me – Deborah! – through the door.

The knocking kept on, quick raps and short pauses. My heart thudded high in my chest. It wasn't my sister or any of her family. They'd announce themselves. They wouldn't pound on the door this way. Neither would my neighbors.

Trouble.

I was in the kitchen part of the front room. The only thing between trouble and me was a door. A door I wasn't sure was latched. It was late afternoon. The light in the cabin was dim. Six paces from the door, I couldn't tell if earlier I'd bothered to slide the bolt into the catch.

My pulse rushed. It was a man out there. I knew that as if the door had turned to glass and I could see through it. For almost four years, men came to my cabin carrying trouble on their backs, each one haunted and looking over his shoulder. Mine was the first cabin in Junction they came to.

They showed up during the spring, they appeared in the summer and early fall. But never now, never in January when snowstorms reared up with little warning and filled mountain passes, blurred landmarks, and covered trails. In this part of Utah Territory, there were long stretches between towns and outposts. Caught in the open, toes and fingers froze. People lost their bearings and even though I didn't like thinking about it, some went missing.

Few people traveled to Junction in January, not if it could be helped.

The knocking was faster, louder.

I was a woman alone.

Behind me, on the cookstove, butter sizzled and popped in the skillet. I moved the skillet off the burner, then got my paring knife. January, I kept thinking. Never before in January.

My chest rattled from the force of my heart. Maybe this man wasn't like the others. Maybe he carried a bigger kind of trouble.

Answer the door, I told myself. Even if it wasn't the right time of year. Even if this felt wrong. Hurry. I couldn't let him give up and go to the next cabin. That was my sister's and I didn't want her pulled into this. Grace and her husband, Michael, had three little boys and expected their fourth child in the spring. They didn't need trouble on their doorstep.

The knife in my hands, my feet began to move. I bumped into the kitchen table; the kerosene lamp on it rocked. I reached out with my free hand to steady it, then circled around the table. My wool skirt wrapped around my ankles as if to hold me back but a few paces later, I was at the door. It wasn't latched.

Fumbling some, I slid the bolt into the catch.

'Who is it?' I called through the door. The knocking stopped. I said, 'What's your business?'

Silence. Then, 'I'm on my way to my brother's.' A man's voice. 'By Pleasant Creek.'

His words came out in broken pieces, his teeth likely chattering from the cold. I understood him, though. His words were a code that told me he was a brother. A Latter-day Saint. But still, I thought. January. It didn't fit the pattern of the past four years.

Through the door, he said, 'I only need directions. Then I'll be on my way.'

This time of year?

I said, 'Pleasant Creek's a good ways off.' This was my part of the code. It told him he'd come to the right place. Yet, it gave nothing away.

The man said, 'So I've been told. By my brother.'

He'd just reaffirmed that he was a Latter-day Saint, a brother. If he wasn't, though, if he intended to trick me or if he was a cattle rustler or a thief, I'd said nothing suspicious. I was saying and doing like I would for any stranger.

'My brother Joe lives there,' he said.

This was a reference to the Prophet Joseph Smith. Still, I held back. Something wasn't right. As soon as I opened my door, I'd let in his trouble. Yet if I didn't, he'd go to the next cabin, my sister's. She and her family were new to Junction. They didn't know anything about the men who came to my door asking for help, and I intended to keep it that way.

'Sister,' he said through the door. '*Wherefore, if they should have charity they would not suffer the laborer in Zion to perish.*'

Scripture from the Book of Mormon.

I slipped the knife into my apron pocket and with the toe of my boot, I pushed aside the small rolled rug that I kept at the threshold to block the draft. I opened the door a few inches. Cold air gusted in.

He wore a long coat. In the shadow cast by his wide-brim

hat, his features were lost but I could see his beard. He wasn't a tall man but he was broad through the chest. I felt his wariness. I felt him taking my measure. His safety was in my hands. And mine was in his.

I looked past him. His horse stood without moving, its head drooped. The day's light had begun to fade. Snow clouds hung heavy. This man wouldn't be going to Pleasant Creek today. Not with darkness coming on soon.

My nerves churned. Turn him away, I thought. Send him on to Nels Anderson who lived past my sister's place on the other side of the creek. Nels would put him up for the night. I'd be done with him.

I couldn't. Right now, I was the only one who knew about him. If he was what he claimed to be, if he was like the other men who came here, I had to follow the plan.

'It's bitter out,' I said. I nodded toward his horse. 'The barn's in the back. There's feed and water. And blankets to warm your horse.' I paused. He's dangerous, a voice whispered in my head. Don't let him in.

Yet, he knew the code. He was a brother. A Saint. It'd be wrong to turn my back on one of my own.

I gathered myself and said, 'I've got dinner on the stove and there's some to spare.'

'Heavenly Father, thank you.'

More code. This was how we Saints began our prayers.

My smile was tight as he turned to take his horse around to the barn. I closed the door and bolted it. I wasn't going to take the chance of him coming in without my say-so. I knotted my shawl closer to the base of my throat. My husband's rifle was mounted on the wall near the door.

He could be both a Saint and an outlaw. There were some Saints who robbed and took what wasn't theirs.

I'd used Samuel's rifle only to scare off snakes and wolves but I took it off the wall mount and propped it in the kitchen corner. I put the skillet back on the burner and added the venison I'd been cutting into chunks. I wiped my hands on a dish towel to settle the shake in them. Using the paring knife, I sliced a potato and added it to the skillet. It was simple food but he wouldn't complain. The men who came to my door never did.

Polygamists, the newspapers in the east called these men. Felons, the federal government branded them. People who were not of our faith – we called those people gentiles – didn't care one bit that plural wives and multitudes of children were thought to increase a man's blessings in Heaven. Gentiles called plural marriage an abomination. They said it was vile and passed laws to get rid of it. Waving the Bible – the very same Bible as ours – they sent federal deputies to Utah Territory to arrest men who had plural wives. If the men were convicted, and most were since the judges and juries were gentiles, they went to prison. From their jail cells they were made to pay hundreds of dollars in fines. If they didn't have the money, their wives sold their homes, businesses, or farms to pay the debt. Homeless, these women and their children were left to the mercy of others to take them in.

That was why some of the men said they ran, why they came here to hide in Utah's canyon country. They did it for their families.

I stirred the stew and put the lid on the skillet. I could be arrested for helping this man who might be accused of being a felon. If I got caught, I could go to jail and lose my home. I was willing to help him, though, and the others who came to my door. But not because I believed plural marriage was holy. I did it for their children.

An icy draft blew through a thin crack that ran alongside the kitchen window. I drew my shawl closer and filled the bread basket with the biscuits I'd made earlier. I set the basket on the center of the table. I got the table lamp and put it on the cooking counter with the two other lamps. When the man came back, I didn't want to see his face.

In my recollections of the men who came to my cabin, they were all alike. They memorized the route, and the names of towns and outposts where they could count on a meal and feed for their horses before traveling south toward the deep canyons in Utah Territory. Their unshaved faces were drawn with worry and tiredness. The last eight miles they'd just traveled was enough to bring any man to his knees. It was what we called the Wastelands, our only direct route in and out of Junction. Massive rock formations rose like castles from far-off lands. In places, boulders piled on top of other boulders and the earth itself was splintered with deep cracks too wide for a horse to jump. A trail came and went as it wandered around rocks and dipped down into deep rocky ravines and dry washes. It didn't take much to get lost, even for those of us who lived here.

The men didn't tell me their names. I didn't tell them mine. One by one, they sat at my kitchen table, their shoulders tight and their gazes darting toward the door. I imagined what they were thinking. I was thinking it, too. The hunters, federal deputies, were out there.

My cabin's two windows were small, and it was the only time I was glad that even on sun-filled days the light inside was poor. I needed to keep their features in shadow so I could forget them after I sent them to Floral Ranch on Pleasant Creek. The ranch, even deeper in the canyons than Junction, was owned by a family. It was eleven miles off, a far distance in the canyons. That was what made it a sanctuary for the men with plural wives.

More men than I cared to count had come through Junction looking for Floral Ranch. But not once had a hunted man come to my door in January. Until now.

———

The man sat at my kitchen table facing the door while he ate. His gaze darted from the window in the parlor half of the room to the window in the kitchen. The table between us, I stood by the cooking counter with my arms crossed. His dark beard covered the lower half of his face, making him look like so many others who'd sat at my table.

I never ate with the men. Even when my husband, Samuel, was home, I didn't. It would be too familiar, too close. The same was true for talk. I said only what was needed and the men followed suit. When the deputies showed up with their hard-edged questions, I had to be able to tell them I didn't know anything about the people they were looking for. I had to be able to look them in the eyes when I said it.

The hunted men were always skittish but this one nearly hummed with nerves. He flinched each time the fire in the cookstove popped. He kept looking over his shoulder toward the open door that went to my bedroom. Things weren't right here, I could almost hear him think. There should be a husband. The gold in my wedding band caught the lamplight and I felt sure he'd noticed it. He might think I was a widow but that probably didn't feel right to him. The cabin, small as it was, should be filled with children, some nearly full grown. I wasn't young but I wasn't old, either. I was thirty-six and my brown hair hadn't begun to gray. I could still have little ones, even a baby in my arms.

I looked to be a woman on her own. Little about me fit his notion of what a Latter-day Saint woman was.

He didn't know what to make of me. I saw that in the narrow-eyed way he watched me as he ate. He didn't know if he should trust me. I could tell him I wasn't going to turn him in. I didn't care about the reward money that was probably on his head. I could tell him I wasn't a convert but was born into the church. I'd grown up seeing my father's outrage when Saints turned against Saints. I could tell him I married when I was nineteen and since then, I'd prayed for a child but not all prayers were heard. I could say I was alone because my husband was a wheelwright who had gone to southern Utah for his work and been forced to come home through steep mountains to the north of here.

I kept still. The less I said, the better. The less he knew about me, the safer I was.

The man took his food in gulps. His right leg jittered. The jangle of the spur on his boot worked on my nerves. Even if he were a cattle rustler or a thief, I wouldn't turn him in. That'd only stir up the interest of the government. All I wanted, what all of us in Junction wanted, was to be left alone.

January, I thought, the word circling in my mind. Lawmen never gave chase during the winter. The reward money to capture a man with plural wives wasn't worth it.

I watched his hands as he ate. A cattle rustler, I thought. A train robber. A killer.

The hair stood on the back of my neck. I inched a little closer to the rifle in the corner. Stay steady, I told myself. He was a Saint. He'd quoted scripture.

I kept my gaze on his hands. The cabin's light was dusky, and I couldn't make out scars or nicks on his hands but they were broad. His knuckles were swollen. Farmer's hands, I thought. Not a train robber's. Just a man with more than one wife.

Most men in the church didn't have plural wives. Those who did usually could afford only two. Maybe this man had wives by the dozen. There might be so many children he wasn't sure of their names. That might have so angered the government that his arrest couldn't wait until the spring.

Or he was an outlaw. One who quoted from the Book of Mormon and when I'd set his plate before him a few minutes ago, he'd bowed his head and prayed his thanksgiving before eating.

Out the windows, it was full dark.

The stew gone, the man ate a biscuit, his leg still jittering. He ate another biscuit. As he did, his leg went still and his shoulders began to slump. Weariness pulled at his eyes. Unexpected pity rose up in me. He might have been traveling for a couple of days. This could be the only hot food he'd had in a good while. Last night he might have slept out in the open. And in the cold of January.

The food gone, he took a deep pull of air. Then he was a flurry of movement, pushing away from the table, getting to his feet, and me backing closer to the rifle.

'I appreciate the hospitality,' the man said. 'If you'll tell me how to get to Pleasant Creek, I'll be on my way.'

He stood across from me with the table between us. If I could, I'd send him to the ranch on Pleasant Creek this very moment. It wasn't that simple, though. Nothing in the canyon country was. It was a place with few straight lines. Most everything called for a plan and here in Junction, we had one for helping the men. It called for measured caution. We took one step at a time.

'I've never been to Pleasant Creek,' I said. 'I don't know

the way. But there's a guide who knows. He'll take you in the morning.'

'I have to go now.'

'It's too late, too dark. The guide won't chance it at night.'

'I'll take that up with him. Where can I find him?'

'He won't take you, not at night. The ground's rocky. The horses could snap an ankle. The landmarks are hard to read even in daylight. So's the trail. Ravines are deep and unexpected. You could fall to your death.'

'Why didn't you tell me this before? When I first got here while it was still dusk.'

One step at a time, I told myself. Don't let him shake you. Stay with the plan. Do like always. He wasn't the first one in a hurry who didn't want to listen. Using code, I said, *'Bear with patience thine afflictions, and I will give unto ye success.'*

His eyes narrowed, studying me. He didn't know how to answer, I thought. He wasn't a Saint; he'd tricked me. I put my hand in my apron pocket and gripped the paring knife.

He said, *'Bear with patience thine affliction.* Alma. Or Mosiah.'

These were books in the Book of Mormon. He knew I was testing him and that I didn't trust him.

We eyed each other. Finally, I said, 'I will give you success but you have to listen to me. You came to my door. A stranger. You asked for help. I'm trying to give it to you.'

The man shifted his weight. A floorboard creaked. He looked down at his clenched hands. He opened them, spread his fingers wide, then clenched and opened them again.

I said, 'You have to stay here tonight in my barn. Before daybreak, I'll send you to the guide.'

'Send me now. I'll sleep in his barn.'

The table was still between us but I felt pressed to the wall. Don't lose your wits, I told myself. Think.

'We welcome strangers,' I said. 'Like you. Many times we have and will keep on as long as there's need.' I picked my words with care. I couldn't give anything away. Even if I did trust him, I wouldn't tell him anything about how we helped men. I couldn't tell him I'd send him to the guide, Nels Anderson, only when Nels was ready to take him to Floral Ranch. Until I sent the man on, I was the only one who knew he was here. If he was found in my barn, I could be arrested. But no one else here was part of it. Only me.

I said, 'We're neighborly people in Junction. But we ask that visitors listen to what we say about the canyons. And about travel.'

He gave me a hard look. I held his gaze. My hand gripped the paring knife in my apron pocket. He looked toward the front door, then at the windows. His gaze came back to me. 'All right. I'll stay in your barn.'

'Yes,' I said. 'Yes. Good.' My words came too fast. I took in some air to calm my nerves. I said, 'I'll wake you before dawn.'

'I'll be ready.'

'Good.' I didn't know why I kept saying that. There wasn't anything good about any of this. I said, 'Horse blankets are in the barn. There's hay in the loft where you can settle down. You won't freeze.'

'God willing.'

'God willing.'

He gave me a quick nod, then walked toward the door. The tinny sound of his spurs marked his footfall. He took his long coat down from the peg and shrugged it into place. I watched him fasten his coat buttons. It'd be cold in the barn but I wasn't about to let him sleep on the floor by the cookstove. He was trouble. I was a woman alone.

The man wound his scarf around his neck. He watched me as I watched him. He tugged on his gloves and settled his hat. Still looking at me, the man started to open the door, then stopped. His gaze flickered toward the kitchen corner where I'd propped Samuel's rifle.

His attention went back to me. 'There's something I have to tell you.'

He was going to confess, I thought. He was going to tell me what he'd done. I put my hand up, palm out. 'No. Don't.'

'I have to. It's only right that you know.'

I shook my head to stop him but he kept on. 'People are looking for me and they're bound to come this way. They're not all that far back, maybe ten miles. Close enough that I saw their campfire last night. When they get here, it could go rough.'

Fear shot through me. 'How many are there?'

'Two. Or three.'

'Ten miles back? That's all?'

'Thereabouts. If they find me, I'll tell them I broke into your barn. You didn't see me. You didn't know I was here.'

I nodded. It was all I could do.

He pulled his hat lower, ready to go. His sudden agreeableness to stay the night in my barn might be a trick. He could be planning to get his horse and try to get to Pleasant Creek on his own in the dark and with snow clouds covering the stars and the nearly full moon. He could get lost, end up backtracking and turning in circles. He wouldn't even know he was doing it. But others would, come daylight. He'd leave a trail a child could follow. Even if the ones after him didn't find him, if he'd fallen into a deep gully and no one saw what was left of him, they'd come back to Junction. They'd know he was here first. They'd accuse every family here of helping him, a man with plural wives. Or a man who'd done something far worse.

I couldn't chance that. With the guide, he wouldn't get lost. With the guide and during the daylight, it'd take four to five hours. By the time the deputies got here, there'd be no trace of the man.

'The men behind you are ten miles back,' I said. 'Eight of those are hard miles. Like you know. We call that stretch of barren land the Wastelands. They won't come through it in the dark. They might try, but they won't keep going. No one travels it at night, not even us. They'll wait for dawn.'

He cocked his head, studying me. He didn't trust me. Like I didn't trust him.

'The Wastelands scares them,' I said. 'Especially at night. It always does.'

'Always?'

'Always.'

'I have your word on that?'

'You have my word.'

His nod was quick, and I didn't know how to read it. He opened the door. It was snowing. He drew back, hesitating. Then he tucked his chin low and went outside, closing the door behind him.

Snow. There'd be footprints. A man's. No one would think otherwise. His boots were bigger than mine. Boots worn by a man wanted by the federal government. Someone I'd agreed to help.

Tracks. From my door to the barn.

CHAPTER TWO

DEBORAH – THE DOLLAR BILL

January 11, 1888

By the light of three lamps, I washed the man's dishes. Getting rid of his presence in my cabin was easy enough. Wiping him from my thoughts was a different matter.

January. Snow. His footprints going from my cabin to the barn.

I wanted Samuel, my husband. I could face this trouble if he were home.

The snow might be a blessing rather than a curse. It might convince the government men to turn back. I scrubbed harder on the cup the man had used. The water in the pan slapped against the sides. The Wastelands trail was faint and hard to follow in good weather. The snow would make it even harder. The deputies might decide to let this man go. Finding him wasn't worth the risk.

I didn't believe that. If they had the grit to follow him this far, they'd want to see this through.

Do the same, I told myself. One step at a time. Get rid of the man's presence in the cabin. That was all I could do at this moment.

The man could already be gone. He could have slipped away behind the barn to keep from having to ride past the cabin where I'd hear him. He might be gone but his tracks wouldn't be.

I dried the dishes and put them on the shelf. Beside it, my calendar was tacked to the wall. The room was too dark for me to make out the numbers but I knew the date. Wednesday, the eleventh of January. As Samuel had done every year of our marriage, he'd left home on the first of September to mend and make wheels for settlers in outposts in southern Utah and northern Arizona. 'Look for me by the first of December,' he told me the day he left.

That was one hundred thirty-three days ago. All that time, and I hadn't gotten a letter from him. It wasn't like him. He always wrote even though the letters took weeks to get here.

Samuel was forty-one days late. The ache I carried for him swallowed me whole. Day after day, I told myself Samuel was on his way home. Nels figured Samuel had to backtrack away from the rockslide and come a longer way. It was winter but that wouldn't stop Samuel. We'd been married nearly eighteen years and he always came home. The weather might slow him. But it wouldn't stop him.

The weather hadn't stopped the man who was hiding in my barn. It hadn't stopped the men who were chasing him. They were only ten miles behind.

I moved one of the lanterns from the counter to the kitchen table. Something was tucked partway under the bread basket. I moved the lamp closer. It was a dollar bill.

Not touching it, I sat down at the table. Most of the men left money. Usually it was dimes and quarters, and once in a while it was a bill like this one. I didn't see the money as a way to buy my silence. Instead, it let the men hold fast to their pride even though they were forced to hide and accept help from strangers. The money was how they let me know they were accustomed to paying their way. They were honorable men who took care of their families, tended their farms, and saw to their businesses. They came to my door unwashed and hungry but they were men of the church who had plural wives as Abraham and Jacob in the Old Testament had. These men practiced the revelation the Prophet Joseph Smith said the Lord had made known to him. Plural marriage was holy, the Prophet said the Lord told him. It assured those who practiced it a place in the celestial kingdom.

Samuel and I had come to believe that wasn't so. Our parents believed otherwise. Samuel's stepfather had two wives. My father had had three wives. The first one was Alice. She died years ago but she stayed a part of our family. My older half-sister and two half-brothers were her children. My father talked about Alice during my growing-up years so we wouldn't forget her or her faith in the church. She and my father had been baptized by the Prophet Joseph Smith soon after they wed in Ohio. From there, they followed the Prophet west and when he was murdered in Missouri, my father and Alice followed Brigham Young to the Utah Territory.

'There were over six hundred of us in the Kimball wagon party,' my father told us every anniversary of Alice's death. His voice was somber but pride underlined his words. He was a big man, barrel-chested, and his arms were strong from his years of tanning leather. He wore his thick dark beard high on his cheekbones. He'd say, too, that Alice was cheerful during that last and final journey. She was always smiling. She was going to Zion. But in Nebraska, Alice took a fever and died. 'I buried her by the Platte River,' he'd say. 'Close to Chimney Rock. I marked her grave with a wood cross. Her name's carved on it.'

My father usually went on to say that Sister Zena, a woman in the wagon party, took his youngest child, Asher. 'He wasn't yet a month old and Sister Zena was able and willing to feed him. Another family, the Bufords, said they'd look after Sarah. She was seven. Someone else said they had room for Paul. He was just a little fellow, newly turned three. Those were all good people but Sarah and Paul? I couldn't give them up.' Here, he'd shake his head. 'I don't mind saying it was no easy thing driving the wagon while seeing to them. The trail's a hard place for children. Some got in the way of wagon wheels and were run over. Others were kicked by mules. Two times that I know of, a child wandered off and got lost. But I took that chance. I had to. It was bad enough I couldn't keep Ash. Alice would understand that. A newborn must be nursed. But she'd expect me to keep Sarah and Paul with me.'

Caring for the children slowed him. His wagon dropped to the back of the party. He hadn't been forgotten, though. An unmarried young woman, nineteen years old, brought supper every night for seven days, walking from her parents' wagon back to his. It wasn't only supper she brought us, my father would say. 'She gave us comfort. She held Sarah and Paul when they cried for their mama and sang lullabies until they were asleep.' Once the children were settled for the night, she went back to her wagon. My father got down on his knees and prayed for strength to face the next day. 'One night, Alice came to me in a vision,' he'd tell us. 'I saw her like she was standing right there before me. "Our children need a mother," I heard her say. "And you need a wife."'

Eight days after burying Alice, my father married the young woman, Margaret, who sang his children to sleep.

She was my mother.

I was born a year later in Salt Lake City. My father called me his daughter of Zion. I was the first of his many children born in Utah Territory.

'God's plan,' my father said about the birth of each child. 'God's plan,' he said when Brigham Young directed him to leave Salt Lake and open a tannery in Parowan. 'God's plan,' he said when a revelation from an angel told him to marry another wife.

'A joyful revelation,' my mother said as Sarah and I cleaned the house to prepare for the arrival of the new wife. Sarah was fifteen and I was seven. 'Because of this, I'll have a place in the celestial kingdom,' my mother said as we washed the walls in the kitchen. 'It's glorious to think of.'

Her voice was high-pitched. Loose strands of brown hair fell from the knot she wore at the nape of her neck. She worked quickly, down on her hands and knees to wipe dust from the corners. 'Girls, God has given us so much,' she said while we washed the windows. 'Your father was baptized into the church by the Prophet Joseph Smith and now Brigham Young has sanctioned this holy revelation.'

My father brought Sister Caroline to our house on the day of their wedding. She was yellow-haired and her waist was smaller than my mother's. Her fingers were smooth. Her knuckles weren't yet swollen from hard work. Her dress was a pattern of black-and-white plaid with sleeves that flared and then gathered at the cuffs. The lace collar was wide and reached all the way to Sister Caroline's shoulders. My mother wore her Sunday best but beside Sister Caroline, her dark blue dress looked plain and old-fashioned. The sleeves were too narrow and the crochet collar was heavy and coarse.

My mother planned for Sister Caroline to sit at her end of the long kitchen table. The wives' end, she had decided to call it. My father shooed away that idea. He had Sister Caroline sit beside him in Paul's usual place on the opposite end of the table. My father helped her get settled on the bench and as he did, his hand lingered on her shoulder. His thumb stroked the curve of her upper arm.

For a moment, everything went still – my mother at the opposite end, my older half-brothers and sister, my two younger brothers sitting on the table benches – all of us startled to see my father touch this woman in this way. Sister Caroline smiled up at him, then glanced toward my mother. My father moved his hand, pulled out his chair, and sat down. He bowed his head. That brought us back to ourselves, and we bowed our heads.

'Heavenly Father,' he prayed. 'We thank you for the food on this table and for bringing your daughter Caroline into our home.'

After dinner but before the table was cleared, my father and Sister Caroline left to take a walk. Distress flashed across my mother's face when they returned and my father whispered something to her. She turned away when he took Sister Caroline into the bedroom he usually shared with my mother. 'The promise of the celestial kingdom,' my mother said more to herself than to Sarah and me when she undressed in our bedroom and slept with us.

She slept with us until the house my father built catty corner to ours was finished and Sister Caroline moved there. I thought this would cheer my mother. She would again sing while we baked bread and scrubbed floors. Our family would be like before. It wasn't. My father spent most of his time at Sister Caroline's house.

'A blessing,' my mother said when Sister Caroline had her first child. 'Your father is favored by God and we have the promise of the celestial kingdom.' Those were her words but with the birth of each of Sister Caroline's children, my mother turned quieter, a faint echo of who she'd been.

My father spent one or two nights a week in our home. My mother had more children. When he was with us, he asked about our school lessons and scooped up his youngest child to hold on his lap. There was an emptiness, though, to him while he ate dinner at our table and then later joined my mother in the bedroom. I believed his thoughts were elsewhere. When he was with Sister Caroline, he looked to be a younger man. His wide smile parted his graying beard and his laugh came easy.

Suitors began to call on me when I was seventeen. I didn't have much to say to the young men who claimed they got down on their knees every night and prayed for revelations from God. I wasn't ready for marriage. I wasn't ready to follow in my mother's footsteps. Or to be a second or third wife.

I was eighteen when my father told me it had been revealed to Ed Yardley, a farmer, that he was worthy of a plural wife. 'He's asked permission to speak to you about this,' my father said. 'With the intention of marrying soon.'

Soon meant within the month. I ducked my head as if considering Brother Ed's revelation but panic beat in my chest. There was nothing wrong with him other than that he had a wife and one child.

I felt my father waiting for an answer. I couldn't tell him I didn't want to be a second wife. I couldn't say I didn't want to wound a first wife the way my mother had been.

'Deborah?' my father said.

I raised my head and I met his gaze. 'Mother needs me. Zeb's just a few months old. I can't leave her now.'

'You're a fine daughter to your mother. But you just had your eighteenth birthday. It's time for you to have your own family, and Brother Ed's a good man. His revelation has been sanctioned.' My father smiled. 'You'll have the promise of the celestial kingdom. And Deborah, he's agreed to build you your own house.'

'Mother needs me,' I said again. 'I can't leave her. When Zeb is older, I'll agree to marry.'

My father must have seen the wisdom of this. By then, my mother's home was a household of nine children. Sarah, my older stepsister, had married and moved away years ago. I was the oldest daughter still at home. My mother would struggle without my help. My father must have realized this since nothing more was said about the matter. Within the month, Ed Yardley, my potential husband, married another woman.

Now, years later, a hunted man was in my barn. His dollar bill was on my kitchen table. The risk I took to help him and others like him was far greater than the worth of a dollar. If I was caught, the deputies might burn my orchards. They could arrest me. I took the risk anyway. Not because I believed in plural marriage. I didn't. I told myself I did it for the men's children and that was so. It wasn't just that, though. These men were like my oldest stepbrother, Paul. He was in the federal prison in Salt Lake. His tannery had been taken from him and his two wives and seven children were dependent on the charity of neighbors and family.

I picked up the dollar bill. It was crinkled as if it had once been clenched in a tight fist. I put it down, left the table, and went to the front window. The night was bright with falling snow. It was quiet. There was no sound of the man.

I strained to see lamplights at my sister's cabin on the other side of the plum orchard. Her cabin was too far, three-quarters of a mile off. Yet I felt the presence of Grace and her husband with their three little boys. I felt, too, the weight of the other six families in Junction.

Tracks in the snow. Lawmen ten miles from here. The man in my barn. If he were still there.

I got Samuel's rifle and put it by the bed. The dollar bill went into the canning jar that served as my bank. I placed the jar inside my top drawer. I brushed out my hair and braided it, but stayed dressed. Sleeping in my clothes would save time in the morning when I got up before dawn to send the man on. That was what I told myself. In truth, I was uneasy. A man slept in my barn. I was alone.

A chill coursed through me and not just from the winter night. I turned down the quilts, ran my hand over the cold bed linens, and went to the kitchen. The glow of the fire around the rim of the cookstove door guided me to it. Using potholders, I took out the two warming stones I kept heated in the oven. I wrapped them in dish towels and, one by one, carried them to the bedroom. I slid them under the quilts at the foot of my bed so their heat could warm the linens.

Samuel gave me the stones when we first came to Junction five and a half years ago. 'This one's sandstone,' he'd said, holding a flat red rock in the palm of his open left hand. His fingers were spread to support it. We were in the kitchen, and the cabin's hewn logs were so fresh that they still smelled of the earth. Samuel'd been digging irrigation ditches for the plum trees we'd just planted, and he'd come in for noon dinner. Using his free hand, Samuel ran a finger over a band of white that circled the stone. He said, 'This part is probably gypsum. Somehow it layered itself into the sandstone.' He nodded toward the kitchen window. 'I want to show you something. Come over here in the light.' I stood beside him at the window with my shoulder against his. He held up the stone with both hands and angled it, turning it. 'See that? The gypsum?' I did.

It was clear as glass in places and cloudy in others. It shimmered like ice on a frozen lake.

'I've never seen anything like it,' I said.

'It puts on a good show. But I've got one even better.' He put the first stone on the kitchen table and got another one from his knapsack. It was smaller and rounder than the first one. Its colors went from faded yellow to light brown. To me, it was ordinary in this cliff country that was filled with rocks.

'Found it in the river,' Samuel said. 'It was the yellow that caught my eye. It looks to be sandstone but it's different. It's harder, stronger, made to last. Like our homestead here, Deborah.'

'And our orchards,' I said. 'Trees that show we were once here.'

Samuel looked at the stone he held, then put it in the palm of my hand. 'You're still young,' he said. 'There's time yet.'

For a child, he meant but didn't say. My yearning for a baby was one of the reasons why I'd agreed to leave our home in Parowan. Coming here was a fresh start. In Parowan, no one knew what to do with me. I was a long-married woman who didn't have children. People there had come to disapprove of my marriage to Samuel. His way of looking at the world was bigger than the church's. My inability to bear children was testimony that Samuel was not a firm believer. In Junction, I was far from the whispers and knowing looks. I thought a child might be possible here.

Now with Samuel not yet home, I used the stones to warm our bed.

Snow spit against the two windows. I checked the bolt in the door latch again. In the bedroom, I held a lantern and studied the map that was pinned to the wall near the clothes pegs. Nels had drawn it for me when he came home with the news about the rockslide. 'Please show me the route Samuel's taking,' I'd said. 'So I know where he is.'

I put my finger on the map place where Nels had printed the word ROCKSLIDE. From there, I traced the trail, a dotted line, south and then west. Nels had drawn the map to show cliffs and plateaus. Dry washes were zigzags and creeks were shaded dark. The Fish Lake Mountains were capped with snow. The dotted line that went through the mountains showed a wide and smooth pass. In the right-hand corner, Nels had drawn a compass to show the four directions.

Years ago, Nels spent time in this part of Utah. That was before there were any settlements or outposts. It was the summer Samuel and I married, and Nels came by himself. Rocks cluttered the land, and the mountain passes were steep. It was a country determined to keep people away. Yet he had drawn a wide and smooth pass on the map.

It wasn't a route Samuel usually took. It was longer and the mountains were higher. I wanted to believe Samuel knew how to find the trail and then the pass. I wanted to believe it was as wide and smooth as Nels drew it to be.

My prayer for Samuel was urgent. 'Heavenly Father, keep Samuel safe. Guide him along the trail. Keep him warm, fed, and his feet steady. Bring him home.' Then I prayed the deputies would turn back and that tomorrow Nels would deliver the man safely to Floral Ranch.

Dressed in my day clothes, I turned down the lamplight and got into bed. The heat from the stones should have been a comfort but nothing eased the bad feeling that came at me from every direction.

No letters from Samuel. He was forty-one days past due getting home. It was snowing. Deputies were on the other side of the Wastelands. A man was hiding in my barn.

Or maybe he'd run off. Maybe his tracks showed plain as day that I'd opened my door to him and gave him shelter. A hunted man wanted by the United States government. In January.

And Samuel wasn't home.

SAMUEL

One hundred and four days ago

September 29, 1887
Utah Territory

Dear Wife Deborah,

I trust this Letter finds You well. I write this from under the Wagon. My Campfire is more Smoke than Flame. The Rain these last Days saw to that. Kindling is so heavy with Water the notion came to Me it would be handy to have your Wringer.

Is it Raining at Home?

There is no telling when You will get this. I intended to write You when I was in Escalante. But I worked from Morning to Night. When I encounter Some One going North, I will ask Him to carry these Words your Way.

I left Escalante 2 Days back and am going South to Henrieville. Snort and Wally got the Wagon through the River Crossing. The Rain caused It to be high and Muddy. I would be proud of those 2 if They had done it without Complaint. If You were here You would say it is the Nature of Mules to wheeze and bellow.

Escalante has more Houses and Streets than it did last Year. Do not let that disturb You. I did not get lost. There were so many broken Wheels that needed fixing that Men tracked Me down. One fellow waited for

*Me outside the Privy. If You were here We would laugh
about that.*

*If You were here We would listen to drops of Rain fall
from the Trees. With you beside me it would be a
cheersome Sound.*

> *Your Husband,*
> *Samuel Tyler*

CHAPTER THREE

DEBORAH – TRACKS

January 12, 1888

It was dark the next morning when I walked to the barn. The snow was up to my ankles and was coming down fast. The air shimmered with it and lit my way.

My boots crunched the snow. Tracks.

The hems of my skirt and wool coat whisked over the snow. My slouch hat was low, and my neck scarf covered my mouth and nose. The parlor clock had chimed five times just before I left the cabin, but I'd been awake most of the night thinking the worst. The man in the barn was a thief. He was a murderer.

Whatever he was, I had given him shelter. That was how the deputies would see it.

Wet flakes clung to my eyelashes. I held my skirt up with one gloved hand and carried a cloth sack in the other. Snow worked its way into the eyelets of my ankle-high boots and dampened my wool stockings.

He was a Saint, I told myself. A man with plural wives. He was like all the others who had asked for my help.

He might have struck out on his own. He'd leave tracks. Tracks that would tell the deputies all they needed to know.

The barn door creaked open. I stopped.

Up ahead, a dark shape moved. It was the man. He was

leading his horse. My nerves jangled. I was on my own, and no one knew he was here.

I tamped down those thoughts. He wouldn't hurt me. He hadn't gone off on his own. He had done what I'd told him to do.

Or maybe I had just caught him trying to sneak off.

He'd stopped walking. I went toward him, the snow breaking. I wanted him to hear my footfall. A man hiding from lawmen doesn't like to be surprised. When I reached him, I wasn't able to make out his features but I felt his stretched nerves. His bearing was tight.

My voice low, I said, 'Good, you're ready.'

'Been ready for a long while.' His voice was as tight as his bearing.

I said, 'It's nearly three hours before full daylight.' I pointed toward the creek in front of my cabin. 'From here, follow the Sulphur west but don't get too close to it. The bank's steep. When you come to a bridge, cross it. The guide lives in the cabin on that side.'

'How far's his place from here?'

'A mile, maybe a little less.' I held out the cloth sack. 'Here. Food.'

'You've done enough. I can't take more.'

'You aren't taking. You paid your way.'

He hesitated.

'Take it,' I said. 'Now go.'

'All right,' he said. 'All right.' He took the sack and put it in the saddlebag. The leather in his saddle crackled in the cold as he mounted his horse. He worked his feet into the stirrups and said, 'They'll see the tracks.'

I looked up at him. I couldn't see his eyes in the dark but sensed what he was thinking. We needed wind to sweep the ground bare in places and make the snow drift in others. That was unlikely, I thought but didn't say. We didn't get much wind here on the floor of the canyon.

I said, 'Go. Please.'

'I'm gone.' Then, 'May our Heavenly Father watch over you.'

'Over us all.'

He flicked the reins. His horse turned away from me and moved off toward the creek.

My eyes watering from the cold, I watched him. He was a shadowy form on horseback in the falling snow. The man angled east at the creek bank and after that, I couldn't see him. I turned away and walked toward the barn. The weight of the bad feeling I'd had since last night rode heavy on my shoulders.

———

The barn wasn't like I expected it to be. I thought it would need tidying. I expected to have to clean the stall where his horse had been. That wasn't so. The horse blankets were folded and stacked on one of the storage shelves. He'd cleaned the stall his horse had used. The wheelbarrow was filled with horse droppings and soiled straw.

Holding a lit lantern, I made my way up the loft ladder. I tripped a few times, my boots catching my skirt. Below, my cow mooed to let me know I hadn't paid any attention to her. Or maybe she was telling me a stranger had been in her barn. In the loft, the straw crunched as I walked from one side to the other. As best as I could tell, all signs of the man's presence were gone.

He'd done what he could to leave the barn as he'd found it. He was looking out for himself and by doing that, he looked out for me.

Back on the barn floor, I hung the lantern on a wall nail. Buttercup mooed again, deeper and louder. 'I know things aren't right,' I said. 'And I'll see to you when I can but there's something I have to do first.'

Gripping the handles of the wheelbarrow that the man had filled with horse droppings, I pushed it through the barn door. It rocked from side to side as I made my way to the manure heap a little ways from the barn. Samuel had our two mules with him, and it'd do me no good if the deputies found droppings in a barn that didn't shelter a horse.

The snow-covered manure heap rose up before me. There, I emptied the wheelbarrow. By now, I thought, the man should be close to Nels' place. The deputies, ten miles back, might be waiting for daylight before venturing into the Wastelands. Once in the Wastelands, it was eight miles of dips and cracks in the earth. Eight miles of massive rock pillars and buttes with rubble at their bases. The trail wasn't a straight line. It meandered and climbed before it descended close to my cabin. These were hard miles that could take five to six hours in fair weather.

Pushing the empty wheelbarrow, I walked toward the barn. Today's weather was anything but fair. It was snowing and had been since last night. The trail in the Wastelands had to be covered like the ground was here. Surely the deputies wouldn't risk the Wastelands before sunrise. Most probably they weren't from this part of Utah; they wouldn't know the landmarks. They'd be forced to travel slow. It could be dusk before they got here. At the soonest. Or it could be tomorrow.

Nels had time to deliver the man to Floral Ranch and be back by then. In good weather, it was four hours to Floral

Ranch and four to get back. I figured the time, then added two hours to account for the snow. Nels would be home by four o'clock. At the latest.

Inside the barn, Buttercup bellowed her complaint when I pushed and pulled her to another stall. 'I know this isn't how we do things,' I said. 'Don't blame you for not liking it. I don't either. All the same, I have to keep a level head.'

I got the pitchfork. In Buttercup's empty stall, I pitched the soiled straw into the wheelbarrow. Nels, I thought, would be startled when the man showed up at his door. Nels might have a bad feeling about him like I did. Not that we'd ever speak of it. The next time I saw him, there'd be only a slight widening of his eyes as he looked my way. A quick duck of his head would tell me he'd done his part to hide the man.

If things went well. If God willed it so.

It was Samuel who had known what to do when the first man came to our cabin asking for help. It was in the spring, nearly four years ago. The man's sudden appearance at our door took me by surprise. Grim-faced, the man spoke in code like this latest one had. I was bewildered that Samuel knew what he was talking about. 'There's no easy way to get to Pleasant Creek,' he'd told the first man. 'It's on the other side of a range of buttes. It's rough country.'

We'd been in Junction for a year and I'd not heard of Pleasant Creek. 'Samuel,' I said. 'What—'

He shook his head, stopping me. 'Don't ask, honey.' He turned his attention back to the man. 'I'll take you. It's a pretty spot, and I won't mind seeing it again.' Samuel saddled Wally, one of our mules, gave me a quick kiss, and rode off with the man.

It was late when Samuel got home that night. His supper had dried out from the long wait on the stove. I was relieved to see him but was put out, too. I'd been worried sick all day. Samuel was caught up in some kind of trouble, and it didn't help matters that he wouldn't answer my questions.

'Deborah, honey, make like you never saw him,' he said when I set his supper before him. 'Don't lodge him in your memory. Don't ask me about where I took him. Or how I know about it. If another one like him shows up and I'm not here, send him to Nels.'

'There'll be more?'

Now, Buttercup's stall clean enough, I put fresh straw down. When that was finished, I pushed the wheelbarrow outside. The air wasn't lit with white flakes. It had stopped snowing, and it was darker than it had been earlier.

I needed a light to guide me to the manure heap. I went inside the barn, got the lantern, and went out. Before me, in the lantern's light, pockets of horse prints glittered in the ankle-deep snow.

They were frozen in place. I knew there would be prints. It'd take a long, heavy snowfall to fill them. I knew they'd show but seeing them laid out from the barn and going toward the creek made my heartbeat knock in my ears.

I had to cover them.

Hurry, I told myself as I carried the lantern a handful of yards ahead of me and left it in the snow. In the dark, I went back for the wheelbarrow and pushed it toward the light. Like before, I took the lantern up ahead, then returned for the wheelbarrow. Over and over I did this, the word *hurry* filling my thoughts.

Finally at the heap, I emptied the wheelbarrow so the flat cow patties were on top of the horse's rounded droppings. The deputies wouldn't be fooled, not if they looked close. But if it snowed again, all the droppings would be covered. If it stayed this cold, the deputies might not bother to walk back here.

Hurry. I headed back to the barn doing like before, carrying the lantern up ahead and then going back for the wheelbarrow. Think of a plan, I told myself. Think what to do about the frozen tracks. First, though, there were the chores that couldn't be put off. There was time, I convinced myself once I was inside the barn. I propped the wheelbarrow against the side wall like always. The lantern now hung on a nail, I settled myself on the milking stool by Buttercup. My hands shook while I stroked her swollen udder to get her ready to be milked. Rushing made mistakes. That was what my father, a tanner, said about curing leather. Do it right the first time.

'You had a crowd here last night,' I said to Buttercup, still stroking her udder. 'Don't let it worry you.' When she was finally ready, I worked her teats. The warm milk pinged against the side of the first pail. My father had also said that if you have dealings with gentiles, bend the truth if you have to. God wouldn't think less of you.

When the first pail was full, I reached for the second one. Think of a way to cover the tracks, I told myself as my hands went through the motions of milking Buttercup. Think.

The milking finally finished, I covered the two pails with lids and put them on the flat-bottomed toboggan. I put feed out for Buttercup, broke the thin ice in her water trough, and left the barn. Pulling the toboggan with one hand and carrying the lantern with the other, I plodded my way to the cabin. A plan began to take shape in my mind.

At my cabin I brought in one of the milk pails. The other stayed outside on the toboggan. I busied myself by making the bed and building up the fire in the cookstove. I had to wait until it was close to daybreak before I could begin to cover the tracks. I didn't want to carry a lantern. I couldn't risk being seen.

When the tips of the buttes that faced east began to show, I left home, pulling the toboggan with the milk pail on it. I followed the man's horse tracks to the creek, shuffling and kicking the icy snow, doing what I could to disguise the prints. The milk was my excuse for walking from my barn to Nels' place on the other side of the creek. When the deputies got here late today or tomorrow, they'd question me about the shuffled tracks. I had to be able to tell them they were mine. I'd say that I owed a neighbor milk in exchange for the cord of wood he'd chopped for me earlier this winter.

At the creek, I turned east. My plum orchard was to my left. The deputies might burn the trees if they caught me helping a felon. My sister and her husband's cabin was on the far side of the orchard. The deputies might accuse Grace and Michael of having a hand in this. I couldn't let that happen.

Behind me, the toboggan crushed the kicked snow making the tracks harder to read. It worried me that I couldn't cover the ones Nels and the man would make once they left Nels' place. I couldn't think of a reason for going on past his cabin, not one the lawmen would believe.

One step at a time. I was doing what I could.

My pulse thudded in my ears. My shoulders ached from pulling the toboggan while I shuffled and kicked the snow. I didn't believe in plural marriage, but for the life of me, I couldn't begin to understand lawmen who were willing to do work that tore families apart. That was the way of gentiles, though. Before Saints came to Utah Territory, gentiles claimed our leaders conspired to take control of the small towns where we settled. We bought too much land, they said. The courts, the mayors' offices, the schools, and newspapers were in our hands. The worst, though, was plural marriage. It was immoral, they said. It was a perversion that must not be allowed to spread.

Farther up the creek, a dog barked. Each bark splintered the quiet and ricocheted off the cliffs. It might be Nels' dog. I strained, listening. The bark was too high-pitched to be Sally's. It was another neighbor's dog that was somewhere well past Nels' place. Noise carried here on the floor of the canyon. The dog might be barking at Nels and the man as they rode past. Alerted, the owner would try to figure out the reason for the disturbance. He'd see Nels with a stranger.

My nerves flared. The fewer who knew, the better. This was especially so for children. They had a way of reporting what they'd seen and repeating what they'd overheard. Some of the deputies were not above drawing children aside from their parents and questioning them.

The barking faded. My breathing was loud in my ears. The sunrise was gloomy, and thick gray clouds shrouded the upper reaches of the cliffs. As I made my way along the river toward the bridge, a circle of yellow lamplight showed in my sister's side window. It was like a whip driving me on. I had to keep Grace and her family of little boys safe.

Close to Grace's, I hunched low and hurried. Don't anybody see me, I thought. It was early, no one should be outside.

Unless it was later than I thought. Unless someone needed to visit the outhouse. I tucked my chin to my chest like that would keep me from being seen. The milk pail clinked on the toboggan. The snow cracked like thunder as I covered the tracks. Grace will hear me, I thought. Her husband, Michael, or the boys will see me.

Holding my breath, I went on. No one called my name. None of the boys came running.

Once past Grace's cabin, I didn't let myself turn around to look. I kept on following the man's tracks. The wood bridge rattled as I crossed it. The creek was iced over close to the banks but ran clear in the middle. To the east, the Fremont roared where it converged with the creek. I drew in some air. I couldn't smell smoke rising from Nels' cookstove chimney. He and the man had been gone long enough for the fire to burn down.

I headed toward the cabin, shuffling over the hoof prints, then stopped. Nearby, another set of hoof prints, not the ones I was walking over, came from the cabin and veered east. Something was wrong. Nels and the man should have left together. There should be two sets of prints.

Staying where I was, I looked around. I didn't see a second set. Nels had sent the man off on his own.

He wouldn't do that. He'd never done it before.

This was January, though. Something about the man might have felt wrong to Nels. Maybe he refused to help him.

I couldn't believe that. Nels didn't take chances. He wouldn't want the man to go back over the bridge to Grace and Michael's. Or to Len and Laura Hall's place a half-mile down the river. He wouldn't want them pulled into this.

Think. Slow down. I peered at the tracks. They weren't the same as the ones I'd shuffled over. These prints were wider apart. It was a different horse.

Nels' horse. A single set. I looked around again. No second set of horse tracks. Yet, I'd followed the man's tracks that crossed the bridge. His tracks ended here.

I went on to the cabin. A jumble of prints covered the area in front of it. Most were boot prints. The paw prints were

Sally's, Nels' dog. If a person didn't know different, it looked like a place where someone had gone about his business without concern for his tracks. The boot tracks and paw prints went to and from the front door to the woodpile on the side of the cabin. Some led toward the outhouse that was in the back and on down a ways. Tracks went toward the water well by the barn, and some went around the corner of the cabin to the trash heap. The snow was trampled like it should be when a person went about his morning.

That must have been Nels' intent. I pictured him, tall, wiry, and yellow-haired, doing all this walking around his cabin on purpose. He wanted the deputies to think nothing was amiss. He'd done it to cover the man's tracks.

Just one set of horse prints, though, that led away from the cabin. Something was wrong.

'Brother Nels,' I called out, standing close to the cabin, the barn off to my right. 'You here? It's Sister Deborah.'

No answer. Nels was a widower and didn't have children. He lived alone and even though I listened hard for his voice, I knew he wasn't here. Everything about the place was quiet. The air felt empty like I was the only one breathing it in. The lamp in Nels' window wasn't lit and smoke didn't rise from his cookstove's chimney. His dog would come bounding if she were anywhere in hearing distance.

Stay with the plan. Don't look around. Someone might be watching. Deliver the milk.

Pulling the toboggan, I went to the front door and knocked, my gloved knuckles making dull thuds. 'Brother Nels,' I said, my voice loud. 'I've got your milk.'

No one was here.

Deliver the milk. That's your excuse for walking over the tracks. But I couldn't leave the milk outside by the door.

It'd freeze. Once it was brought inside and thawed, the milk would curdle. If the deputies showed up here before Nels got back, they'd find it peculiar that a pail of milk was outside by the door. No one would do such a thing in this weather.

I thumped the sides of my right boot, then the left, against the cabin wall to knock off the worst of the snow. I had to make it look like Nels was here when I arrived. I had to fool the deputies into believing this was an ordinary day. Then I could go home like none of this happened.

Carrying the pail, I opened the door. It was dark inside. The man might be hiding here.

'Brother Nels?' I said. 'Anybody?'

No answer.

I'd known Nels since my marriage to Samuel. He was Samuel's stepbrother and was younger by a year. Samuel was twelve when his mother married Nels' father. The two boys were as close as blood brothers, and when Nels staked the first claim in Junction nearly six years ago, Samuel and I followed him a few months later. As well as I knew Nels, though, I'd never stepped a foot inside his cabin without Samuel with me. It wasn't something a woman did.

I went inside. The cabin was cold. My skin prickled with unease. I kept the door open for light. Hurry, a voice drummed in my thoughts. Don't get caught here. It's nearly full daylight. The deputies are on their way. Hurry.

I tried to shake the voice away. Rushing made mistakes. There was time.

My footfall was loud as I walked to the kitchen table. The cabin was empty but I felt I was being watched. I told myself that no one could hide here. It was one room with two chairs at the kitchen table and a low-slung bed placed sideways along the back wall. The cookstove was pressed against the south wall. A few dishes were stacked on the cooking counter. A skillet hung from the wall nail. No one was here. Just me.

I put the milk pail on the table. I took off one of my gloves and touched a pan of water on the cookstove. It was cold. Nels hadn't eaten this morning. The bed was unmade with the blankets tossed to one side.

An empty wash basin was on the counter. I took it outside and scooped up some snow to line the bottom. Back inside, I placed the basin on the floor and put the pail of milk in it to keep it cool. I started to leave, then stopped. The tossed blankets, the cold fire. The person who lived here had left in a rush. That was how the deputies would see it if somehow they got here before Nels was back.

Rushing made mistakes. I took a deep breath and willed myself to slow down. I found a few pieces of split wood in the corner of the kitchen, put them in the cookstove, and blew on the embers until a fire took hold. It wouldn't last more than a few hours but at least it wouldn't look like a fire that went cold during the night. That done, I went to Nels' bed.

The hollow in the middle of the pillow where he'd rested his head was a deep shadow. I smoothed the top sheet, leaving my gloves on to keep distance between me and the bed clothing of a man who was not my husband. I untangled the three dark blankets. The wool was coarse and I didn't want to think what it was like for Nels to sleep in this bed alone for almost six years. Just before coming to Junction, his wife, Lydia, died during childbirth. They had been married for fourteen months.

His cabin, one room, was smaller than Samuel's and mine. It made me think Nels built it believing he'd never remarry. A pencil drawing of Lydia was on the back wall near the foot of the bed. Nels had drawn it. There were other drawings, too, tacked on the walls but only the one of Lydia was framed.

Hurry, the voice in my head said. Get out of here.

I layered the blankets on the bed, one on top of the other, and pulled each one close to the pillow but left them lumpy in places like a man might do. One look and anyone could see a woman didn't live here. The sparse kitchen, the lack of a dress on a wall peg, and the coarse blankets rather than quilts said this was the home of a man who lived on his own. It wouldn't look right if the cabin was too tidy.

I gave the room one last look, then left to go home.

The empty toboggan behind me bumped on the uneven trampled snow as I walked over my shuffled tracks. The single set of horse prints worried me. It didn't make sense.

I crossed the bridge. Grace's cabin was up ahead. It must be around seven o'clock, and Michael and the boys were probably seeing to their milk cow and horse. Grace would be cooking breakfast. She might look out the front window. Even though the sunrise was dull, she could see me. She'd find it peculiar. She'd come out to see what I was doing.

There'd be no getting away if any of them saw me. My nephews, Jacob, Joe, and Hyrum, would come running. Their curious faces would look up at me, their cheeks patched red from the cold and their breaths showing as quick puffs of white air. 'Where're you going?' they'd ask. 'Can we come too? There's time before school starts.' Jacob, the oldest at seven, would want to pull the toboggan. So would Joe, he was six. Hyrum was three and would beg for a ride.

Grace and Michael had moved here from Parowan last October, a week after the last man had shown up at the cabin. I didn't tell them about the men and I didn't tell them about Floral Ranch. It was better if they didn't know. Ignorance protected them if deputies questioned them. Neither did I talk about this with any of the neighbors. I had to protect them, too.

Sooner or later, Michael and the boys were bound to see my shuffled tracks. There was nothing I could do about that. At this moment, I couldn't risk them seeing me. When the deputies came, they had to be able to say they hadn't seen the person who had made the tracks.

I needed to stay out of sight. To my left, the creek had cut a deep channel in the land. I gave the toboggan a push. It plunged over the top of the bank, down the drop-off, and stopped on the rocky creek bed. Slipping, the snow spilling around me, I went down after it. I couldn't be seen from here.

I pulled the toboggan over the icy rocks that edged the creek. When the deputies saw the change in the tracks at the top of the bank, I'd tell them I'd slipped and the toboggan got away from me.

A part of me wanted to warn Michael and Grace that deputies were on the way. It'd scare Grace and the boys to have deputies at their door. Michael wouldn't understand the purpose of their questions and their demands to search the cabin and barn. It hurt me to think of the boys' scared faces. I couldn't warn them, though. Ignorance was the best defense.

I passed their cabin. When I figured it was safe, I pulled the toboggan up the bank and followed my earlier shuffled footsteps home.

So many risks, I thought. So many lies I had to tell.

When the deputies asked about the single set of horse prints at Nels', there'd be no need to lie. My ignorance was real.

Nels' barn. The image of it flashed in my mind just before I got home. I couldn't see it from here but I looked over my shoulder toward his place. 'I want my barn to be airy,' Nels had said when he and Samuel built it. 'For the summers. Even if it does take a little extra doing.'

Like all barns, the front wall had double doors that opened the width of a wagon with room to spare. It was the back wall that was different from most. Nels, a carpenter by trade, put a door there.

It came to me as clear as if I'd been there. Nels had directed the man to leave from the back of the barn while he left from the front. A steep cliff rose up behind the barn. Nels told the man to take the narrow rocky path along the cliff's base. The cliff was a buffer from the snowfall and the ground was apt to be bare in places. The prints wouldn't be so easy to read there. I pictured Nels telling the man about some kind of landmark, a particular rock formation or maybe a bend. 'Wait there,' I could almost hear him say. 'You'll reach it before me but I'll be along. There's a place where I can cross over in the creek to meet you. That might throw off the trail.'

It would, I told myself. When the deputies got here – maybe late this afternoon or tomorrow – they'd see the single set. If Nels was back by then, and he should be, they'd question him. He'd come up with some kind of story. He'd gone hunting for winter provisions, he might say. But he hadn't had any luck. That could fool the deputies. Or maybe they'd follow the single tracks but they would have doubts.

Doubt was a powerful force. It could slow a person. It could make her question all she once believed was true.

Off in the distance the school bell rang. It was eight o'clock, later than I thought. Michael, the schoolmaster, always walked with Jacob and Joe to the schoolhouse. They had missed seeing me by a handful of minutes.

I caught my breath and began to walk. The upper half of the cliffs was lost in the bank of heavy clouds. The air was so still the bare branches of my plum trees looked frozen in place. *Heavenly Father*, I prayed. *Send us more snow and give us wind. Cover the tracks, blow them away. Hold the deputies back. Give us time.*

CHAPTER FOUR

DEBORAH – THE IN-BETWEEN

January 12, 1888

Home, I fried venison, heated milk, and set out biscuits for my breakfast. The parlor clock's tick was loud in my ears. Eight-thirty. Nels and the man might be close to Floral Ranch.

Breakfast eaten, I left the table and looked out the kitchen window's thick wavy glass. A fox stood sideways between two plum trees. Its gray coat was flecked with snow and its bushy tail brushed the snow-covered ground. Its head was turned toward the cabin. It was looking at me.

It was after the chickens in the coop. Before I could do anything to chase it off, it raised its head as if sniffing the air, then looked over its shoulder toward the Wastelands.

My skin prickled. The fox looked again at me. I stepped back from the window. The fox turned and wound its way through the orchard until it blended into the snow.

A warning. Foxes were night creatures. I'd never seen one during this time of day before. Just like I'd never had a hunted man come to my door in January.

Don't lodge the man in your memory, I told myself. He was gone. I'd never see him again.

I washed the breakfast dishes and when that was finished, I carried a pail of heated water to the coop. Drinking it would help warm the chickens in this cold. I studied the snow as I walked, expecting to see the fox's tracks near the coop.

There weren't any. The fox hadn't come to do harm but to warn. Deputies were on their way.

I looked toward the trail that came from the Wastelands. Nothing. Inside the coop, the rooster and the six hens, their black and white feathers fluffed against the cold, cackled when I came inside the fenced-off yard. Big Tom stood up and beat his wings. 'I know,' I said. 'You're put out with me for running late.' The water in their nearly-empty pan had a thin coat of ice on the top. I changed the water and before I'd finished, the hens were out of their nests and circling the pan. 'Be fair-minded,' I said to Pretty Girl who bossed the hens. 'Don't take what's not yours.'

I scattered corn on top of the snow in the yard. Sure that I heard a horse nicker, I whirled around. Nothing.

The chickens clucked and pecked at the corn poking holes in the snow. If the fox had been around, they weren't riled up. I needed to do the same. I had to go about my business like this were any other day.

A sudden screech made my pulse rush. Just a bird, I told myself. A hawk. Or its prey. I cleaned out the coop's soiled straw and was certain I heard men's voices.

It was the nearby poplar tree, its upper branches scraping in the light wind. My nerves rattled, I put fresh straw down inside the coop. 'Keep warm,' I told the hens and Big Tom when I left. I got Buttercup from the barn and brought her out to the barnyard. She nosed the snow and at the water trough; I kept looking over my shoulder as I worked the pump, believing heavy footsteps crunched the snow behind me.

Not yet. Too soon. It'd be dusk or maybe tomorrow before the deputies got here.

Back in the cabin, I got one of Samuel's rocks that he kept on top of the bedroom dresser. It was black with whitish-yellow lines that flowed through it. I ran my forefinger along the edges. They were jagged as if they'd broken off from a bigger rock. 'It's a wonderment to me,' Samuel had told me when he brought it home several years ago. 'Don't know what it is. I found it and others like it up on the plateau. It's not limestone like most.' He licked his forefinger and wiped the rock so that it shined. 'Makes me think it's not from here. Maybe it rose up from the belly of the earth.'

I laughed, then saw how Samuel was studying the rock, turning it one way and then another. 'Could such a thing happen?'

'Maybe not. But until I know different, I like to lean toward the side of maybe so.'

Samuel saying such things was what drew me to him. I was nearly nineteen and he was a few months short of twenty-four when I met him. Like now, he was a wheelwright who traveled to small towns in the back country of Utah and the northern parts of Arizona. He came to Parowan every year to mend wagon wheels and made new ones when the old couldn't be fixed. During the first years he came to Parowan, I'd never had an occasion to speak to him although I'd seen him at church services.

That changed in early April of 1870. I'll never forget the month or the year. The day was cold, and there was a wet snow on the ground. My father had hired Samuel to replace two wagon wheels but Samuel had been able to fix them. Pleased about the savings, my father brought Samuel home for dinner. It was a Tuesday, the one day of the week my father visited us and stayed the night with my mother.

Samuel was a short man just a few inches taller than me. Most women wouldn't call him handsome. His nose was too broad. But his grin came easily and his dark brown hair, in need of a trim, curled around his ears. A cowlick swirled and poked up at the back of his head. He was clean shaven, and that set him apart from my father whose gray beard came down to his collar.

There were twelve of us at the long kitchen table. My father was at one end and my mother was at the other. I won't forget that either, how we were all together, Samuel a part of it. My seven brothers and Grace stair-stepped from ages twenty years to sixteen months. For the most part, we were fair-headed with hazel eyes. Samuel sat in the middle of one of the side benches with my brothers beside and across from him. Grace and I were across from Samuel and at the end by my mother. I had Zeb on my lap. He was sixteen months old and didn't like to sit still. He whined and arched his back wanting to be let down but it was dinner and he was expected at the table. I fed him a piece of biscuit to chew while my father said the blessing for the meal. When we raised our heads, my mother gave the younger boys and Grace stern looks as she always did when my father visited. They were to speak only when spoken to.

'Tell us about your travels,' my father said to Samuel as we passed platters of sliced ham and boiled potatoes around the table. 'How are things in St. George?'

'Doing well, I'd say,' Samuel said. He spread a sliver of butter on his slice of bread. 'Three farmers had new wagons built and I take that as a spritely sign. They're talking about last year's wheat crop and how it was a good one. This year's might do the same. That is, if the rainfall isn't too much or too little. If the sun isn't too bright or it's too cloudy.' He smiled, bringing out a dimple in his left cheek. 'You know how farmers are. Always on one side or the other of worry.'

My father's laugh was a deep rumble. 'How well I know,

Brother Samuel. My father farmed and there was never a moment's peace about the weather. It's why I'm a tanner. Rain or shine, there's work.'

My mother eased back into her chair. The corners of her mouth hinted at a smile. My father was enjoying himself, I could almost hear her think. He was content to be with us. The boys were all behaving themselves. They chewed with their mouths closed and their gazes fixed on Samuel, a stranger to our table. Even Zeb had settled down, busy with the mashed bites of boiled potatoes I fed him. My father went on to tell Samuel about the hides he'd gotten from a trader in Panguitch. After that Ash, my older half-brother, laid out his plans to move to Springdale in a month's time. 'Brother Brigham called upon me to start a tannery there,' Ash said. Above his beard, his cheeks flushed red, showing his pleasure at being chosen by the Prophet Young.

'The people there will be glad to have you,' Samuel said. 'Springdale's a fine settlement and the Virgin River runs fast even during the summer. You'll do well there.'

'He surely will,' my father said. 'He's a fine tanner like Paul. That's my oldest son. His tannery's up in Provo. Brother Brigham called him there a year back.' My father's eyes were bright with pride. 'What about you?' he said to Samuel. 'Have the apostles called upon you to settle down and set up a wheelwright shop? Help build a new town for the Saints?'

For a moment, Samuel's gray eyes darkened. Then he shook his head and his eyes cleared. 'I'm not sure that's in me, Brother Daniel, staying in one place.'

My father's eyebrows raised. A restless man, I could almost hear him thinking about Samuel.

Samuel said, 'I like seeing how the land can change in a day's travel, how in the morning I can be in the mountains but by the end of the day I'm in the desert. But it's the in-between places I like seeing most of all.'

'In-between places?' my father said.

'Sounds foolish, I know. But it's where junipers give way to aspens, or where the rocky ground shifts into black soil. I'm always on the lookout for the exact place where the mountains ease into hills and where those hills slide into low swells.' He paused, then said, 'In-between places.'

This was when I knew Samuel was different. He hadn't answered my father's question about being called by the church but had talked around it. My father might have noticed but didn't ask again. The talk went back to Ash's move to Springdale and how he planned to help build a wardhouse as soon as the four walls of his tannery were in place. Samuel nodded and said that was a solid plan. Not once, though, did he say anything about doing work for the church. Neither did he say anything against church work.

Supper ended. While Samuel thanked my mother and father for the good cooking and fellowship, I put Zeb on the floor and told Grace to mind him so I could get Samuel's coat. He shook Ash's hand, and he shook all the boys' hands. This made the older boys stand tall while the younger ones' mouths formed small circles. It pleased them that Samuel treated them like grown men. I held out Samuel's coat to him and by then there was a clamor around us. Seventeen-year-old Saul said he wanted to show Samuel a fishing hole at the creek. The younger boys said they wanted to go too, even if there was still snow on the ground. Their voices climbed over each others', loud and some of them high-pitched. Through it all, Samuel grinned. Still holding his coat, I stepped closer to him and in a low voice said, 'You've caused a stir.'

'The notion of fishing can do that.' His voice was as low as mine.

'It's not that,' I said. 'It's what you said about in-between places. You've given me something to think about.'

'I have?'

'You have.'

Samuel looked at me like he'd not really noticed me before.

My mother clapped her hands once and told the boys to hush, they'd forgotten their manners. The clamor around us settled but the younger boys gave each other little pushes, the floorboards squeaking as they jostled. Samuel nodded at me, his eyes steady, and when he took his coat from me, our hands touched. In that moment, there was no one else in the room but Samuel.

The next day he asked my father for permission to call on me. My father approved. He told me Samuel was a good man and it was time for him to settle down. 'He'll make a fine church elder. All he needs is a steady hand to guide him.'

Samuel lingered in Parowan and during our four-week courtship, spring overtook winter. The sun's gathering warmth melted the snow, the frozen ground turned muddy, and the linden trees budded. Samuel walked me home after Sunday church services and called on me two evenings a week. I was light with happiness when I was with him. We sat on the parlor love seat, our knees turned toward one another but with Grace usually sitting between us. If she wasn't there, I'd put my left hand flat on the love-seat cushion and he'd put his right hand beside mine, the sides of our hands touching until my brothers came into the parlor. They had fossils to show Samuel. Samuel obliged them by running his forefinger over the creatures outlined in the rocks. 'From ancient times,' he'd tell the boys. 'Don't you wonder what color they were when they were alive? And what they ate and where they nested?' That'd set the boys off, guessing about such things. Grace did, too, if my mother hadn't already called her to bed. Just when I thought I'd been forgotten, he'd turn to me and wink as if we shared a great secret.

Those winks made me laugh.

'I like shaping wood into spokes,' Samuel once said while we walked the three blocks home from church. My family was on all sides of us, Sister Caroline and her four children, too. 'There's something about working with wood, it's hard to explain. It's the grain, I guess you could say. It tells me the wood knew another life before it was cut.'

'Like the leather I use to make gloves,' I said.

'You're a glovemaker?'

'Oh, I don't know if I'd call myself that.' I paused and considered the word. 'But I suppose I am. My gloves are sold in the store here in town. Paul, my brother who's in Provo now, he taught me how to measure hands and stitch leather. I like the work. It quiets my mind.'

Samuel stopped walking. I did, too. We turned toward each other, an arm's length between us. Saul and another one of my brothers, Jothan, weren't far behind us. Samuel said, 'And that matters to you, a quiet mind?'

I smiled. 'I live with seven brothers.'

'And you're still standing to tell the tale.'

That made me laugh, too.

Now, alone in our bedroom, I held the black rock that Samuel called a wonderment. I studied the map that I had asked Nels to draw for me so I could trace Samuel's path home. I wanted to hear Samuel's voice. I wanted his embrace. I wanted to stop waiting.

Carrying the rock, I left the bedroom and stood before the parlor clock. The pendulum swung from side to side. It was a few minutes before ten.

Nels and the man might be at Floral Ranch by now. Or almost there. The deputies could still be on the far side of the Wastelands, unable to find the snow-covered trail.

I placed the rock back on the dresser, put my shawl on, and went outside. I wrapped my arms around myself and breathed in the cold. It had started to spit snow. I studied the land, looking for the fox but not seeing it. Maybe I'd imagined it earlier. Nerves were known to do such things. I pulled my shawl tighter around me. No signs of the deputies. Not yet.

On the other side of the plum orchard, Grace was home with three-year-old Hyrum. Michael and the two older boys were at the schoolhouse. Today was Thursday and like always on Thursdays, Grace would be baking. I should do the same.

I went inside and hung up my shawl. The minute hand on the clock had barely moved. Once Nels delivered the man to the family at Floral Ranch, I believed he'd stay long enough only to water his horse. He'd want to get back before the deputies got here. We all needed to be going about our business as if this were an ordinary day. The family who owned the ranch – I didn't know their names and didn't want to – would surely want Nels gone, too. They'd want to get the man hidden. It wouldn't go easy for them if they were caught hiding a man charged with a felony.

A thin layer of frost covered the inside lower half of the kitchen windowpane. I scraped the pane clean with my thumbnail. Snow was coming down harder. Good, I thought. It'd slow the lawmen. It'd slow Nels too but he knew the landmarks and the shape of the land.

Jacob, Grace's oldest, was in sore need of new gloves and

if I could, I'd sit myself down and make him a new pair. Doing so would settle my mind but I'd run out of leather and dark-colored thread a month ago. All of us in Junction were running low on supplies. When Samuel left in September, we'd given him our lists of what we needed him to buy: bolts of fabric, buttons, shoelaces, metal nails, a new map for the school-house, kerosene, sacks of flour and bottles of molasses. As he did every year, he'd bargain for the best prices as he traveled from town to town.

I left the window and went to the parlor. A quarter past ten. Surely Nels had delivered the man to Floral Ranch and was on his way home.

Stay busy, I told myself. Do something. It was Thursday. Baking day. In the kitchen, I heated water on the stove and got my large bowl from the shelf, then the jars of yeast and salt, the bottle of molasses, and the small sack of flour.

I measured each ingredient with care. The closest town on the far side of the Wastelands was Thurber and prices were dear at the small general store there. Eight days after Samuel was due to return but hadn't, a neighbor, Len Hall, told me he'd make the twenty-five-mile trip to Thurber for supplies the families of Junction could not do without.

'There's no need,' I'd told Len. 'Samuel'll be home any time.'

This was before I knew about the rockslide.

It was the flour and salt that Len bought in Thurber that I used now. My hands did the work, heating water, measuring the yeast and adding the molasses, then the flour and salt. Kneading the dough over and over, I watched the snow out my window slacken, then start up again. January, I thought, my back aching from the work and from pulling the sled earlier. What had the man done that the deputies couldn't wait until spring?

Maybe it wasn't what the man had done. The government might have come up with a new reason to go after Saints. That was what gentiles did. Before Saints came to the Great Salt Lake, we settled in Illinois and Missouri. The gentiles there thought Joseph Smith was a madman, and the Book of Mormon was the work of a false prophet. They said we were like swarms of locusts. They burned our churches and they burned our crops and homes. Then, thinking it would put an end to us, they killed Joseph Smith and his brother, Hyrum.

I patted the dough in a bowl to let it rise, covered it with cheesecloth, and rinsed my hands. The clock's tick drummed a slow but steady beat. Twenty minutes past eleven. The deputies couldn't get here before late afternoon. Surely Nels was on his way home.

Unless the snow was deeper at Floral Ranch than it was here.

Snow was what held Samuel back, I told myself. The rockslide forced him to come through the mountains so high the air was said to be thin. The snow was bound to be far deeper than here on the floor of a canyon.

I dried my hands on my apron and studied the map that Nels had drawn for me. I traced the trail through the mountain pass in the Fish Lakes with my forefinger. *Heavenly Father,* I prayed. *Watch over Samuel. Deliver him home.*

Today was the twelfth. Nels said Samuel would be here by the second week of January. That was this week. But it was only Thursday. He could come home today. Or tomorrow. Or Saturday or Sunday.

I put my shawl and gloves on, and went outside to get firewood that I kept stacked against the front of the cabin.

I looked through the falling snow for the fox. There weren't any signs it had ever been here.

On the other side of the orchard, more than likely Grace was in her corner kitchen. A woman with a husband and three boys was never far from the kitchen. Although her belly had begun to swell with the baby she expected in April, Grace was so thin her shoulder blades showed through the back of the dress. Her sleeves might be rolled to her elbows as she scrubbed bread pans, her yellow hair tied in a knot at the nape of her neck. Hyrum might be on the floor building a fort with his wood blocks.

At the schoolhouse, Jacob, Joe, and their classmates could be fidgeting at their desks. Their bellies might rumble as they wait for Michael to take his pocket watch from his vest, tell them they may put their lessons away, it was time to go home for the noon meal. The children who lived too far stayed at the school and ate the food their mothers packed for them this morning. The mothers, my neighbors, were probably in their cabins cooking, stirring pots of stew or warming slices of ham. Their faces were red from the heat of the cookstoves and small children might clutch and pull at their skirts. Husbands and older sons would soon stop their chores and go home to noon dinner.

None of them knew trouble was coming.

CHAPTER FIVE

DEBORAH – THE ARRIVAL

January 12, 1888

One o'clock. Nels should be back by four. At the latest. In the distance, the school bell rang. The noon meal was over and it was time for the pupils to return to school. It was a call to me, too. Since Grace and Michael's move to Junction last October, it was my custom to go to their cabin at this time. Hyrum was the only child home during school hours and that made for less commotion. It usually didn't take much for me to convince Grace to get off her feet while I washed the dishes and tidied the cabin.

Today, I wanted to stay home and keep watch for the deputies. Grace, though, would find it peculiar if I didn't visit her.

The deputies were hours away, I told myself. It might even be tomorrow. There was plenty of time. I left home and walked through the plum orchard toward Grace's cabin. It was still snowing and had already filled the irrigation ditches that ran along the rows of trees. In places where the ground wasn't sheltered by the dense bare branches of the trees, it looked to be some eight inches deep.

The tracks I'd shuffled over this morning were filling in. Just like the tracks made by Nels and the man would be. This snow would slow them getting to Floral Ranch but the deputies weren't traveling any faster. Nels would get back home long before the deputies arrived.

Close to Grace's now, I looked across the creek toward Nels'. No smoke. The fire I'd made this morning in his cook-stove had gone out. I looked behind me and toward the Wastelands like I might see the deputies coming. No one was there.

Put it out of your mind, I told myself. Don't let Grace see that anything was wrong.

At her cabin, I knocked on the door. 'It's me,' I called.

'Sister,' Grace said when she opened the door. I was barely inside when three-year-old Hyrum flung his arms around my legs. He buried his face into my coat that was cold and damp with snow.

'Who's this?' I said, my gloved hands patting the top of his head. It took all I had to work up a smile and make my voice normal. I looked at Grace. My smile faded. She was pale and the circles under her eyes were darker than they'd been yesterday.

Hyrum burrowed against me. I said, 'This can't be Hyrum. Why, this boy's too big. It must be Joe. Or now that I think about it, this must be Billy Cookson.'

This was one of the games he and I played. I'd mistake him for one of his brothers or for one of the older neighbor boys. Like he always did, Hyrum let go of me, put his head back and looked up at me. His smile was stretched wide across his freckled face. His blue eyes sparkled.

'It's me,' he said, his voice pitched high with excitement. 'I'm Hyrum!'

I studied his face like I wasn't sure. After a moment, I shook my head with wonder. 'So it is.'

It could be any other day. Grace fussed at Hyrum telling him to give me room while I took off my coat. As usual, the dishes from noon dinner were still on the kitchen table. Dirty pots and pans were on the cookstove and counter. The cabin, only a few feet wider than mine, smelled of bread. Two loaves cooled on the kitchen counter.

I hung up my coat and when I turned around, Grace surprised me by pulling me to her. 'Deborah,' she said, close to my ear.

What's this? I thought but didn't say. I put my arms around her like I'd done so many times when she was a little girl. I was twelve when she was born and our mother looked to me to help raise her. Now, as Grace leaned in to me, I felt her swollen belly. Her fourth child in seven years. Her arms still around me, I rubbed Grace's back. The points of her backbone were sharp beneath my fingertips.

'Deborah,' she said, the word now sounding like a plea. Her arms tightened around me.

She knew about the man, I thought. She'd seen him. Or she'd seen me pulling the toboggan to and from Nels'.

'What's wrong?' I said. I had to ask. We both expected me to even though I dreaded the answer.

'Nothing,' she said. Grace let go of me and began to clear the table. She turned her face away but not before I saw the weariness in her eyes. Even her yellow hair looked worn out. Strands had come loose from the knot tied at the nape of her neck and fell around the sides of her face.

She knew, I thought.

'Hyrum,' I said, forcing my voice to be cheerful. 'You ready to go outside for a spell?'

He gave a little jump. 'I'm going to build a fort. A big one.'

'Well then, let's get you ready. Grace, don't touch those dishes. Those are mine to do. Now, get off your feet. You hear me?'

She gathered up a smile. 'You always did tell me what to

do.' That made us laugh like everything was as it should be. I shooed her into the parlor half of the room and made her sit down in her rocker. I turned my attention to Hyrum and tried not to worry about what Grace might have seen or what she knew.

Hyrum and I climbed up the ladder to the loft. I saw to it that he used the chamber pot kept by the boys' bed. I'd empty it later. When he finished, Hyrum counted the rungs in the ladder as we climbed down it. In the parlor, Grace sat in the rocker and watched as I helped him get into his leggings, his small hands on my shoulders for balance as he stepped into each pants leg. He chattered about building a snow fort. 'I'll hide behind it. With snowballs. It'll be this tall.' He let go of my shoulders and put his arms high above his head.

'Won't that surprise your brothers?' I said, now getting Hyrum into his coat and fastening the buttons. His eyes widened at the thought of that and when at last he was dressed with only his blue eyes showing above his neck scarf and below his cap, I sent him outside. 'Mind you stay by the kitchen window so I can see you,' I told him. He said he would. Packed into his layers of clothes, he lumbered outside. 'By the window,' I called to him as I stood in the doorway.

Hyrum nodded and began to make his way around the corner of the house, kicking straight-legged at the snow. Inside, I went to the kitchen window and when he appeared, I knocked my knuckles against the cold pane of glass. He waved at me and then fell to his knees to go about the work of making a fort.

I turned toward Grace in the parlor. 'That child,' I said, seeing to it that there was a smile in my voice. 'So busy.'

She put one of her hands on her stomach. 'Three boys. I'm due a girl.'

'Mama said much the same when expecting you.'

'Did she?'

'She did. Of course she welcomed the boys.'

'Of course.'

Ball to heel, Grace rocked the chair back and forth over the green-and-blue braided rug. She didn't look at me but kept her gaze on the portrait of Joseph Smith that hung on the wall. She knew about the man I'd sheltered, I thought. Please don't ask.

The clock on the small marble-topped table in the parlor showed half past one. Two and a half hours before Nels should get back from Floral Ranch.

Grace's gaze was still fixed on the portrait of Joseph Smith. I busied myself with the dishes and hummed her favorite hymn – 'Come, Come Ye Saints' – to fill the quiet. I cleared the table and scraped the food scraps into a bucket that was used for such a purpose. My back to Grace, I worked and kept watch on Hyrum out the window.

After she and Michael moved to Junction last October, she and I fell to talking whenever we were together. We talked about the boys and we talked about the lessons Michael was teaching the children at the schoolhouse. We talked about Mama and Father back in Parowan and about our brothers and sister and their families.

Then the nature of our visits changed. It was in November. While Hyrum played outside and I tidied the kitchen, instead of talking, Grace read to me from the Book of Mormon. The passages – *But wo, wo unto him who knoweth that he rebelleth against God!* and *If ye will not nourish the word, looking forward with an eye of faith to the fruit thereof, ye can never pluck of the fruit of the tree of life* – made my cheeks burn. I understood why Grace read those lines.

In Parowan, Michael and Grace lived their lives according to the church teachings. Junction, though, wasn't like Parowan. Junction was what Samuel called an in-between place. Most of us ignored the practices that gave us pause. Yet we called ourselves Latter-day Saints. On Sundays, many of us gathered in the schoolhouse and listened to those who felt called upon to preach. We said the Blessing of the Bread and upheld the sacrament of the Lord's Supper. None of us, though, said anything about needing a bishop. A bishop would guide our spiritual lives. He'd organize us into committees. He'd assign duties that would bind us together in a firm grip. We didn't want that. We each lived our faith as we saw fit. We didn't judge our neighbors.

I was taken aback when Michael and Grace moved here. They were pious, firm believers. Without questioning them, I accepted the story that they came here so Michael could be our first schoolmaster. But in my heart, I believed that something painful must have happened. They must have needed distance from the church.

I didn't ask. That was how we did it in Junction. Even when it was family, we stayed out of each other's business.

In November, when Grace started the practice of reading to me, I understood she disapproved of Junction.

Then in December, the nature of our visits changed again. Samuel hadn't come home as expected. 'Stay with us,' Grace said when he was fourteen days overdue. This was before we knew about the rockslide taking out the trail. 'You shouldn't be alone. Not at this time.'

'Why's that?' I'd said, the words snapping.

She flushed. 'It's just . . .' Her voice broke. She gathered herself. 'This isn't like Samuel to be late. And no letters this whole time. I'm worried about him. I can hardly bear to think what might have happened.'

'Then don't.'

Since then, she had not brought up Samuel's absence but our visits had become brittle. Grace read from the Book of Mormon and glanced at me from time to time as if she expected me to break into small pieces. As the days went by, I watched her stomach swell and her face hollow. Today was different, though. Today, she didn't read. Our tongues were tied in a way they hadn't been before.

A pot of water simmered on the stove. I poured it into the dish basin. Steam rose up, and I breathed it in. I wanted it to burn away the cold fear that had settled in my being. Grace knew about the man I'd sheltered. When the deputies came and questioned her, it'd show on her face.

Her rocker made a soft swish on the braided rug as she rocked back and forth. I began to wash the dishes. Outside, Hyrum patted snow into a rounded heap.

The air in the cabin was heavy with unspoken thoughts.

I said, 'Surely wish the sun would come out.'

The rocking chair went quiet. 'Michael's troubled,' Grace said.

'What?' I turned to face her. Water dripped from my hands. I wiped them on my apron.

'I can't keep it to myself any longer. Michael's troubled by what goes on here.'

Michael knew about the men and Floral Ranch. Someone told him. Or he'd guessed. It was a small town. Even if we didn't talk about certain things, that didn't mean people didn't know. Not that Michael would be against what we did for the men. He'd believe that we did it to uphold the revelations and covenants of the church. The risks, though, would make him uneasy.

Grace said, 'He believes the people in Junction have strayed from the church.'

Relief swept through me. She didn't know about the man.

'It pains us,' she was saying. 'We didn't want to see what was before our eyes. We didn't want to think it about anyone here.' Her words ran past me. I leaned against the counter, my relief leaving me weak. Grace didn't know. She hadn't seen anything out of the ordinary.

Grace said, 'I see it upsets you, too.'

'Yes,' I said, although I'd lost hold of what she was saying.

'Michael isn't the only one who's concerned. The stake presidents are, too. So's Father.'

Her words began to take on a new meaning. 'Father?'

'Yes. Father most of all. You and Brother Samuel have been here for more than five years. Some of the others almost as long. All those years, Deborah, and there still isn't a bishop. Or a wardhouse. Or a chapel. There's concern the people here have left the church.'

'Father said this?'

'And the other stake presidents.'

They could declare us apostates. We'd be shunned by our families. That was if Nels got the man safely to Floral Ranch. If we weren't caught and arrested.

Grace looked at me, waiting. Finally I said, 'No chapel by name, that's true. The schoolhouse serves as our church and wardhouse.'

'But no bishop?'

What had once puzzled me, was now clear. I looked over my shoulder. Out the window, Hyrum scooped up snow in his gloved hands and patted it on top of what was beginning to look like a low wall. I turned back to Grace. 'Did Father and the other stake presidents send you and Michael here? To give them a report about us? Is that the real reason you moved here?'

She said, 'Can you see Hyrum?'

I looked again out the window. 'Yes. He's right here.'

'Come sit down. Please.'

Every part of me felt wooden. Michael was sent to bring us back into the church. I should have known.

I sat down in the upholstered chair across from Grace. She tucked the loose strands of hair behind her ears. Her neck was splotched with patches of red, her nerves showing. She couldn't meet my eyes.

I said, 'What do Father and the others say about us?'

Grace twisted her gold wedding band. 'He's worried for you, for your soul. And for everyone here. You need a bishop. He and the others are sure a bishop will heal what's wrong in Junction.' She paused. 'There are rumors, disturbing rumors.' Her glance flickered to the portrait of Joseph Smith, then back to me. 'We've heard that some of the fruit grown here is distilled for spirits.'

'Spirits?'

'Alcohol.'

'You can't listen to such talk. Those are rumors.'

'Then you've heard this talk, too?'

'I don't pay rumors any mind.' I brushed my hand over my skirt as if to rid myself of rumors, then stopped when I saw the shake in my hand. Father and the others might declare me an apostate. They could declare me dead to them.

Grace said, 'I said much the same to Michael. These rumors were probably started by gentiles. But no bishop? No one can ignore that.'

'Was Michael sent to be our bishop?'

'And to be the schoolmaster. The children here are in dire need of instruction. As we all are.'

'You should have told me this before.'

'I wanted to. But I couldn't. I didn't want you to think I thought bad of you. I don't. It's the others . . .' Her voice trailed off. Her eyes watered. She wiped her cheeks. 'Michael's talked to all the men here more times than I can count. He's willing to serve as bishop. He brought it up again last Sunday after worship. He could have been talking in tongues from the way they looked at him. They're not even willing to put it to a vote. Did you know that?'

'No.'

'Doesn't it concern you?'

'We're all Saints here.'

'Everyone?'

'Yes.' Then I said something about Hyrum. I got up and went to the window. He was still busy building his fort. I should have guessed the truth about Michael's decision to come here. He was devoted to the church. I hadn't let myself think about it, though. I wanted to have Grace and her family close. She was more like a daughter than a sister. When Samuel and I were first married and lived in Parowan, she and I were homesick for each other. Samuel set up a cot for her in a small room off our kitchen so she could live with us. I watched her grow up. I witnessed her courtship with Michael and then her marriage. My heart ached when Samuel and I moved to Junction. Every week I wrote her long letters. Last summer, I rejoiced when Grace wrote with the news that Michael wanted to be Junction's schoolmaster. It was an opportunity to shape the minds of young pupils, he'd believed. For me, it meant Grace and I were reunited.

I left the window and sat down across from her. 'Grace. We're different here. But in our hearts, we're all Saints.'

She pressed her fingertips to her lips, then put her hand on her stomach. 'If the men fail to elect a bishop by spring, we'll receive orders to go to another outpost. One that will welcome us.'

'But you can't. I . . .' My words tripped. 'You've only been here a few months. As for a bishop, I'll speak to the women.'

'The men won't take a vote, Deborah. It's not important to them. But it is to us. We're concerned for the boys. Jacob and Joe ask questions. They want to know who our bishop is. They want to know why the Millers and Brother Nels don't always come to Sunday services. This isn't how we want to raise our children.' She stopped and glanced again at the portrait of Joseph Smith, then, 'We want you to come with us.'

'What?'

'It'd worry me no end to think of you here in a place without a bishop. Michael agrees. And the boys are fond of you.'

'No.' I stood up. 'This is our home. Samuel's and mine.'

'But Brother Samuel is gone so much. If you're with us, you won't be alone.'

'Samuel's usually gone just three months.'

'But this year . . .' Her words faded.

'He's on his way home. There was a rockslide, you know what Brother Nels said. Samuel's been forced to take a longer route.'

'Deborah.'

I went to the window. Outside, Hyrum had found a stick and was waving it around like a sword. I'd heard the pity in Grace's voice. I was a woman who didn't have children. My husband traveled and left me on my own. Worst of all, I lived in a place that had strayed from the church.

Grace said, 'Hyrum's all right?'

'Yes.' My throat was tight, it was hard to breathe. Trouble came at me from all directions. Father's doubts about me. Grace leaving. Nels and the man who had stayed the night in my barn. Samuel not home.

'I'm sorry, Sister.' Grace had come to the kitchen and stood beside me. She put her arm around my waist. I turned in to her and embraced her. 'Do you want to leave?' I said as we held onto one another.

'The biggest part of me does.' Her voice was a whisper in my ear. 'For the children.'

I should have known this, too. I pressed my cheek into Grace's hair. I couldn't think about her leaving. Right now, there were bigger worries. Spring was months away. So much could happen before then.

She said, 'Please come with us.'

'No. Samuel and I aren't leaving.' I let go of her and stepped back. 'We won't talk of it again. It's better that way.'

This was what we always did. We didn't talk about the things that hurt us. Or the things that might. It was as if silence could stop pain and fear.

'I've distressed you,' Grace said. 'You're white as a sheet.'

I shook my head. 'Please. Let's not talk about it.' With that, I turned and rapped on the window. Hyrum looked up at me. I waved at him signaling it was time to come in. Then I walked away from my sister and went to the door to wait for Hyrum.

———

The snow sucked at my boots as I walked home through the orchard. An ache burned in my chest. Grace was going to leave Junction.

I wasn't alone, I told myself. Samuel will come home. Any day.

I was almost at my cabin when I saw something in the distance move. I stopped and blinked hard. It was a man on horseback coming from the direction of the Wastelands. One man. Not two or three.

Samuel. My knees buckled. I caught myself. A sense of airiness washed through me. I began to walk to him, the snow falling around us. I tried to call out his name. I couldn't get my throat to work. I hurried to him, my hand raised, snow breaking under my boots.

Samuel didn't return the greeting.

Something was wrong. Samuel would call out to me. He would slide off his horse and come running. This man didn't. He kept riding, not changing his pace, not saying my name, just riding, coming toward me.

It wasn't Samuel. My feet stumbled to a halt. Not Samuel.

A great pain welled up inside of me. I pressed a hand to my breastbone to push against the hurt of disappointment.

My breath shuddering, I flicked away the tears and watched this man who wasn't my husband. His horse plodded but he rode high in the saddle with his shoulders back. He was some forty paces away and kept coming.

Fear overrode the pain in my heart. The man's coat was dark. His hat was wide-brimmed, and the lower half of his face was covered with his scarf. I felt his boldness as he looked at me, my barn, and then my orchard. His chin tilted up. His gaze seemed to pierce the buttes. An enemy.

His gaze shifted back to me. I felt the hardness of his stare. I wanted to run. A deputy. Or an outlaw.

Don't let him see you're scared, I told myself. Treat him like you would any stranger who showed up in this manner.

His horse wheezed. His saddle creaked as he rode toward me. My pulse skipped. He was a lawman, not an outlaw. Lawmen didn't wear uniforms like army men. They didn't have to. There was something about them – an air of authority, the determined set of their shoulders – that showed what they were. Like this one. He'd come through eight miles of the Wastelands. Against all reason, he must have started out in the dark. Snow covered the trail but that hadn't stopped him.

He was closer now. At any moment he'd see the tracks along the creek that I tried to cover.

None of this was of my making, I thought. None of it. This was my property, my home. Leave me alone, I wanted to say. I've done nothing to you.

'Stop right there,' I heard myself call out.

He pulled up on the reins, halting the horse but not moving otherwise. We studied each other. A long rifle rode crossways behind the saddle horn and in front of the man. I said, 'Who are you?'

He pushed his scarf down to his chin. 'Name's Fletcher.' His breath was a white cloud but his tone was deliberate. 'Marshal Thomas S. Fletcher with the United States Government.'

He reached inside his coat and took something out. He held it up for me to see. It was a metal star. His badge. I stood looking up at it, my thoughts tumbling. He'd said he was a marshal. But marshals didn't hunt men with plural wives. Their deputies did.

He held the badge out without speaking. Finally, he put it back inside his coat.

'You got a husband?' he said.

'Yes.'

'I have matters to discuss with him.'

He spoke with an accent, the kind that stretched words long. He was from the South, I thought.

I said, 'He's working.'

'Doing what? Where is he?'

'He's working in another town.'

'Another town. Is that what you people call Floral Ranch?'

'What?'

'Don't you act ignorant with me. Where's your husband?'

'He's a wheelwright. He travels from town to town. What's this all about?'

'I'm looking for Lewis Braden. Where is he?'

'There aren't any Bradens here.'

'You sure about that? You sure your husband's not hiding him?'

'I don't know what you're talking about.'

The marshal coughed, then cleared his throat. He said, 'I find that mighty peculiar. I've been tracking Lewis Braden since Tennessee and have good reason to know he's here. Or been here. I've got a warrant for his arrest.'

I took a step backward.

The lawman said, 'I'll have myself a look around the place.' He pointed to my barn. 'I'll start there, then the cabin.' He tipped his head back, squinted his eyes against the falling snow, and looked up at the buttes. My teeth chattered. I clamped my jaw tight. His gaze swept over the orchards before turning back to me.

He said, 'Who lives here with you? Other than your husband who happens not to be here.'

'Just me.'

'Nobody else?'

I shook my head.

'You a Mormon?'

'Yes.'

'There're others of your kind here?'

'Yes.'

'Where?'

'They live along the creek.' I pointed past my plum orchard. The marshal didn't bother to look. He squinted, looking at me like he didn't believe a word I said.

Samuel, I thought. I'm scared.

The marshal stood up in his saddle, stretching, then sat back down. He clicked his tongue twice and flicked the reins. 'Don't do anything foolish,' he said as he rode past me and toward the barn.

SAMUEL

Eighty-nine days ago

> *October 15, 1887*
> *Utah Territory*

Dear Wife Deborah,

I trust You are well and the Apple Harvest is good for Nels and the Others. Is Buttercup minding her Manners? I believe She is ornery only for Me. I am in Johnson. It is a new Outpost. There are more Hoot Owls in a handful of trees than People.

There are two Familys. The Church sent Them in May. All ready there is a Childs grave in a hard patch of land They call a Cemetery. Rain is rare in these parts. The Creek is down to a trickle. Afternoons the North Clouds turn black. The familys wait and pray Wind will blow the Clouds this way. It never does. I fear for the people here. I do not see how they can hold out much longer.

Do not worry about me. My bones got so wet from the Rain up by Escalante that I will be a long Time drying out.

In the Morning I go North and some West to Mt. Carmel. It will not take long to get there. Likely You will hear Snort and Wally complaining all the way from here. They have loud opinions about creek beds that lack water. I am still carrying my first Letter to You. But I am sure to come across Some One that will get both of these to You.

This Sun baked Country is not meant for Familys. It was wrong of the Church to send them here. It makes Me glad for Junction. But the Cliffs here are something to behold. They rise up in great Swirls of pink and white Rock. The Stars hang low. They make a Man believe He can jump up and touch Them. If You were with Me I would try to do that just to hear You laugh.

Your Husband,
Samuel Tyler

CHAPTER SIX

DEBORAH – THE TROUGH

January 12, 1888

The marshal crowded my cabin. I felt this from the moment I let him inside after he'd had his look around the barn. It was like the ceiling had dropped lower. The walls felt tight around me and it wasn't just because of his size. Or because I was alone with him. It was how he looked at me, his dark eyes shadowed with suspicion.

He stood just inside the door, his coat shimmering with snow. He held his hat in one hand. His rifle was in the other with the barrel pointed down.

I backed away from him so that the kitchen table was between us.

The marshal eyed Samuel's rifle that was propped in a kitchen corner. From there, his gaze went to the two parlor chairs and the small picture in the parlor half of the front room. My pulse was so loud in my ears that I couldn't hear the clock's tick. Hurry home, Nels, I thought. Be home before this lawman gets to your place.

The marshal studied the open door that went to the other room.

'There's no one else here,' I said. 'But you may look around.' It took everything I had to keep my voice steady. It wouldn't pay to be meek. That might tell him how scared I was and that I had something to hide. I said, 'If you would, please wipe your boots on the door rug. The floor's newly washed.'

'I know my manners.'

'Yes. Of course. I didn't mean any offense.'

He raised his eyebrows but didn't say anything. He did as I asked. After the small rug was streaked with icy clumps of snow and mud, the man took a few long strides across the room and stood in the doorway of the bedroom. He looked in, seeing, I believed, the dresser with Samuel's rocks beside my comb, brush, and hand mirror. There was also Samuel's Sunday suit that hung on a wall peg to consider. My two dresses and nightclothes were on pegs too, and on the floor were the butter-colored shoes I wore to services during fair weather.

Still in the doorway, the marshal crouched down. The tail of his long coat bunched on the floor. He was looking under the bed, I thought. He held the stock of his rifle under one arm so that it was now pointed at the bed. Then it came to me that he wasn't going to go into the room. Something held him back. Maybe he understood it wasn't right to go into a woman's bedroom.

The marshal put a hand on the door frame. His knees popped when he straightened. He turned to face me, the rifle barrel down. Dark patches shadowed his red-rimmed eyes, and crisscrossing lines ran to his cheekbones. His deep brown hair was creased and mashed from his hat. Even in the poor light I could see the gray in his mustache and that his cheeks and chin were in need of a shave. A patch of skin along his right cheekbone was slick and yellow. Frostbite.

He said, 'Where'd you say your husband was?'

'He's a wheelwright, he goes from town to town south of here.'

'This time of year?'

'He's due home any moment.'

'He's got other wives in those towns?'

'No.'

'You expect me to believe that?'

'It's true. We don't practice plural marriage.'

'Just like your claim about not seeing Lewis Braden is true?'

I felt my face flush. The air in the cabin was all of a sudden overheated and close. I said, 'I haven't seen this Lewis Braden. I don't know anything about him.'

'You have a horse?'

He'd found the pile of horse dung, I thought. I'd tried to cover the dung but he must have seen it. I said, 'I borrow my brother-in-law's horse from time to time.'

'Where's he live?'

'On the other side of the plum orchard.'

'He's home? Or maybe he's away like your husband is. Maybe they're both taking Braden to Floral Ranch.'

'My brother-in-law's at the schoolhouse. He's the school-master.'

The marshal put his head back like he was looking down his nose at me. Air caught in my throat. It was hard to breathe.

He said, 'Tell me about Floral Ranch.'

I could lie and say I'd never heard of it. But patches of truth might make the lies harder to find. I said, 'I've never been there. The travel's too hard.'

'Tell me what you know.'

'A family lives there, that's what I've heard. They have orchards. But I don't know them, they don't come this way. They trade in towns on the other side of the canyons. The far east side, not our side. That's what I've been told.'

The lawman's gaze pierced me. He knew I was lying, I thought. Before I could stop myself, I touched my forehead. It was damp with sweat. Say something, I told myself. Something any woman might say. I put my hand on the back of the chair to steady myself.

'This man you're looking for,' I said. 'If he comes this way, is he dangerous? Could he hurt me? What's he done?'

'He's got a pack of wives.'

'A pack?'

Anger flashed across his face. He took a step toward me. I backed away, bumping into the cooking counter. 'Three wives,' he said. His thick drawl had gone hard. 'That's what Braden calls them. Wives. The last one's a girl, just sixteen.'

I didn't know what to say.

'I know he was here. There's water in two troughs. One's in the stall used by that cow of yours. One animal, two stalls with water. I find that mighty odd. A trough without an animal to water should be dry. Or, seems to me, if there's water, it should be all the way iced over, no animal there to do any drinking. But it wasn't. Only a layer of ice along the edge, ice as thin as a slip of paper.' He paused. 'You know why that is?'

'It's for my cow. I filled both this morning.'

'You hauled water to two stalls when one would do? You think I believe that?'

'It's true.'

He shook that off. 'Another animal was in the barn. One that isn't there now. Lewis Braden's horse. He paused, disgust showing in his eyes. 'Isn't that so?'

'No.'

The marshal slapped his hat against the side of his leg, then put it on. He walked toward the door. His hand clenched his rifle and his footfall was crisp with anger. He opened the

door. Snow-filled air rushed in. He looked at me. 'You're covering for Braden, it's how you people do. You're good at that.
But where I come from in Tennessee, we don't do harm to
women. Not like you people do. Neither do we lay the blame
on others. Lying is what you Mormons do. That book of you
all's is a pack of lies. You all lie about how your men charm
young women. You all lied about what happened at Mountain
Meadows.'

The air left the room. Thirty years ago, gentiles in a wagon
train on their way to California were killed where they had
camped not far from Cedar City. The place was Mountain
Meadows.

The marshal said, 'You reckoned I didn't know about that,
didn't you?'

'I had nothing to do with any of that.'

'Like you don't know anything about Lewis Braden.'

I couldn't find words. He said, 'Where I come from, we
don't force women to do things against their will. We don't
shake them into talking. Not even women who lie.' Then he
walked out into the weather, the door left open.

———

On my knees, I put a rag over the wet muddy footprints on
the door rug. The palms of both hands flat on the rag, I
pressed hard. I wanted to get rid of the marshal's presence in
my home. Just like I wanted to get rid of the trough I hadn't
thought to empty.

I pressed harder on the soiled rug. Somehow the marshal
came through the Wastelands faster than I'd figured. Somehow I had overlooked the trough. If we got caught, it was
my fault.

The marshal was probably following my shuffled tracks

this very moment. He'd stop at Grace's and question her. From there, he would follow the tracks to Nels'. It was half past two. Nels wouldn't be back yet.

Mountain Meadows. Bringing that up was the marshal's way of unnerving me all the more. Horrible things had gone on there. I was six when it happened, and Mountain Meadows wasn't all that far from Parowan where I lived. Only a handful of children from a wagon party traveling from Arkansas to California survived the massacre.

Paiutes had done the killing. I'd grown up believing that. The Indians were provoked by the members of the wagon party, church elders said. The gentiles had poisoned the Paiutes' drinking water.

Rumors and the surviving children told a different story. They said white men, painted to look like Indians, killed the travelers. White men who were Saints. Saints who believed gentiles were poking their noses too much into the church's business.

Twenty years after the massacre, one Saint was tried and convicted for the killings. His punishment was the firing squad.

Whispered rumors said there were others. One man couldn't kill a wagon party of over a hundred people. Other Saints, it was said, were guilty of killing innocent women and children.

Since Mountain Meadows, the United States had turned against us all the more. They claimed we knew more than we were saying. They claimed we lied to protect guilty men. They believed that all of us who lived in this part of Utah were responsible for the deaths.

Saints tried to forget the massacre. Some gentiles hadn't. The marshal was one of those. And now he had caught me in a lie.

The dirty rag in my hands, I rocked back on my heels. It didn't fit that he was a marshal. Marshals didn't hunt outlaws. They ran their states' courts and jails. Their deputies did the tracking.

A marshal. Trouble like never before. Whatever Braden had done to bring this on, it was bad.

And where were the marshal's deputies? He wouldn't come here alone. They were out there somewhere. They might be watching me.

The minute hand on the clock had barely moved. Nels was probably at least an hour from Junction. It was snowing but likely the tracks I'd trampled early this morning showed as a trail of soft-edged indentations. The marshal might be at Grace's cabin. I'd told him I had family there. He might think they had something to do with hiding Braden. The marshal would push his way inside with his questions. He aimed to catch Braden and because of my carelessness, he knew Braden had been here.

I'd never had dealings with a marshal before. Only deputies. Grace hadn't dealt with either.

The marshal might expect me to try to send a warning of some kind. He could be watching me. Or his deputies were. It hurt to think of Grace and Hyrum alone with a lawman but I had to keep away from them. I couldn't do what the marshal might expect. I'd made one mistake, and maybe I'd made others. I couldn't make any more.

Never again, I told myself. I went back to cleaning the rug, pressing hard on the watery tracks. 'You've come to the wrong place,' I'd say to the next stranger who showed up at my door. Charity was a virtue and the Book of Mormon said it was the pure love of Christ. I believed that. But it was someone else's turn to help the men with plural wives. I'd done it long enough.

My hands went still. There wouldn't be a next time. Not if the marshal caught Lewis Braden. I'd be arrested, convicted of helping a felon, and my property taken from me. My name would be in gentile newspapers. There would be sly hints of my depravity.

I could go to jail. Nels, too. I couldn't bear the thought of Samuel coming home and finding me gone.

All because of Braden, a man I didn't know until yesterday. Three wives, the marshal said about him. He made it out to be something filthy, as if the women were forced to marry against their will. It wasn't like that. Braden would have asked church elders for permission to have more than one wife. The elders would consider his devotion and service to the church. They'd ask if he had the means to support more wives and children. 'Are you willing to marry this man, Sister?' they'd ask the third woman just as they had asked the second wife.

'Yes,' the third woman must have answered. Her good fortune might have made her rejoice. Marriage to a man with plural wives was said to ensure everlasting life in the celestial kingdom.

I balled the wet rag, stood up, and went to the parlor window that faced the plum orchard and Grace's cabin. The snowfall was dense and I couldn't see past the first row of trees. If the marshal was at Grace's, her hazel eyes would be wide with bewilderment and fear. Hyrum might be crying as he held onto her skirt. But her bewilderment was her protection and so was the truth. She didn't know about Braden, her husband was at the schoolhouse, and I had visited her this afternoon like I always did.

Lewis Braden's third wife was sixteen, the marshal had

said, his tone bitter. That was young but some girls knew their minds early. Grace had. She'd married Michael the day after her sixteenth birthday and would have married him sooner if our father had allowed it.

It wasn't the same. Grace had been sixteen to Michael's twenty. Braden looked to be in his early thirties, much older than his third wife.

Her age riled the marshal, I thought. Not plural marriage itself. Otherwise he would have said something about the other two wives. It was the girl that had him worked up. Maybe it wasn't only because she was young. There must be something different about her. Or about Braden.

The marshal's bitterness about Mountain Meadows was different, too. No other lawman had ever said anything about it. Maybe he knew someone who'd been killed there. Or it could be he was like other gentiles who used the massacre as one more thing to hold against us.

I left the window. In the kitchen I put the rag in the empty laundry basin. Questioning Grace would slow the marshal, I thought. From there, he might go to the schoolhouse to speak to Michael. By the time he got around to following the tracks that crossed the bridge, Nels could be home. The marshal would find everyone where they should be, nothing out of place.

Except for the water in the trough. And anything else I overlooked.

Time hung. Three o'clock. No deputies. Not yet. The marshal must have left Grace's by now. He might be at the school-house questioning Michael. Or he might be looking around Nels' place.

Four o'clock. I thought by now Grace or Michael would have come to my cabin. I thought they'd tell me about the marshal. They hadn't. And Nels. Surely he was home by now. The marshal could be questioning him this very moment.

Five o'clock. I choked down some venison and bread. I didn't understand why gentiles and Saints couldn't live together in peace. When I was a child and first learned about the murders of Joseph and Hyrum Smith, I asked my mother, 'Why'd they do this to the Prophet and his brother?' We were in the kitchen and she was peeling potatoes. She put down her paring knife and looked into my eyes. 'Because the angel Moroni revealed to the Prophet the existence of more holy scripture. Because he was the one who found the scriptures, the golden tablets. Gentiles don't know what to make of that. Why would God send an angel to a farmer's son? It scared them. And when folks are scared, they're not in their right minds. They're likely to do anything.' She paused, her eyebrows pulled close. 'Don't ever lose sight of that, Deborah, should you have dealings with gentiles.'

Half past five. I needed to milk Buttercup and take warm water to the chickens. I couldn't get myself to move.

———

It was a few minutes past seven when Nels pounded on the door, calling my name. 'There's been an accident,' he said as I let him in. In the lamplight, his gray eyes watered from the cold and his wheat-colored eyebrows and mustache were crusted with ice. 'Get your coat,' he said. 'Hurry.'

'An accident?'

'It's a lawman. His head's hurt bad, maybe cracked.'

My heart knocked against my ribcage.

'He's at my cabin. Now hurry.'

'Your cabin? He's here? What happened?'

Nels took my coat from the wall peg and thrust it at me. 'Hurry.'

I couldn't move. I couldn't get Nels' words to make sense.

'Wouldn't bring you into this if I didn't have to,' he said. 'But when other lawmen get here, there should be a woman tending the hurt man. That way they'll see we're doing what we can. We can't give them one more thing to hold against us.'

The marshal, hurt. At Nels'. The marshal who knew Braden had been here. They'll burn our orchards down.

'It can't be me looking after him,' Nels was saying. 'I've got to get Braden hid.'

'Braden? But you took him—'

'He's at my place.'

I reared back as if I'd been struck. 'He's here? With the marshal?'

'I know it. It's bad. Now let's go.'

Black spots floated before my eyes. Our homes taken from us. Junction deserted. Samuel not able to find me.

Nels' hand was on my arm, propping me up. I blinked the spots away and saw the deep worry lines between his eyebrows. I said, 'Tell me what happened.'

'Not now. Later. We're wasting time.' His tone was sharp and shook me into doing what he wanted. I got ready, my thoughts scattered, while Nels put the flames out in my lamps. The cabin went dark and then we were outside.

Nightfall had come on quick but the snow cast a glow. It was still coming down but was heavy with ice and even though the brim of my hat was wide, it stung my face. I slitted my eyes against it. Nels' horse, Bob, was at the hitching rail off to the side of the cabin. Straining to see, I stepped high in the foot-deep snow, holding up my coat and skirt with both hands. Nels grasped my upper arm.

His horse wore only a blanket and Nels helped me up. He hoisted himself up behind me and put his arms around me to take the reins while I held onto the mane. Bob pressed forward, wanting to get home but the deep snow slowed him. Behind me, Nels felt tight with nerves. He looked over my left shoulder and leaned in to me so that I leaned forward, too, helping Bob fight against the snow.

We followed the creek east. It wasn't all the way frozen over and in the middle it roared as it rushed over the rocks. All afternoon I thought Grace would come to my cabin and tell me the marshal had questioned her. She'd demand to know what was behind all of this. But Grace hadn't come. Just like nothing else had played out as I'd imagined.

I strained, looking into the dark. We weren't close enough to Grace's to see a light in her window.

'Me and Braden split up this morning,' Nels said from behind me, his voice startling me. 'Because of the tracks. Couldn't have double prints. I had to throw off the marshal.'

I nodded.

'Braden got lost. I had to backtrack, find him. Lost a lot of time.' His words came out in quick puffs. Like a confession, I thought.

'Then the snow took up harder. I couldn't read the landmarks for the cut to Floral Ranch. We were going in circles and his horse was near to give out. Once I got my bearings, Braden and I turned back. Didn't want to get caught out in the dark, not in this weather. Not without shelter.' Nels paused, then, 'That's when it happened. When we came across the marshal. He was on the ground. Hurt bad.'

'How bad?'

Nels didn't say anything. I thought he hadn't heard but then he said, 'He's got a knot the size of an egg on his head. He can't walk, can't hardly talk.'

'Oh Heavenly Father.'

I felt Nels nod. I said, 'Could he die?'

'Maybe.' Then, 'If he pulls through, he'll talk.'

My breathing was shallow and quick. It was like the marshal was here, standing over me and bearing down with accusations that I couldn't deny.

'Sister Deborah, we couldn't leave him.' I felt Nels take in some air, then let go of it. He said, 'He could have frozen to death. If the coyotes didn't get him first.' Nels' words came slow. It was like he was sorting through them, deciding what to tell me. He said, 'Leaving the marshal would work on me. Braden said the same. So we brought him back, hard as it could go on all of us. We had to.'

Nels' horse dipped and staggered, the snow-covered ground uneven. His arms tightened around me. Bob steadied and lurched forward. I wanted the marshal to go back to where he'd come from. I wanted it to be yesterday so I could close my door against Braden and tell him I couldn't help.

If only Nels and Braden hadn't found the marshal. If only nature had been allowed to take its course.

Nels went on, 'If we'd left him, we'd be no better than our enemies.' He shifted his weight. 'The marshal's a gentile but he's still one of God's children.'

My face flamed with shame. I pushed away my ugly thought about nature taking its course. I swallowed hard, then said, 'You did right.'

Nels went quiet. My thoughts darted and clashed. The

marshal. An accident. Our enemy. But one of God's children. And I had to take care of him.

———·———

'There's ice under the snow,' Nels said about the bridge when we got to it. He dismounted, took the reins, and began to walk us across, sliding some while trying to keep Bob from going too fast and falling. I clutched the mane and my legs gripped the horse tighter.

'Brother Nels,' I said, raising my voice so he could hear me over the crunch of his footfall and the rush of the creek below us. 'I did something bad.'

He was a dark figure against the snowfall but I saw him turn his head quickly toward me to let me know he'd heard. I said, 'This afternoon when the marshal came, he found water in a trough where there shouldn't have been any. I didn't think to empty it but the marshal saw it. He knew Braden was in my barn. He knew to keep looking.'

Still walking, Nels looked over his shoulder at me. 'It doesn't matter. A man like him would have pressed on.'

I wasn't so sure about that but I kept it to myself. I said, 'Maybe things aren't as bad as you think. When you found the marshal, he was bad off. And probably half-frozen. He might not have recognized Braden.'

Nels didn't say anything.

I said, 'The fall could have made his eyesight fuzzy. If he gets better and talks, he might not remember seeing Braden. Isn't that so?'

Nels stopped. The horse skidded to a halt. I leaned forward on Bob and waited for Nels to tell me there was a chance we'd come out of this all right. Surely even a gentile jury knew water in a trough wasn't enough to condemn us.

His back to me, he began to walk, leading Bob off the icy bridge like he hadn't heard me. Nels had, though. Otherwise he would have mounted the horse for the last of the way to his cabin. Instead, he stayed away from me, trudging through the snow like he didn't want to hear any more questions.

A great trembling took hold of me. My teeth chattered. I clamped my mouth shut but couldn't stop the shaking that came from deep inside of me. Nels was keeping something from me. Something that could ruin us.

CHAPTER SEVEN

DEBORAH – THE BRIDGE

January 12, 1888

Ruin. Blood thumped in my ears. The bridge behind us, everything happened in a rush: Nels' brown dog bounding through the snow to meet us, Braden letting us in, the overheated one-room cabin, the musty smell of wet wool, the stench of vomit, the marshal in Nels' bed with the blankets pulled to his shoulders, and Braden backing up to the kitchen table to make room for us.

'Is he . . . ?' Nels said.

'Still the same,' Braden said. He glanced toward me where I stood by the door. I looked away from him. I didn't want to see his face in the lamplight. When more lawmen came, and I was sure there'd be more, I had to be able to tell them I didn't know the man they were looking for.

'Has he said anything?' Nels said.

'Tries but I can't make out what it is.'

Nels gave Braden a narrow-eyed look. He didn't believe him, I thought. Nels said, 'Is he moving any?'

'Not much other than his foot. Sometimes it jerks.'

Nels went to the back wall, stood over the bed, and looked down at the marshal. The marshal, his head on a pillow, was on his back. He didn't look anything like the man who earlier today showed me his badge.

Nels took his gloves off and turned the blankets down far

enough that I saw the marshal had on his vest and shirt. He'd been put to bed still dressed. The stink of vomit hit all the harder. I tried not to breathe it in but it filled the too-warm cabin and overtook the musty smell of wet wool. All at once waves of rank sweat came at me. I backed up even closer to the door, grateful for the drafts of cold air around the frame.

The marshal mumbled, then groaned. A shudder ran through me.

Nels placed the palm of his right hand on the marshal's chest and bowed his head. He was either measuring the marshal's heartbeat or praying. Before I could decide which, Nels pulled the blankets back up, went to the kitchen, and got the cloth bag that hung from the wall. 'Let's go,' he said to Braden, his back to him as filled the bag with the cans of food stacked on a shelf.

'No,' Braden said. 'I'm not hiding. Not after what I did.'

Nels' hands stopped. He turned around. 'That's not what we agreed to. Get your things.'

'Can't. This is all my doing. Come dawn, I'll go back and turn myself in. Tell them what happened.'

'No, you won't.'

I didn't know what to make of this. It didn't make sense that Braden had come this far and now wanted to give himself up.

Braden said, 'I prayed about it, Brother. God has spoken. He told me I have to do what's right.'

'Is that so?' Nels put down the bag and stepped close to Braden, the two men square to one another. Braden was broader through the chest but Nels was taller. 'And did God say that when you turn yourself in, when you tell how the marshal came to be laid up in my bed, that it's not only your hide but ours?' Nels nodded toward me. 'Hers, mine, and likely everybody else's in Junction.'

'I'll tell them you had nothing to do with it. This is between me and him. I'll tell them I was by myself when I found him, that I brought him here for help.'

'You think they'll believe you?' Nels kept his voice low. The marshal, bad off as he was, might be able to hear. 'They've had us in their sights for a long time. They know we help people like you, they just haven't caught us. If they find you here or if you turn yourself in, they'll come after us. You'll have more on your conscience than just the marshal. Now let's go. We're wasting time.'

'When he gets better, he'll talk.'

'Then they've got us. If he gets better. Right now, I'll take that chance. And so will you.' Nels inclined his head toward me. 'Or you'll have this woman's fate on your head. And others'.'

Braden looked at me, then at the marshal. Nels' face was set. He glared at Braden, his eyes dark with anger. I'd never seen Nels this way before. Something had happened that I didn't know about. Whatever it was, Braden had to get as far away from the marshal and Junction as possible.

'Go with him,' I said to Braden. 'Please.'

He shook his head. 'God said otherwise.'

'You have wives? And children?'

'Yes.'

'Think of them. What's best for them? You in jail? Or free to come home when this quiets down?'

Braden's gaze was fixed on the marshal.

'My father once hid from gentiles. In Nauvoo.' My words surprised me. It had been years since I'd thought about this story that my father told about his first wife, Alice. 'It was the night the Prophet Joseph Smith and his brother were murdered. My father had been warned the mob was coming for him next, he and the Prophet were friends. My father's wife begged him not to fight them. He was outnumbered. She convinced him to hide in a neighboring town. He didn't want to but did it anyway. When the gentiles came looking for my father, his wife let them in the house. She told them she hoped they'd find her husband. He'd taken up drink, she said. Likely he was in a saloon somewhere, spending money they didn't have. Her words were so bitter the gentiles left. It burned my father's pride to have his wife lie for him. But he did it for his family, for his children.'

Braden ran his hand over his beard. For a moment I thought I'd made matters worse. Then something began to slide inside of him, a slight sinking of his shoulders.

'Let's go,' Nels said.

Braden turned to me. 'You'll look after him?'

'I'll do what I can.'

'Promise me, Sister. Tell me you'll take care of him.'

'Yes. I promise. Now go. Please.'

Braden looked at the marshal, then at me. 'All right,' he said, reaching for his coat that was draped on a kitchen chair. 'I'll do it your way.'

Nels gave him a sharp look. He worked his right hand into his glove, then the left hand, the fringe on the cuffs swinging. He said, 'The marshal's horse is in the barn.' His words were directed to me but he was watching Braden get his coat on.

Nels didn't trust him, I thought. He knew something about him that I didn't.

His voice low, Nels said to me, 'I'll be back as quick as I can but if the deputies get here first, tell them I found the marshal like this.' I leaned close to Nels, straining to hear. 'Say

99

I found him on the bridge in the snow. His horse must have spooked and thrown him, the bridge creaking the way it is. The horse showed up in my yard and I went out looking for the owner. I brought him here, fetched you to look after him while I've gone off to get help from Sister Rebecca.'

'Yes,' I said. 'All right.'

'Say it back to me.'

I repeated the lies, stumbling over them only once. After I got them out, Nels said, 'The part about me going to Sister Rebecca's is true. She'll have herbs, something we can give him.'

'Go. Please go. Now.'

Nels' gaze flickered to the marshal. 'Fools.' His voice was low. I took that to mean all of us. Braden for having plural wives, the marshal for chasing him in January, and Nels and me for getting caught up in trouble that wasn't of our making. Nels gave the marshal another glance, then got the sack of food supplies, opened the door, and whistled for his dog. Sally shot into the cabin, her coat covered with snow.

'She'll look after you,' Nels said to me. 'You'll be all right.'

'I know. Now go. Go.'

Nels' nod came quick. 'Stay,' he told Sally. I held onto her collar as Nels went outside. Braden, behind him and at the threshold, stopped and turned around, snow blowing in through the open doorway.

'Didn't mean for this to happen,' he said and before I could say anything, he went out into the night.

I let go of Sally and latched the door. Just that quick, I was alone with the marshal.

I turned around to face the bed, standing where Braden had just been. *Didn't mean for this to happen.* His apology was heavy with guilt. But it wasn't directed to me, I realized.

He hadn't even glanced at me. He was apologizing to the marshal.

———•———

Sally growled. She stood a few feet from the marshal, watching him, her nose twitching and her neck stretched long. 'It's all right,' I whispered. One of her ears flickered. She kept staring at him.

It wasn't all right. Yesterday Braden was running from the marshal. Now he wanted to turn himself in. Now he'd apologized. It didn't make sense. The only thing that had changed was that the marshal was hurt.

Still wearing my coat, I got a lamp and went closer to the bed. Sally came with me. I put my free hand on her neck. She quaked with tension. My own nerves hummed. This couldn't be the same man who this afternoon had accused me of helping Lewis Braden. His eyes were closed. One side of his face drooped. Dark patches of dirt smudged his cheeks. The weather lines around his eyes were deeper. His nose was thinner as though pain pinched his features. In the dim light, everything about him was gray – his skin, his mustache, and the flop of hair on his forehead.

He scared me now more than he had this afternoon. It was one thing if he died in his sleep. It was another if he took to struggling to breathe. He could choke. His chest could rattle with death. I wasn't a nurse. I didn't know what to do. His dying could be slow and hard, and I'd be alone with him.

Or he could get better. He could say that he'd seen Braden.

I angled the lamp to see the marshal better. If there was a wound on his head, I couldn't see it.

Maybe he hadn't hurt his head. Nels might be wrong

about that. He and Braden had found him like this. They hadn't seen what happened. Years ago, one of my younger brothers, Solomon, hit his head on a tree branch when riding a horse. Blood poured from the wound on his forehead, scaring my mother and father. He howled when it was stitched together and for a few days he had to stay in bed. His eyes didn't work quite right and the ache in his head was so powerful he cried each time he moved. As bad as Solomon was, though, he never looked to be on the edge of death.

Something scraped against the outside of the cabin. I went still. Sally turned her head, listening, then went back to watching the marshal. The scraping kept on. My skin crawled. Someone was out there.

Sally didn't pay the scraping any attention. A familiar noise, I thought. Then I realized it was a tree branch from one of the lindens by the side of the cabin. The wind had picked up. Not enough, though, to blow away the tracks.

I put the lamp on the kitchen table, took off my coat, scarf, and hat, and hung them up. The marshal's were on the peg beside mine so that the sides of our coats overlapped. My skin crawled. When he left my cabin this afternoon, I believed I'd never see him again.

I straightened his tall boots that had been splayed on the floor. I strained to hear his breathing above the tree's scrape against the cabin.

Sally sniffed the marshal's coat, snorting and blowing air. There must be a reason why Braden wanted to turn himself in. Something made him feel the need to apologize to the marshal.

Stay busy, I told myself. I was better off not knowing. Nels was protecting me from the truth.

I pulled my shawl tighter around my shoulders. In the

corner close to the door, Sally sniffed the propped-up rifle, then the curled gun belt on the floor. These were the marshal's, I thought. A rifle and bullets. This was how he intended to protect himself.

Don't think about what might happen if he started to talk. Don't think about how it could be if he got worse. Stay busy.

I found some rags in the kitchen, got down on my hands and knees, and began to wipe up the watery footprints that marked the floor. It seemed this was the only thing I knew to do. First, I'd wiped up the marshal's snowy tracks in my cabin. Now I was wiping up Nels' and Braden's. And mine.

Nels hadn't said where he was taking Braden for the night. He didn't want me to know. But in the cliffs that rose up behind Nels' cabin, there were carved-out pockets with rock overhangs. One of these could shelter Braden and his horse from the weather. Getting there wouldn't be easy at night with the snow and now this wind. The trail was a series of steep switchbacks but Nels knew the way. Sheltering in a pocket would be cold for Braden but he'd be all right. He'd have to be. None of us could take the chance of hiding him on our properties.

I kept cleaning the floor like I could get rid of the trouble we were in. I wiped up the footprints just like this morning I'd tried to cover Braden's tracks. All at once, the marshal groaned, long and deep. I sat back on my heels. Sally growled, quivering. Under the blankets, his right foot jerked and twitched. This afternoon he told me his name but I had pushed it from my memory. His title, marshal, was enough. It was all I needed to know about him.

His foot twitched again. I should do something to ease his suffering. I should bathe his face and put a damp cloth on his forehead. I should loosen his clothing to make him more comfortable. Sister Rebecca, a freckle-faced woman with red curls that were forever escaping from hair pins, was the person who took care of our sick. She would know what to do. She'd get him out of his clothes and wash him herself. She had remedies for every kind of ailment and if the remedies didn't help, she'd sit at the bedside and knit, the clicking of the needles a soothing melody.

Sister Rebecca, though, was expecting a baby soon and shouldn't be asked to travel the mile and a half from her cabin to here in this weather. Generous-hearted Rebecca wasn't the one who was alone with a gentile, an enemy who came here to do us harm. I was, and I couldn't bring myself to touch him.

He might die. He might live and talk. Braden and Nels would be tried by people who claimed ours was a false and corrupt religion.

They could make me testify against Nels. And Braden. They could twist my words. They were good at doing that. Because of me, Nels and Braden could be condemned not only for breaking the law but for doing harm to the marshal.

They could be shot by firing squads. Or hanged.

Still sitting on my heels and holding the dirty cloth, I rubbed the throb in my temples with my free hand. Braden made me promise I'd take care of the marshal. Was he such a godly man that he put his enemy's welfare before his own? And ours?

If only Nels and Braden hadn't found the marshal. If only nature had been allowed to take its course.

Stay clear-headed, I told myself. Nels' plan to hide Braden could work. The story about finding the marshal on the bridge was believable. The man laid up in Nels' bed was a stranger; we didn't know who he was.

Unless the marshal talked.

Nels' plan depended on the marshal's death. Horror coursed through me. I got myself up off the floor. The room shifted. I sat down at the table. A few yards from me, the marshal's face blurred, then came into sharp focus. The lines of pain around his nose and mouth had deepened, I was sure of it. Nels' plan depended on him dying in bed, attended by a woman who'd done her best for him. It depended on lawmen finding me with the marshal. It depended on me taking care of him like he was one of God's own and not our enemy. Caring for him made us look innocent. It made it look like we didn't know about Braden or why the marshal was here.

The marshal began to shake, quick bursts of spasms. His teeth clattered, loud clicks. The cabin, earlier overheated, had gone cold. I got up from the table, stoked the fire in the lower part of the cookstove, and blew on the red embers until they flared into flames.

The oven door's hinges squeaked as I closed it. I didn't want the marshal to die, I told myself. Neither did Nels. But if the marshal did die . . . I broke off the thought. To want someone's death was horrifying. It went against God's word. It went against everything I'd been taught.

'Be better than your enemies,' my father often said. 'Rise above them and forgive them their trespasses. Be merciful and show charity. But never forget who your enemies are. Or what they've done.'

My mother's lesson came from the Book of Mormon. *If ye do not remember to be charitable, ye are as dross, which the refiners cast out.* My father, I understood, was referring to gentiles and the wrongs they inflicted on us. My mother, I came to believe when I was older, was referring to my father's third wife. Sister Caroline had taken what was dearest to my mother, yet my mother never caused her any harm. She never said a word against her. When Sister Caroline was weak and suffering through childbirth, my mother tended to her. When any of Sister Caroline's children were sick, my mother brought her food.

This was different. We – Grace and her family, Nels, me, every family in Junction – could lose everything. If the marshal talked.

If he died? And I'd done nothing to ease his suffering during his last hours on earth? No prayers, no words of comfort. I would be no better than my enemies. I would be as dross, cast out by the refiners, and rightly so.

The marshal kept shaking. I should do something. I glanced around the cabin like I'd find the answer in one of the dark corners.

A flood of anger took hold of me. Braden was wrong for bringing his trouble here. The marshal was wrong for coming here in January. He should have known better. This was canyon country. It couldn't be trusted. Especially for those who weren't from here and didn't know the land.

Samuel. He was wrong, too. Anger welled up inside of me. Year after year, he went off to fix and make new wheels. He did it so we'd have money set aside for whatever might come up. Samuel going off meant he expected me to take care of the orchards. He expected me to keep the cabin in good repair. He expected me to answer knocks on our door when strangers asked for help. Samuel should be home. He should be helping me with this. I shouldn't be waiting every minute for his return. But I was. Because of his work, he'd left me by myself. Now I was alone with a marshal.

I crossed the room, my footfall pounding. Sally, lying under the table, sprang to her feet. I jerked open the front door, went outside, and slammed it behind me. Never again.

I'd never let Samuel leave again. I'd make that clear the moment he got home.

I plunged into the knee-deep snow, going toward the bridge. None of this was ever going to happen again. I'd see to that. I'd never open my home to another strange man. My shawl flapped in the wind. The night sky was lit up with falling snow. Good. Cover the tracks. Cover everything that has gone wrong. Make this all go away. I tripped, caught myself and pressed on, getting away from Nels' place, getting away from the marshal. I'd done more than enough. I was going home.

SAMUEL

Seventy days ago

November 3, 1887
Utah Territory

Dear Wife Deborah,

I do not have much Time. A Church Elder passing through is tapping his Foot waiting for Me to write this. He is going to Marysville. He will see to it that You get it and the 2 other Letters.

This Outpost is so fresh new the Familys have not come up with a Name for it. It is 5 miles South of Mt. Carmel. There is only 1 married Man but He has 2 Familys. Some of his Boys are big but not full grown.

They need 3 wheels. I am teaching the oldest Boys how to fix them. Me a teacher. Think of that. This Country is so rough with Rocks the Boys need to know how. Some Places are not made for people. Some Places should be left alone. This is one of those.

I am lonesome for You. But not for long. Look for Me by December 1. You will know Me by the Grin on my Face.

Your Husband,
Samuel Tyler

CHAPTER EIGHT

DEBORAH – THE BARGAIN

January 12, 1888

Samuel left me on my own. The words bore down, circling tighter and tighter in my thoughts. I stumbled through the snow, going home, putting Nels' cabin and the marshal behind me. My anger at Samuel swelled. He'd left me to fend for myself.

On the bridge, I slipped. My arms flailed, trying to keep me upright. My feet spun. I fell on my knees. Pain shot through me. My eyes teared.

All at once, my anger unclenched and was gone.

Samuel. Shame burned in my heart. None of this was his doing. It was wrong of me to blame him. He intended to be home weeks ago. He'd be here if the rockslide hadn't taken out the trail.

Still on my knees, I got ahold of the bridge railing and pulled myself to my feet. I cupped my hands around my eyes and looked up through the falling snow. Dense clouds covered the stars and moon. Samuel will be home this week. That was what Nels had figured. This was only Thursday. Tomorrow, he'll be here. Or the next day or the next. If this snow doesn't slow him.

It wouldn't, I told myself. Samuel knows his way. He always comes home. Shielding my eyes again with my hands, I looked up at the sky. The night clouds kept me from seeing the stars and moon that were guiding Samuel to me but they were there.

Just like the marshal was laid up at Nels' even if I didn't want to face it.

Nels counted on me to stay at his cabin. The deputies had to find me taking care of the marshal. It was the one thing that could go in our favor. It was the one thing that might keep them from rounding all of us up and driving us out of Junction.

Far off on the other side of the creek, my cabin was dark. I turned around. A yellow light showed in the window of Nels' cabin. I began to walk back toward it. I did it for Nels and for everyone in Junction. Most of all, I did it for Samuel. I had to be in Junction when he came home.

———

Inside Nels' cabin, the stench of vomit made my stomach twist. Sally pawed at me, panting with nerves. I told her it was all right, and I was surprised by the strength in my voice. The marshal was still breathing but near the foot of the bed the blankets had fallen on the floor. Sally must have pawed at them while I was gone.

One of the marshal's legs, from the knee down, was exposed. The cuff of his trouser had ridden up. His stocking was dark and the skin on his leg glowed a shiny white in the pale lamplight. His leg twitched, restless. His cheeks were sunken and so were his eyes. The frostbitten yellow patch of skin on his right cheekbone had turned into a red, mean-looking blister the size of my thumbnail. He was helpless but he was still the enemy.

And one of God's children.

I went close to the bed. I picked up the ends of the

blankets that were on the floor. The marshal's foot caught my attention. Across the top of his stockings, at the toes, the yarn was a darker cast than the rest of the material. There'd been a hole but it had been mended.

This wasn't the marshal's handiwork. The stitches were like the ones I did for my gloves, tidy and precise. A man wasn't likely to take the time to sew the stitches this even. He wouldn't make the edges so smooth. This was a woman's work. It had been done by someone who took pride in her skill. His wife. Or a daughter, maybe a sister. She'd seen to it that there weren't any uneven places that could rub his skin raw.

The woman cared about the marshal. She might be waiting for him to return home. She didn't know he was hurt.

Sudden tears burned the backs of my eyes. Samuel. Something might have happened to him. He could be hurt. He could be unable to speak for himself and in need of help. He might be at the mercy of strangers who saw him only as trouble. They wouldn't know that Samuel could read rocks and in them, he saw layers of the past. They wouldn't know that he liked in-between places, or that he was a wheelwright and knew the names of each family in every outpost in the Utah Territory. They wouldn't know that he belonged here, with me.

The marshal's teeth rattled. His family didn't know he was hurt. Like I didn't know what was happening to Samuel.

All at once I was hurrying as I would want someone to do for my husband if he were cold and suffering. A stranger to Nels' kitchen, I fumbled as I filled a small pan with water from a pitcher and set the pan on the stove to heat. I opened the oven door. The hinges' long, shrill squeak made me grit my teeth. I peered inside the hot oven that was lit by the fire beneath it. Most of us kept our warming stones in our ovens and there were two in Nels'. Using dish rags, I took out the first stone, then the other, dropping them on top of the cook-stove with a clatter, my hands burning.

I flapped my hands to cool my fingers. This was a trade. A bargain. If I took care of the marshal, someone would do the same for Samuel. If I showed charity to my enemy, Samuel would come home. If I took care of the marshal, the deputies would leave us alone. My husband would come home, and find me here. Everything would be as it should. I couldn't bear to think of it any other way.

Trying to ignore the sting in my fingers, I wrapped the stones in the dish towels and carried them to the end of the bed. Sally stayed at my heels. 'I have warming stones for your feet,' I said to the marshal, watching his face. 'Just want you to know. I don't want to surprise you.'

His eyes opened. Scared, I reared back. Beneath his mus-tache, he worked his lips. The left side of his mouth hung low. I told myself he was helpless. He couldn't hurt me.

Gathering myself, I said, 'I'm here to take care of you. I won't hurt you.'

His eyes closed. I took that as a sign that he believed me. I settled the warming stones on either side of his feet. The reek of vomit was sour and strong. One of God's children, I reminded myself. Do as you would want others to do for Samuel. Do what you must to look innocent in the eyes of the deputies.

I ran the palms of my hands down the sides of my skirt. My right hand bumped over Samuel's rock that I had put in my pocket this afternoon. I took it out and held the flat side against my cheek. After a moment, I put it back into my pocket, then covered the marshal with the blankets.

In the kitchen, I dipped a finger in the water heating on

the stove. It was warm enough. I soaked a dish rag, then wrung it out. *Heavenly Father*, I prayed. *In your wisdom, help me with this.*

I went to the marshal. 'I'm going to wash your face. If that's all right with you.'

His eyelids flickered open. He looked at me. My heart thundered in my ears.

His eyes flickered closed. He moved his head. A nod. He'd understood what I'd said to him. Maybe he wasn't as bad off as he looked. He could be tricking me. At any time, he could sit up and accuse me of helping Braden.

Help me, Heavenly Father. Help me.

The marshal's face was tight with pain. His eyes were squeezed shut. Just moving his head to nod had caused him misery. It wasn't a trick; he was as bad off as he looked.

Years back when my brother Solomon hit his head on a branch, my mother had me hold a rag soaked in cold water against the knot on his forehead. 'To get the swelling down,' she'd said. 'To keep it from pressing against his skull.'

A knot or bump didn't show on the marshal's face or the sides of his head. Maybe he'd landed on the back of his head.

'I'll do my best not to hurt you,' I said. His right eye opened halfway, then closed. I waited a few moments. He stayed still. This could be Samuel, I told myself. Take care of the marshal like you'd want someone to do for Samuel.

'Now I'm going to move the blankets a little to keep from dribbling water on them,' I said. His lips twitched. I waited a moment before lowering the blankets to his waist. His shirt was a dull white in the lamplight and he had on a light brown vest. A gold chain, attached to a watch in the left vest pocket, draped through a buttonhole, and then into the pocket on the right side. Dark stains spattered the front of his vest. There was some near the collar of his shirt. He'd been sick on himself but it'd been a while ago. The stains looked dry.

'Now your face,' I said. If the marshal heard me, I couldn't tell. Gathering myself, I began to wash the dirt from his face. It'd been maybe a week since he'd shaved. His whiskers were gray but his hair was still a deep brown. The frostbite blister above his cheek surely caused him pain. I wrung out the cloth and then washed his face again. For Samuel, I thought. For the woman who did the marshal's mending and who waited for him.

The water was warm but he shivered as I washed his cheeks and forehead. I patted the blister with the warm cloth.

His lips moved. He said something. It was garbled. I stepped back from the bed. He said it again: I still couldn't make it out. The muscles in his face bunched as he tried to talk. His right eye was open wide. The marshal tensed, as if gathering energy, then said, 'Mary Louise.'

His words drifted into a moan.

'Mary Louise,' I said. He might have nodded, I couldn't tell. He lapsed back into himself and went quiet. Mary Louise. The woman who waited for him. The one whose mending had been done with care.

His wife. It had to be. A man hurt bad and far from home would call for his wife.

All at once I felt her presence; it was like she was watching me. I tried to shake the feeling away but couldn't. There were things she wanted me to do for her husband. Like I would want done for Samuel.

I went to the marshal. 'One more thing,' I said, my voice a whisper. 'Your vest and shirt. They're soiled. I'm going to clean them.'

The marshal's eyes opened, then closed. This was his way, I believed, of telling me he understood.

Using the washrag, I wiped at the stains on his vest and shirt, doing my best to clean up the worst of the vomit. Show charity to your enemies, I told myself as I bent over the marshal doing this work. The washrag bumped over the watch that was in his vest pocket. Be kind. No matter how hard. Like Samuel would expect me to do.

On the last day of August, the day before Samuel went off to do his wheelwright work in scattered outposts, I told him I wanted to trim his hair. 'Can't send you off unkempt,' I said, making him sit on the kitchen chair that I'd brought outside, the scissors in my hand. 'Your customers won't have you to dinner or let you sleep in a spare room.'

'It'd cause a ruckus,' Samuel said, a smile in his voice. 'Sure as day. A shaggy-headed wheelwright? Folks living in outposts have never seen the like.' I'd laughed at that but there was a hollowness to it. I was lonesome for Samuel already.

I trimmed his hair, working around his neck and ears. His dark hair was coarse and had a mind of its own. A swirl on the top of his head and toward the back sprang into a cowlick. I brushed his hair across my fingertips as I cut it. It was as thick as it had been on the day I met him.

'The apples are coming along in Nels' orchard,' Samuel said, filling the silence made by the ache of his leave-taking. 'It'll be a good harvest. We'll have apple pie all winter long.'

'I'll have one waiting for you on December the first,' I managed to say.

'I'll come home wearing a bib tucked in my collar and a fork in my hand.'

'And a collection of new rocks in the other.'

'Mrs Tyler, you know me inside and out.'

We went quiet. I clipped at his hair and before us, the red-rock cliffs with their streaks of white glistened in the sunlight. In places, the cliffs were sharp and craggy. In others, the edges were rounded and worn. Nearby, the creek was a low murmur. A wren perched on a rock raised its head and sang. From somewhere farther up the creek, another wren sang back.

Samuel put his hand on my free wrist. I stopped trimming his hair. 'Deborah,' he said. He looked up at me. 'I've been a test to you, all my coming and going. You've never said a word against it.' He'd caressed my wrist, his fingers skimmed over my skin. 'You're a good woman, Deborah. None better.'

He wouldn't say that now. A good woman wouldn't want someone to die. A good woman would do one more thing for a man who was helpless.

I put the pan of dirty water and the washrag in the kitchen and went back to the marshal. My voice low, I said, 'Is it the back of your head? Is that where it most hurts?'

His eyes moved under his lids. His lips twitched. He said something. It sounded like yes.

I put my hand to my pocket and felt Samuel's rock. It was warm, like a living thing, giving me courage. I let go of it, got my coat, and laid it on the foot of the bed. Nels' spare trousers and shirt hung on a peg and I got those too.

'I'm going to roll you onto your side,' I said to the marshal. 'Your left side. To get the pressure off the back of your head.'

His jaw clenched. 'It'll hurt,' I said. 'I know. But then it'll be better.'

Before I could think too long about it, I bent over him, put one hand on his right shoulder and the other under his arm, and pulled him toward me and onto his left side. He cried out, a growl from deep in his throat. Sally, behind me, panted and whimpered. Holding onto him with one hand, I grabbed my coat and put it behind him to keep him from rolling back. Still holding onto him, I got Nels' clothes, wadded them and put them against his chest to stop him from rolling forward.

I let go of him. His breathing rasped. Pain creased his face. 'I'm sorry,' I said, and I was. I was sorry he was hurt. I was sorry, too, for the trouble he would surely bring and that everything had gone so wrong.

'Rest,' I said. This was meant for me as much as it was for the marshal. I started to pull up the blankets to cover him, then stopped. His gold watch, attached to the chain, had fallen out of his vest pocket and was on the bed. It wasn't ticking. It had run down.

Samuel didn't carry a watch. Knowing the precise time didn't matter to him. Tracking the sun and watching shadows told him all he needed. My father, though, carried a watch. It was silver and had been his father's. When I was a small child, I was prone to bad dreams. I'd wake up screaming and because my mother usually had my younger brother to nurse, it was my father who came to comfort me. This was when my mother was his only wife and he still lived with us. He'd hold me close and when my heart began to calm, he settled me back in bed. He'd get out his pocket watch, spring it open, and hold it to my ear. 'Let's count the seconds,' he'd say. Together we'd do that, my father taking the lead as the numbers got bigger. After several minutes of counting the seconds, I'd fall back asleep.

The marshal might be comforted by the sound of his watch. I told him what I was going to do. I believed I saw him nod his head. I unfastened the vest button that held the chain in the buttonhole and worked the chain through. When it was free, I pressed the knob on the top. The cover sprang open.

The time had stopped at one minute past twelve. A

photograph was opposite the clock face. I went to the table where the light was better. It was a woman and two young children. She sat on a high-back wicker chair. A boy, about five or so, stood at her knee. A little girl, a few years younger than the boy, sat on the woman's lap.

The marshal's family. The people who waited for him.

I snapped the cover shut. I didn't want to know anything about his family. I didn't want the name Mary Louise to have a face, and I didn't want to think about children. The marshal was an enemy. He could arrest me and take our home from Samuel and me.

If he lived and told what he knew.

My fingers pulled up the knob and began to twist it back and forth, winding the watch. Nels didn't have a clock but it didn't matter. I didn't need to set the watch. My intent was just to make it tick.

The stem tightened. The watch's tick was loud in my ears. Across from me, the marshal shivered. I pushed the stem down and went back to the marshal. I put the watch back into his vest pocket, ran the chain through the buttonhole, and put the opposite end of the chain in the other pocket. I pulled the blankets up to the marshal's shoulders, got his coat, and spread it over him.

The tightness in the marshal's face eased some even though his breathing stayed ragged. Mary Louise couldn't expect me to do more. I'd done what I could. I'd done what was right. Not for the marshal, though. I'd done it for Samuel. A bargain.

———

Across from the marshal, I sat at the table. Sally lay close to my feet with her head between her paws. The marshal looked helpless but he wasn't. He had the force of the federal government behind him. He could ruin us.

Yet he had a wife, Mary Louise. And a son and daughter. He cared about them. He kept their images close.

I had my own way of keeping people close. I kept a record book with a page for each pair of gloves I'd made for my family and for those who I cared about. Each page had the date, the person's name, and the hand measurements. I wrote down a description of the gloves and the kind of thread I'd used. To keep the memory fresh, I made a paste from fish and beeswax, and glued scraps of the leather and thread I'd used to each page.

The marshal muttered, then went quiet. He wanted his wife with him, I thought. He wanted the comfort of her presence. Surely she would want to be with him. Instead, this very moment she was going about her day like it was any other. She didn't know her husband's breathing rasped, he'd hurt his head, and one side of his face had gone slack.

I pushed myself up from the table. I had convinced myself I'd done enough for the marshal. Mary Louise would expect more from me. Just as I would expect more of her if Samuel were in her care.

In the kitchen, I found a clean dishcloth and went outside. I scooped up some snow and wrapped it in the cloth. For Samuel, I thought. And to keep my end of the bargain.

Inside, I went to the marshal. 'This will be cold,' I said. 'I know that. But I'm trying to ease the pain, not hurt you.' His good eye opened, then closed, letting me know he understood. Bending over him, I pressed the snow-filled cloth to the back of his head. Hurt as he was, he hadn't lost his senses. I felt sure the marshal knew where he was and who I was. Just like he had known this afternoon when he rode toward me, coming from nowhere. He had sat high on his horse with his shoulders set and his rifle in easy reach. I'd known why he came to Junction but I had to make like I didn't so I asked him his business. I asked him who he was.

Behind me, the fire in the cookstove popped. In that moment, what I had told myself I'd forgotten, rushed back. His name was Fletcher.

Don't think about it. Forget it, push it from your mind. Keep him a stranger, nameless.

I couldn't. Telling myself to forget only made me remember all the better. Like it was happening again, I pictured him sitting on his horse. I heard his voice saying his name. Marshal Thomas Fletcher. There was a middle initial but I couldn't remember it.

I pressed the cold cloth against the back of his head, left the bed, and sat down at the kitchen table. Thomas Fletcher.

No, I told myself. Don't let him have a name. I got up from the table. Stay busy. I filled the wash basin with warm water that heated on the cookstove, and put the washrag I'd used to clean the marshal in it. Using a sliver of lye soap, I worked up a few suds. I couldn't find a washboard. Instead, I rubbed the rag against itself, back and forth, the water slopping some onto the counter.

Thomas Fletcher. His name echoed in my mind. I couldn't shake it away. His name made him a person. His wife was Mary Louise Fletcher.

I stared down into the wash basin. The water had turned brown.

I remembered something else. This afternoon, while Thomas Fletcher was in my kitchen, he'd said something about where he was from. I'd been so taken aback by his anger that this had washed over me. Now it came back. He was from Tennessee.

I rubbed the rag together even harder. The dirty water splashed over the sides. Three years ago, at a place called Cane Creek in Tennessee, Saints gathered in a farmhouse for church services. A mob of men, Tennesseans, surrounded the house. They said the Saints had seduced Southern women into living lives of disgrace and perversion. The mob wanted revenge. Days later, when their anger had played out, four Saints had been killed. One gentile was dead. The few Saints still in the county were given thirty days to pack their belongings and get out.

Earlier, the marshal told me they didn't hurt women in Tennessee, not even ones who lied. But at Cane Creek, a woman was shot and her two sons were killed.

I balled the washrag and put it on the counter. I pitched the dirty water out the door and scooped up snow with it to wash it clean. Then I brought in more fresh snow to heat on the oven so I could rinse the rag.

The marshal. Tennessee. That drummed at me. And not just because of Cane Creek.

I puzzled over it. Each state and territory had a marshal. The President of the United States picked the marshals. Marshals and their deputies could make arrests only in their own jurisdictions. At last word, Frank Dyer was Utah's marshal.

Saints made certain to know the name of Utah's marshal. He was our enemy. I hadn't heard of Fletcher but that didn't mean anything. Most marshals didn't stay more than a few years. President Cleveland must have sent Thomas Fletcher to be Utah's next marshal. We were slow to get news here.

The water on the stove simmered. I poured it into the basin and put the rag in the water to rinse. The marshal's breathing rasped. His voice had been strong when he rode up to my cabin this afternoon. His movements had been sure when he got out his badge and showed it to me.

His badge. He had taken it from an inside pocket.

I shook out my hands and dried them on my apron. Only his watch was in his front pocket. I would have seen the shape of the badge while cleaning his vest and shirt. I went to the marshal's coat on the wall peg. The marshal's eyes were closed. He wasn't watching me.

I ran my hands along his coat. A soiled handkerchief and a ball of string were in one of the outside pockets. His gloves, worn thin in the palms, were in another. A pocketknife and a cloth pouch partially filled with dried leaves were inside his coat. A narrow silver canteen was in a different inside pocket. I shook it. The liquid inside of it sloshed.

The badge must be in his saddlebags. That couldn't be right, though. This afternoon, the marshal had taken it from inside of his coat.

He'd lost it. It could be in my barn or by the manure pile. Maybe by the chicken coop. If the deputies found it on my property, they'd know he'd been there. They'd know he would have shown me his badge. They wouldn't believe my claim that I didn't know anything about him.

I took out Samuel's rock from my apron. It was the yellow one with brown in it. Samuel said it was different from the other sandstone he found in Junction. It reminded him of our home, he'd said. It was stronger than most. I put it by the wash basin to give me courage.

I dipped the rag in and out of the wash basin to rinse it. The marshal stirred. My heart skipped, then raced. He tried to say something.

'You're all right,' I said even though it wasn't so.

The marshal squeezed his eyes tight.

Be merciful and show charity, my father had said. But don't turn soft. Don't forget who your enemy is.

Thomas Fletcher.

This afternoon I believed the water I'd left in the trough would be our undoing. Now there was the lost badge.

The deputies were out there somewhere. At any moment, they might pound on the door demanding to be let in.

I found a kitchen knife and put it in my skirt pocket.

Heavenly Father, I prayed. *Look after Nels. Help him find a safe place to hide Braden. Help Nels get back before the deputies show up.*

CHAPTER NINE

NELS – THE FALL

January 12, 1888

It was a sorry thing leaving Deborah with the marshal. I didn't like it. But sorry as I was, I had to get Braden hid for the night. So him and me left Deborah on her own and rode our horses to the head of the trail that went up the cliff behind my place.

'I'll follow you,' I told Braden.

'I don't know where we're going.'

And I don't know who you are, I thought. Or what you've done.

I pointed to the cliff before us. If it were daylight and if it weren't snowing, we'd see a cut zigzagging its way up the side. I said, 'The trail'll show itself once we're on it. Your horse'll sense it. There's only one way to go and that's up.'

'Then I'll go on my own. I've already pulled you into enough trouble.'

'True. But I'm going with you.'

I didn't trust him. I intended to keep him in my sights until I got him hid away for the night.

He cocked his head. I expected an argument but he gave a small nod and took the lead. With me directly on his tail, he couldn't turn around in a wide patch in the trail and go back to Junction. I'd already stuck my neck out more times than I could count today, but there was one risk I wasn't willing to take: Braden turning himself in.

I eyed him as we started up the trail. This morning, dawn
not more than a glint of gray light, Braden showed up at
my cabin. A man with plural wives. It didn't sit right. I nearly
didn't open the door. The federal government left men like
him alone in the winter. Braden, though, knew the code.
He talked like a Saint. Deborah must have thought the same.
She'd sent him on to me. Likely she didn't feel any easier
about him than I did but neither of us had much of a choice.
We went and stepped right into Braden's troubles.

Now I was sunk deep. So was Deborah. Leaving her alone
with the marshal tore at me hard.

Blast this weather. It'd kept me from getting Braden to
Floral Ranch. Now I had to hide him close to Junction. Now
the marshal was hurt bad and laid up in my cabin. There
was no soft way to put it. Deborah and I were neck deep in
trouble.

Fletcher being a marshal was another thing that gnawed
at me. I'd never heard of marshals tracking outlaws. They left
that to their deputies. Neither had I heard of a lawman traveling alone in this part of the Territory. There were bound to be
deputies somewhere with him.

The notion of them watching us made my skin crawl.
There was no two ways about it. I had to get Lewis Braden
out of Junction.

Falling snow lit the night. I kept my sights on Braden's
horse's rump and tail that were flecked with snow. My horse,
Bob, shook his head and snorted bursts of frozen air. Bob had
a low opinion, I knew, about being made to follow a slow-
moving horse that was worn out. The trail, a narrow thread
that switchbacked up the cliff, wasn't all that steep, not like
most tended to be in this part of Utah. But in places the snow

was over knee deep and Braden's horse had been ridden hard the last few days.

That wasn't my concern. Hiding Braden was. So was getting back to Junction as fast as I could. I had to be there when the deputies showed up. If I wasn't, they'd say I was helping Braden. Which was so. Anyway, it wasn't likely deputies would come now that it was dark. But nothing about any of this fit with how things had gone in the past.

Ahead of me, Braden's horse stumbled. Braden said something. His voice was too low for me to make out the words. The horse righted himself and lurched forward. Small drifts of snow spilled and loose stones clattered over the side of the cliff. If the deputies showed up now, they couldn't see us but this racket would tell them plenty. That's how it was in these parts. Noise carried and ricocheted from one red rock to the next.

Some two hundred feet above the canyon floor now, we rounded a bend. The wind caught us, gusting, the snow driving into my face. Braden must have said something to his horse. The horse shook himself and his pace quickened a notch, the wind having swept the trail bare.

The path thinned. A misstep, and it'd be a long slide down to the canyon floor. Braden's horse was wheezing like an old man by the time we got to the crest. We came to a standstill. Braden didn't know where to go next. In a low voice, I said, 'Keep to the left. We're going down the backside.'

He nodded. He talked to his horse, coaxing him down the steep trail, rocks and snow tumbling over the side.

If I'd gotten Braden to Floral Ranch, this fix I was in wouldn't be near as deep. But snow had covered the landmarks. I wasn't able to find the cut that went to the ranch. The day's light had gone fast.

Then we encountered the marshal.

I'd tried to figure a way to keep Deborah out of this any more than she already was. She was by herself, Samuel not home. Hard as it was, I couldn't find a path around keeping her out of it. It'd go rough on us all if the deputies found the marshal untended. There'd be no explaining that, a man hurt bad and by himself in a cabin, the owner nowhere around.

Deborah'll be all right, I told myself. She was small of frame but her spirit was sturdy.

We picked our way down the trail, the going slow in the wind. The marshal might die tonight. He might be dead right now. I'd heard the crack when his head hit the ground.

That was something else I couldn't tell Deborah. She was better off not knowing even if it meant telling her a fistful of lies. Like how it was when we came across the marshal. I'd told her we found him in the snow. That was so but he wasn't hurt. Braden and I were riding single file through a tight spot on the trail. Our snow tracks must have made it easy for the marshal to follow us. We had turned back, heading to Junction and me in a foul mood about it. Likely the marshal heard us coming or maybe he'd spotted us somehow. All I can say for sure is he was waiting for us, laying low on top of a flat, long boulder.

'Lewis Braden,' he'd called as we rode by him. 'Stop right there.'

His words echoed, startling me so much that I looked heavenward. The voice of God. An angry God.

It wasn't God. 'I'm United States Marshal Thomas S. Fletcher,' he said. He stood on the boulder making him a few feet higher than us. 'You're under arrest.'

A marshal.

His rifle was drawn and aimed square at Braden who was ahead of me. 'Throw down your weapons. Both of you.'

'Let him go, Brother,' Braden said. 'It's me you want.'

'Like hell I'm your brother. Throw your weapons. Over there.' He pointed the barrel of his rifle to our right.

His deputies had to be somewhere close. We had to be surrounded. I said, 'Only got a knife.' My mouth had gone dry. I said, 'It's on my belt under my coat.'

'Get it,' the marshal said. 'Move slow. Don't give me a reason to shoot.'

I did like he said. My sheathed knife made a soft plunk in the snow. Braden's rifle struck a rock when he dropped it. It clattered, spinning some, but didn't go over the edge of the trail.

The marshal said, 'Ride forward, slow, until I tell you to stop. Don't do anything foolish.'

We did it all like he said to. We stopped when we were a few yards ahead of our weapons. He came down off the boulder, his rifle still pointed at Braden. He had us get off our horses and made us walk a few yards away. The marshal tossed some rope to Braden. 'Tie his hands,' he said.

Braden said, 'He doesn't have anything to do with this.'

'Doesn't look that way to me.'

'Do it,' I said to Braden. The marshal had a rifle aimed at me. His deputies, hidden somewhere, probably did too.

When my hands were tied, the marshal had another string of rope for Braden. 'There's no need for this,' Braden said. 'I'll come with you willingly.'

'Put out your hands. Wrist to wrist.'

'You have my word. I'll come with you.'

'Your word's no good.' The rifle was pointed at Braden's head. 'Put your hands out.'

Braden did. The marshal shifted the rifle under one arm and wrapped the rope around Braden's wrists. I glanced

around for the deputies. They should have shown themselves
by now.

The marshal's face was set as he knotted the rope. There
was a grimness to him. If he took pleasure in capturing Braden,
it didn't show. He gave the rope a tight yank around Braden's
wrist and said, 'Where is she?'

What? I thought.

Braden said, 'She's well.'

'Where is she?'

I said, 'You know each other?' They didn't pay me any
mind. Braden said, 'She'll write you when she's ready.'

'Where is she?'

'She doesn't want you to know.'

'You're lying.'

'It's the truth.'

'You tricked her, filled her head with nonsense.'

'That's not so.'

'Like hell. You lied to her, lured her in. A young girl.'

The marshal's face was flushed red, his anger showing. I
said, 'Braden. What's he talking about?'

They disregarded me. The two men stood so close that if
the marshal used his gun there'd be nothing left of Braden's
head. Their eyes seemed to burn into each other. Then I was
thinking, where were the deputies?

Braden said, 'She came to me. There was no stopping her.
She knew what she was doing, she'd made up her mind.'

'She's sixteen.'

'That makes her a woman.'

'Damn you to Hell.'

The words rang, striking each cliff, condemning. A wild-
ness came into Braden's eyes, a kind of letting go of all reason.

His hands were tied but all at once he swung at the marshal's rifle, knocking it upward.

A shot exploded. My ears rang.

Braden shoved the marshal. The marshal stumbled backward, his feet tangling, his eyes wide with surprise. I expected him to regain his footing, to come back at Braden. But the ground was rocky under the snow. His arms flailing, he slipped, letting go of the rifle and his end of the rope. He fell. His head cracked against a rough-cut boulder, a brittle snap that echoed in the cliffs.

'God Almighty,' I said and that traveled the cliffs, too. Not moving, the marshal lay face up on the frozen ground. His coat was caught around his legs. His slouch hat was to the side of his face. My hands still tied, I pushed past Braden and dropped to my knees in the snow beside the marshal, my balance off with my hands done up.

The marshal didn't move. I bent over him. He was breathing. I looked up at Braden. He shook his head, bewilderment splashed across his features.

I turned back to the marshal. Falling snow wet his face and stuck to his mustache.

'Can you hear me?' I said. I could hardly hear myself. My ears still rang from the rifle shot. I asked him again. He opened his eyes, then closed them against the snow. I used my teeth to loosen the rope around my wrists, tugging and pulling. Finally, I got myself free. I untied the stampede strings of the marshal's hat, slid the hat out from under him, and held it to shelter his face from the snow.

'He'll be all right, won't he?' Braden said. He leaned over me. His breathing was hard and fast.

The marshal opened his eyes. 'You stole her.'

'Stole her?' I said. 'Braden. What's he talking about?'

'That's not how it was. She came to me.'

'Liar,' the marshal said. 'You took her.'

'What's going on here?' I said.

Braden's attention was fixed on the marshal.

'You know him, don't you?' I said to Braden. 'Don't you?'

'He's—' Braden started but just then, the marshal raised his head like he intended to sit up. Pain streaked across his features. His face squeezed up tight as a fist. He fell back, hitting his head again. He bit his lower lip like he was trying to stop from crying out. Water leaked from under his eyelids.

Braden dropped to his knees on the other side of the marshal. 'Marshal.' There was panic in the word. 'Marshal.'

Fletcher's eyes fluttered open. His head was angled my way, and he fixed his gaze on me. He worked his mouth and said, 'Where is she?'

His eyes pleaded with me like I had the answer. 'I don't know who you're talking about,' I said. He tried to say something more but all at once, an oddness came over him. The muscles on one side of his face loosened and slipped out of place.

His right eye stared at me. I saw the panic. I knew what he was trying to say. He was begging for help. Lydia, my wife, had looked at me this same way when the baby took too long and she was nearly torn in two.

'Marshal,' Braden said, across from me. He hunched over his knees and put his bound hands on the marshal's shoulder. 'I didn't mean to hurt you. I didn't.' The marshal's face reddened. Braden moved his hands away. He looked at me and then again at the marshal. 'Heavenly Father, what have I done?'

'Did you steal a girl?' I said.

'No. No.' His bound hands clasped, Braden rocked back

and forth. 'Heavenly Father, I didn't mean to hurt him. Forgive me, forgive me.'

The marshal's words about stealing a girl crashed in my head. And now this, the man hurt bad. I looked up at the cliffs sure that deputies would come pouring down.

The red cliffs were white with snow. Nothing moved. The snow hissed when it fell to the ground. I felt the cold eyes of mountain lions and coyotes watching and waiting. The marshal, I realized, had come here alone.

Braden kept up his chant about wanting forgiveness. The marshal's face dragged on the left side. His dark eyes begged and his mouth twisted as he tried to talk.

If gentiles got wind of the fight, they'd go after Braden full force. And me.

We could leave the marshal. We could let nature do its will. He'd freeze to death if the coyotes and mountain lions didn't get him first. Like none of this had happened, tomorrow I'd take Braden to Floral Ranch. This time I wouldn't miss the landmarks. I couldn't. When other lawmen showed up looking for the marshal and Braden, I'd play dumb. I hadn't seen either of them. Maybe they got lost in the Wastelands. The lawmen would go back there to look for them. I'd offer to help. After that, they'd leave us alone.

Braden's plea to God stopped. A calculating look had come over his face. He watched me. I figured I knew what he was thinking. I was thinking it, too. Leave the marshal.

It'd be easy to do. Whatever got to him first, the lions or coyotes, they'd carry off parts of him. That happened to the dead in canyon country. We could walk away like we'd never seen him. What was left of him might not be found until late spring. We could make like none of this had happened.

But it had. He was alive. I wasn't a religious man, not like

I'd been raised to be. That didn't make me godless, though. I knew to do unto others as I would want them to do unto me. Those who were merciful received mercy.

'We can't leave him,' I said.

The marshal worked his lips, trying to talk. Nothing came out but it didn't matter. I understood he was pleading for his life.

Braden didn't say anything.

'We're taking him back,' I said. Braden turned away and bowed his head. Calling on God for help, I figured. I got up, went back to where I'd thrown down my knife, and found it. Braden was still praying when I got back. The marshal's right eye watched him.

Holding the knife, I said to Braden, 'Put your hands out.'

That stopped his talk with God. Braden raised his head, turned toward me, and put his bound wrists out. I sawed at the rope with my knife. When his hands were free, I said, 'Get his horse.' Braden did like I told him. My plans must have agreed with whatever God told Braden to do.

Now, the marshal was at my place and likely dying in my bed. On the way to the cabin, he'd sunk deeper within himself. He had trouble keeping his eyes open. His words were garbled. I should feel sorry for him. He was bad off. But the marshal not being altogether able to talk would not only save my skin but Deborah's too. Before Samuel had left, I'd told him I'd look out for her. I intended to keep my word.

Ahead of me on the trail, Braden's horse plodded. The cliffs were close here and the darkness was thick. The marshal's words – *you stole her* – played over and over in my mind.

I pulled down my wool scarf, leaned over the side of my horse, and spat. I straightened, then rocked forward a little to ease my sitting bones.

Everything about this gnawed at me. Federal marshals didn't track down outlaws. They ran their states' courts and jails. They didn't run all over the countryside. Their deputies did the hunting.

I'd been dealing with deputies since word got out that Floral Ranch was a hideout. For over four years, deputies waved arrest warrants in my face. They said I'd be next if I didn't cooperate. Some of the deputies were mean-spirited. Some made threats when they didn't like my answers. A few looked to take pleasure in carrying out those threats. Others went about their job grim-faced, like they'd rather earn their living another way.

Not once had a federal marshal come here. Not once did deputies make mention of a particular woman. Their concerns were the men they hunted. Until today.

The girl must be somebody important. Braden knew that. The marshal's accusations made Braden spitting mad but he knew what the marshal was talking about. *You stole her.*

Quit thinking about it, I told myself. The less I knew, the better. That way I wasn't part of it. Or at least not all of it.

I shifted the reins to my left hand. I was fooling myself. I was part of it, neck deep and paired with a man I knew nothing about.

I slowed Bob. We fell a few extra yards behind Braden. Using my free hand, I unfastened my coat's top buttons and reached into my vest pocket. I took out the marshal's badge. I'd found it when Braden and I brought the marshal into my cabin. It must have fallen out of his pocket. It was on the bed caught in the blankets. I'd nearly said something to Braden when I first saw it. He was at the foot of the bed pulling off the marshal's boots and hadn't seen the badge. Before I had much time to think, I put it in my pocket. I had to get rid of it.

On the trail with Braden ahead of me, I stopped. I ran my free hand along the side of the cliff. I found a crevice in the rock, one of thousands in the canyon country. I worked the badge into it and gave it a good push. It dropped into a deep hole inside of the cliff.

I urged Bob on. We left the crevice. I'd never know exactly where it was. Even in the daylight, one crevice didn't look all that different from the others.

It was wrong what I'd just done. I'd stolen a man's belonging and not just any belonging. I'd taken his identity, and him a man not able to speak for himself. It was wrong. But if he died without talking, we had to be able to say we didn't know he was a marshal. We didn't know his business and what he was doing here. Getting rid of his badge might save Junction.

That worked on me. The trouble we were in made me do things I wasn't proud of.

A short, gnarly juniper that poked out upward from a crevice in the butte brushed against me. 'Hold up,' I said to Braden. He came to a stop. 'We're here.'

CHAPTER TEN

NELS – THE HANDSHAKE

January 12, 1888

Braden and I got off our horses and went inside an opening in the side of a cliff. It was dark and cold. The opening was some thirteen feet wide and its depth was close to eighteen feet. On the back wall, someone – an Indian most likely – had painted a red stick figure of a horse. Near the opening, snow blew in and drifted over the rock floor. A few years ago, I told Samuel it looked to be a half-hearted cave since it wasn't very deep. Samuel grinned and said it wasn't a real cave since it didn't go underground. He said it was a weak place in the sandstone. He called it a pocket that had been carved out by rain, wind, and time.

I lit a lantern I'd brought with me. In the flare of the light, Braden's eyes looked as sunken as the marshal's had.

Braden was a Saint, I didn't doubt that. He said all the right things. But there were Saints who rustled cattle and some who robbed trains. Growing up in the church didn't mean a man couldn't do wrong.

Stealing a girl. That wasn't anything like rustling cattle or robbing trains.

Braden left the pocket and went outside. I stood in the opening to keep an eye on him. He went to the edge of the trail and bowed his head. He was either praying or plotting, I didn't know which.

Watching Braden, I went outside and took up trying to get his horse in the pocket. The animal had turned stubborn, though, and wouldn't move. Braden didn't seem to notice. I tussled with the horse thinking how most of us in Junction didn't agree with plural marriage. Samuel said Junction was made up of in-between Saints and that was so. We wanted air between us and the church. Still, at the core we were Saints. We didn't turn our backs on our own. The men who came here could be our fathers, brothers, or friends.

I should have known our luck would run out.

I worked with his horse, my patience on the low end. 'I'll do it,' Braden said, finally coming back to himself. He took the reins from me, then coaxed his horse into the pocket. His voice was low but I saw how easily his horse obeyed, how once he got the horse in place he stroked the sides of its face with both hands. Maybe this was how he'd gotten the girl to go with him.

I said, 'Here's the plan. If the weather breaks, I'll be back at dawn to take you to Floral Ranch. Tonight, don't build a fire. The deputies, if they come, might smell it. Or see it. The neighbors could too. I don't want them knowing about you.'

'God sees all,' Braden said. 'He knows what I've done.'

'The neighbors aren't God. Don't build a fire.'

'I won't do anything senseless.'

Like steal a girl? I thought. And go after a United States marshal? 'I'll get the supplies,' I said and left him where he stood by his horse. I stomped my way through the snow to Bob. Usually I didn't want to know the particulars about the men I took to Floral Ranch. It made it easier when I was questioned by lawmen. But Braden wasn't like the others.

I put my hand on Bob's neck. His ears flickered, then went back. He wasn't happy about the circumstances. 'Me neither,'

I said. If Braden had stolen a girl, only God knew what he might do next. A desperate man could do most anything.

I felt Braden behind me. I turned around. He wasn't there.

He wouldn't harm me, I thought as I looked into the dark night. He needed me to get him to Floral Ranch. Unless he intended to sneak off and turn himself in. If that was so, he'd no reason to hurt me. But maybe that show he'd made in my cabin about turning himself in was just that: a show. Maybe he was up to something I didn't know about.

I trailed my gloved hand along Bob's side until I came to his rump. I untied the rolled horse blankets from my saddle, got my saddlebags, and went back inside the pocket. There, Braden stood by his horse. I eyed him. I felt him studying me the same way. He wasn't sure about me. Nothing about me squared with his notion of a Saint. I wasn't married. I didn't have a herd of children. He might think the same about Deborah. For all he knew, we'd left the church. I might be one of those Saints who turned traitor. More than likely there was reward money on his head. Braden might think that money tempted me. Not finding the cut to Floral Ranch and bringing him here could be me laying a trap for him.

Neither of us trusted the other but we were bound together.

I dropped the blankets on the floor of the pocket. I dug out a bag of feed and the sack of canned meat from my saddlebags. 'Keep moving your feet and fingers,' I said. 'That way they won't freeze.' I handed him the supplies. 'You've got your bedroll and these blankets, so likely you'll be all right. Leastways you probably won't lose anything more than the tips of your ears.'

'I deserve worse,' Braden said. 'By my own hand, I might

have killed him.' There was a break in his voice. 'You hear me, Brother? I might have killed a man.'

I heard him plenty loud. Murder. I said, 'You know him. Don't you?'

'Yes.' He paused. 'He's her father.'

'What?'

'The marshal's my third wife's father.'

His words didn't fit right. The marshal. The third wife. I said, 'She's his daughter? The one he says you stole? That's his daughter?'

'I didn't steal her.'

A marshal's daughter. My blood went hot. Before Braden could say anything more, before I could give him a thrashing for bringing his trouble to us, I went outside. Caught in gusts, snow fell and rose in swirls. I walked away from the pocket.

They'd get us. They'd use everything they had to find Braden.

The snow cracked behind me. I whirled around. It was Braden. I braced myself, not knowing what he might do.

'Brother, I didn't know he was a marshal,' he said. 'Not until after I'd married her.'

'Did you steal her?'

'What kind of man do you think I am?'

'I don't know what you are.'

'I didn't steal her. I was doing mission work in Tennessee with three other elders. That's how I met her.' Braden's words ran like a river out of its banks, spilling and going where they shouldn't. 'She and her older brother saw to the family farm. Their mother and father had business in Nashville. She'd heard other Saints preach last year and believe me, Brother, that young woman was hungry to hear more preaching about the reformed gospel.'

'He said you stole her.'

'That's a lie. She came to us, we didn't seek her out. She came to us. I didn't take her against her free will.'

'But that's what the government says? That you stole her?'

'It's not true. She walked four miles to hear us preach. After the second Sunday, she asked me to baptize her. I did, and Brother, the joy on her face was something to behold. Mary Louise, that's her name. Mary Louise went back to the farm and when she left us, it was like she walked on air. The following Sunday she came to services carrying what she owned in a satchel. Mary Louise knew we were leaving for Salt Lake the next day. She begged me and the three other elders to take her with us to Zion.'

'God Almighty, man. Her father's a federal marshal.'

'I didn't know. She told me her mother and father were good people. But they weren't churchgoers. They didn't even have a Bible in the house. Her older brother wasn't much better. Mary Louise couldn't live like that anymore. Not after the reformed gospel was revealed to her. She said if we didn't let her come with us to Utah, she'd follow behind us, walking. But if we let her ride with us, she'd do the cooking and washing to earn her way. There were four of us, all men. And her. How would that look?'

'She's sixteen. You should've taken her back to where she came from.'

'She'd only run off and try to get to Utah on her own.'

'That would have been her doing, not yours.'

'A girl by herself? In the wilderness? I'd baptized her, she was my responsibility. I asked God to tell me what to do with this woman who wanted to live among us. The other elders prayed with me. We trusted He'd reveal what I must do, and our trust was fulfilled.' He paused. 'God commanded me to marry her.'

'I figured as much,' I said, my words sharp. This was the kind of talk that'd turned me away from the church. It was a reason I'd come to Junction. I'd had my fill of God commanding Saints to do what they'd intended to do all along. I thought I'd gotten away from this talk but it had tracked me down.

I said, 'What are you charged with?'

'Polygamy. Unlawful cohabitation.' Braden paused. 'Kidnapping.'

My pulse roared in my ears. Kidnapping. I fought the urge to put my hands around Braden's neck and be done with him. Deborah and I were helping a kidnapper. 'You know what they could do to us?' I said, spitting out the words. 'They'll put ropes around our necks and hang us. Or put us in front of firing squads.'

'It's why I'm hiding. You've got to believe me. I didn't know her father was a lawman. She wasn't kidnapped. I did right by her. A young woman traveling unchaperoned with four men? It'd look bad.'

'Stay back.' I walked off. The snow was knee deep in places and just up to my ankles in others. I kicked it. The snow spiraled and was carried off by the wind. I was boiling hot at myself for getting caught up with Braden. Kidnapping. It wasn't just him who could be shot or hanged.

Four Mormon men stole a sixteen-year-old girl. That was how a gentile jury would see it. They'd not only pin them for it but they'd say I helped Braden hide. They'd claim Deborah helped, too.

The bastard. I believed his account of how he met the girl. It was what missionaries did. They preached, baptized converts, and sometimes tore up families. Like Samuel's family.

His sister, older than him by five years, didn't want anything to do with the church. She stayed behind in Ohio when Samuel and his mother came to Utah Territory.

A family torn up that way was different than marrying the daughter of a gentile marshal. Poking a hot stick in the government's eye couldn't be any worse. I should turn Braden in myself. I could tell the deputies that Braden showed up with the marshal on his heels and there'd been an argument. It had nothing to do with any of us in Junction. The chase just happened to end here.

The deputies wouldn't believe that. Government men knew about Floral Ranch. They knew about the owner, Ephraim Hanks, who hid Saints. They just didn't know precisely where the ranch was other than it was close to Junction. Anyone with wits enough to put two and two together could figure we had a part in helping the men get there. The government would like nothing better than to round us up and clear us out. It was just a matter of catching us red-handed.

I drew in some air. It was needle-sharp. If the marshal lived and made it known how Deborah had sheltered Braden, how he'd come across me and Braden together, how the fight happened, they'd have us.

I blew the air out. It steamed white in the dark. Swallow your anger, I told myself. Stay with the plan. Like I'd told Deborah to do. Like she depended on me to do.

I went back to the pocket. Braden was outside on the trail, waiting for me. When I got close to him, I said, 'You told me there were three other elders and the girl. Where're the other three?'

'Hiding, like me.'

'Are they coming here?'

'No. We went different ways.'

'I have your word on that? You're by yourself.'

'I'm never alone. God walks with me.'

I felt my temper rise. I swallowed it down and said, 'Other than God being with you, I have your word you're by yourself?'

'You do.'

His word didn't count for much. Not with me. Yet, here I was, in a hard place where there was nothing to do but trust that his word meant something to him. I said, 'Now keep your mouth clamped and listen to me. Nothing's changed other than me knowing about the girl and her father. You understand? Nothing's different. You're going to stay here like we'd planned. I'll go back to Junction to find out what's going on there. I'll come back at dawn and take you to Floral Ranch. This snow has to quit sometime. If we're lucky, it'll let up soon and I'll be able to see the cut to the ranch. If the deputies show up at my cabin during the night, and that's a mighty big if with this weather, but supposing they do, I don't know when I'll get up here. But I'll get here. Or I'll send someone in my place.'

In the dark, I felt him studying me. After a moment, he said, 'You're a good man, Brother. A forgiving man.'

'Forgiveness's got nothing to do with it. I'm doing this to save Junction.'

'I know that. And so does God. He knows you're putting others before yourself.' He put his hand out. 'Brother.'

I clenched my teeth and bit back the urge to be like the marshal and say I wasn't his brother. But I was. He and I were Saints even if I was just a partial one. We were related even if we didn't want to be.

Not wanting to, I shook his hand, binding me to him all the more. A man charged with kidnapping. I had to trust that his story was true and he hadn't stolen the girl. I had to believe he wouldn't lose his head and leave during the night. Braden had to do his own trusting. He had to believe I wouldn't turn him in for the reward money.

We were stuck with each other. The only way out of this scrape was for both of us to do what we said we would.

I let go of his hand and got on my horse. Bob stomped the ground, tired of waiting. Braden watched and just before I maneuvered Bob to turn around on the trail, Braden said, 'God's with us.'

Joseph Smith probably believed that, too. But when he and his brother, Hyrum, were trapped in a jail cell, God did nothing to hold back the men who shot them dead.

My nod to Braden was quick. I turned Bob around on the trail and fixed my sights on getting back to Junction.

CHAPTER ELEVEN

NELS – REMEDY

January 12, 1888

Making my way down the trail, Braden's words – *God's with us* – stayed with me. Gentiles probably believed God was with them. I figured none of us knew for sure where we stood. Like how I didn't know which way matters stood with Deborah. She was on her own with the marshal. I wanted to spur Bob on, make him go faster to get me home. Nature conspired against me. The return was downhill, and I had to let Bob pick his way.

The marshal might be better. He might be accusing Deborah of helping a kidnapper. He might be dead.

Bob stumbled. He was just about played out. Midway down the trail, I got off him and walked. After we got to the floor of the canyon, I got back on. When I turned him away from the direction of my cabin, Bob fought me, rearing his head. 'Quit that,' I said. 'I know you're tired but we aren't done yet.' I had to go see Rebecca Baker, the woman who did our doctoring. It went against the grain pulling Rebecca and her husband, Adam, into this. It meant spreading the trouble. It wouldn't just be Deborah and me caught in this scrape. I had to see the Bakers, though, to make my story about finding a stranger on the bridge stand up. Getting advice from the woman who tended our sick was something I'd be expected to do. When other lawmen turned up, they'd see Deborah and me doing all we could. They might swallow my story.

I shifted the reins to my left hand and flexed my fingers on the right. Snow had wedged its way into the creases of my gloves but my hands were dry. Warm, too. Deborah made the gloves two Christmases back. She and Samuel had had me to their cabin for Christmas dinner. Before we sat down to eat, I gave them a picture I'd sketched with a pencil. It was of their plum orchard. Buds were about to burst open on the trees' bare limbs. Behind the trees, cliffs rose up. I'd made a frame and even though the Christmas ham was ready to be sliced, Deborah wanted the picture put up right then and there. Samuel said, 'Can't argue with a woman when her mind is set.' He got a nail and hammer, and hung it on the parlor side of the front room.

Deborah spent a fair amount of time admiring the picture. 'I could step right into it, it's that real,' she said. 'And look here, how you shaded the ground so it looks to be noon, the sun directly overhead.' She turned to me. 'Did you intend that? For it to be noon?'

'I did.'

'The midpoint. Where things can go on like they've been, or make a turn a different way.' She was quiet for a while, just looking at the picture. Then she said, 'We have a little something for you.' Deborah wasn't as pretty as some women. Her face was all angles with high cheekbones and her chin ended in a point. That changed when she smiled. Her smile made the angles in her face go soft. Her hazel eyes with their bits of blue took on a shine like they were dancing a jig. That was how she looked when she gave me a package done up in brown paper.

I opened it. Inside were gloves. They were buckskin and smelled of oak bark and what I believed was wolf oil. They were a mild yellow color that was bound to darken over time. Across the back of each one, Deborah had stitched three rows of raised cording. Fringe, six inches long, ran along the outer sides of what she called the gauntlet, the part of the glove that flared below the wrist.

Deborah said, 'They're lined for winter wear and the leather'll hold up for hard work. And don't say they're too showy for you.' She nodded toward the fringe.

'No,' I said. 'Not showy. Handsome.'

She bit back a smile and had me try them on for fit. 'I wanted to measure your hands to make sure about the size. I looked in my record book and it's been two years since I made your last pair. Can you believe it's been that long? If I'd asked to measure you, it would've spoiled the surprise.'

I put them on. The leather was soft and had give. Deborah took my right hand. My pulse made a quick turn. Her features were set as she tested the fit, running her thumb and forefinger along the sides of each of my fingers. Her fingers were long and thin. I wanted to take off the gloves so I could feel her touch.

Samuel said, 'Deborah fretted they wouldn't be right. But she has an eye for these things, I told her that.'

She didn't seem to hear him. She felt the palm, pushing the padding. Then her hand went around my wrist just above the gauntlet. She did the same with my left hand, me frozen in place.

'They'll do,' Deborah said. She let go of my hand and looked up at me. I ducked my head and said my thanks, my tongue too knotted to say more.

That was just over a year ago. Not a one of us knew then what was ahead of us. We didn't know a man charged with kidnapping would come to Junction. We never figured on having a half-dead marshal in my cabin. We didn't know

Samuel would run long getting home. We hadn't foreseen that it'd be me looking out for Deborah.

———

Rebecca and Adam Baker's place was dark. The fire in their cookstove had died down enough that I didn't smell it until their cabin took shape in the night. Impatience made me want to pound on their door but they had two children. Stirring up the little ones wouldn't help matters. My knock was light and I took up sweating in the cold waiting for Adam to answer. He and Rebecca had moved here two years ago. Like most of us, they were looking for space between them and the church. Like us, they'd been questioned by deputies about the men and Floral Ranch. Like everyone, they didn't talk about it and made like none of it happened. Now I was about to pull them into it, a family with two little ones and a baby on the way.

Adam called out, asking who it was. I told him it was me and he let me in. Standing in his front room, I said how I didn't like waking him up but I had a man hurt bad in my cabin. 'He's a stranger,' I said, doing my best to keep my voice low. 'I found him on the bridge. He's in a bad way.'

'On the bridge?' Adam said. I heard his wariness. Strangers didn't come here in January. I could tell he knew this wasn't right.

'I figure he took a hard fall and maybe cracked his head. I don't know what to do for him.'

'He's a Saint?'

'I don't know. He can't do much more than mumble.'

Adam ran his fingers through his beard like that might help him fit this all together. He was shorter than me by half a head and younger by a good ten years or so. He glanced toward the back room. I'd gotten him up from his bed. He'd dressed in a hurry. His shirt, unbuttoned, wasn't tucked into his trousers. His curly hair was riled in all directions. If Adam knew for certain that Samuel and I were the ones who took the men to Floral Ranch, he'd put that together on his own. He hadn't heard it from me or from Samuel and Deborah.

Adam pulled on his beard. I felt him wanting to turn me away. He didn't want any part of this. I didn't either. That didn't change matters, though.

A stirring came from above us in the loft. 'Girls,' Adam said. He looked up at the open square cut in the ceiling. A ladder went up to it. 'Go back to bed.' Someone giggled. 'Now,' he said. There was more rustling and then creaking from the ticking in a mattress. Adam waited, listening. When the quiet in the loft finally seemed to suit him, he lit a table lantern. The flame cast a shadow on the kitchen wall. He said, 'Rebecca can't go out, not in her condition.'

'I don't want her to. All I need is for her to tell me what to do.'

'That's all?'

'Brother Nels.' It was Rebecca. She'd come out of the bedroom. Her hair was in a long braid and she was wrapped in a shawl. The light from the lantern barely poked through the dark but from the slowness of her movements, it was plain to see she was expecting soon. She was in no condition to travel the mile and a half to my cabin.

'Someone's hurt?' she said.

I went through the lies again about finding a man on the bridge and then told the truth about how he was in a bad way. Rebecca looked at her husband, her eyebrows raised. Something unspoken passed between the two of them. They knew about the men I took to Floral Ranch, I thought. And now they knew someone was here who could bring us trouble.

'He's alone?' she said. 'At your cabin?'

'Sister Deborah's with him. I went and got her to tend him while I came here.'

She looked up toward the loft. I figured she was thinking about her children and what could happen if she and her husband were caught knowing more than they should.

Rebecca said, 'What's his breathing like? Fast? Or drawn out and ragged-like? Does it stop and start?'

'No, not that. It's ragged mostly.'

'Can he keep his eyes open? Is he making good sense?'

'He mumbles, I can't make it out. He drifts off.'

'Is there a wound?'

'Not that I could see. But there's a fair-size knot swelled up on the back of his head.'

'How big?'

My thoughts shifted back to when Braden and I got him to my cabin. I'd felt the knot when we were settling him in the bed. It'd made my insides lurch. I said, 'The size of an egg.'

Adam blew a short whistle. He and Rebecca looked at each other again. After a moment, she said, 'I don't like the sound of that.'

I said, 'That's how I figure it.'

'Is he feverish?'

'Doesn't seem so.'

Rebecca clicked her tongue like I should know one way or the other. She said, 'Has he been sick? Heaved up his stomach?'

'Could have. He smells like he did.' I couldn't tell her the truth. I couldn't let her know the man wasn't sick when I'd first come across him. I had to stay with the story that I'd found him on the bridge. I couldn't tell how, when Braden and I each took one of the marshal's arms to get him off the ground, he'd spewed out everything he'd likely eaten in the last day or so. I couldn't say how, after that, he took on a bad look that made me think he might die.

She said, 'It matters if he's been sick. Do you know one way or the other?'

I hesitated, then, 'It happened when I moved him. When I picked him up to get him to my cabin.'

In the faint light, I felt Rebecca and Adam give each other another knowing look. They understood I couldn't say all I knew. I was trying to protect them. I said, 'One side of his face sags.'

Rebecca frowned. She looked at Adam. He gave her a quick nod. That seemed to settle something between them.

'The poor man,' she said. She got the lamp and went to the shelf by the cookstove where there were canning jars. She took one and put the lamp down on the kitchen table. She found a piece of cloth and from the jar, took out what looked to be leaves. She wrapped them in the cloth and gave it to me.

She said, 'The best you and Sister Deborah can do is try to take down the swelling. Pack some snow and put it on the knot you spoke of. It'll make him cold so keep him warm with as many blankets as you have. Coats, too. Those are mint leaves.' She nodded toward the folded cloth she'd given me. 'Put them in warm water, soak a rag, and hold it close to his nose. It might ease his pain. His head probably hurts mightily. You can try dribbling a few drops of the mint water into his mouth. If he swallows it, try a little more. But only if he can swallow. Don't let him choke.'

'We won't.'

I told them I had to get back. They agreed. I put the folded cloth in my breast pocket and made ready to leave.

After I said my thanks, Rebecca said, 'Brother Nels, there's one more thing.'

I drew up. She was going to tell me she knew what I was in the middle of. She said, 'If he starts to bleed, there's nothing you can do for him other than keep him warm.'

'Bleed?'

'From his nose or his mouth. Maybe from his ears. There could be a wound inside his head. He could leak blood.'

My belly rolled. The marshal's death could save us but I hadn't let myself think how it might come about. I hadn't thought about the suffering and the ugliness of it.

Rebecca put her hand on my arm. 'Stay steady, Brother Nels. You've kept the poor man from suffering alone in the cold. You've given him your bed and are doing all you can. That and prayer could save him. If they don't, it was God's will. Find solace in that.'

I couldn't look at her or Adam. I stumbled through my goodbye and left before they could read the truth on my face. Whichever way this went, there was bound to be a sorry ending for somebody. There'd be no solace.

———

Deborah's face was pale when she opened my cabin's door. 'You're here,' she said. 'Thank God.' The relief of seeing her tied my tongue. Deborah's eyes began to water. She flicked the tears from her cheeks. I wanted to tuck her close to me. I didn't. She was Samuel's, not mine.

She opened the door wider for me so I could come inside. The flames in the four lamps were patches of light in the room. Sally's tail thumped against my legs beating the snow from my coat. My fingers skimmed the fur on her haunches.

The marshal's breathing rasped loud. He was worse. Or maybe I'd forgotten how bad he sounded.

The cabin smelled like leaves rotting in mud. Deborah's eyes were too big. She looked past me like someone had followed me inside.

'I'm alone,' I said.

'He's settled?'

I understood she meant Braden. 'For now.'

She swatted away more tears. Not knowing what I'd do if she couldn't stop them, I busied myself by pulling off my gloves. Deborah took them from me. Her fingertips ran up and down the braided cording on the back of one of them. She said, 'One side of his face droops.'

I nodded, not saying anything. I unfastened my coat. The marshal's rasping stopped. We went still. Sally did, too.

The rasping started up again. The struggle of it made me grit my teeth. Deborah said, 'It's been like this for a while. He's getting worse.'

The marshal's breathing stopped, then took up again, stuttering.

I didn't know how Deborah had stood it all day.

I hung up my coat and went to the bed. The marshal was on his left side. He'd either found the strength to move himself or Deborah had done it. He was covered in my blankets and his coat was on top. A bunched-up dishcloth was pressed to the back of his head. His coloring was a peculiar gray that lacked life.

'Is he bleeding?' I said.

'No.' She shuddered. 'Thank goodness.' She came and stood beside me. The marshal looked half the size he'd been when he stood on the rock and held his rifle on Braden and me.

Deborah said, 'I wrapped snow in the dishcloth that's

pressed to his head. A knot's bulging from back there. It was all I could think to do to get the swelling down.'

Her words reminded me of the mint leaves. 'Here.' I took them from my breast pocket, gave them to Deborah, and told her what Rebecca had said to do. 'It'll ease his pain,' I added.

'At least it's something,' Deborah said. She took the leaves to the kitchen. The marshal's breathing whistled, wheezing. All because of a girl. Her father, this man, wanted her back. He'd come to find her. He wanted her safe.

Braden, if what he said was true, aimed to keep her safe, too. Bad things happened to a woman in the wilderness if she wasn't claimed by a man. It took months to travel from Tennessee to Utah. It meant crossing mountains. It called for fording rivers that weren't predictable. A person had to sleep out in the open and there were all manner of rough sorts on the trail.

Now the girl's father was fighting for air. I didn't like thinking how that'd be for her once she knew her husband's part in this. It'd be a burden she'd carry for the rest of her life. All because she'd heard preaching and believed.

That was, if Braden's story was true.

———

I left the cabin to get Bob settled in the barn and to break up the icy drinking water in the stall where I'd put the marshal's horse. His horse drooped and stood with one leg resting on the tip of his hoof, more asleep than awake. Doing only what had to be done, I got the saddlebags and packs off the marshal's horse, unsaddled him, and filled his trough and then Bob's with feed.

A heaviness came over my limbs when I put blankets over

the horses. I was empty of sleep and food. It sickened me, but God help me, I wanted the marshal to die. Now that it was before me, though, I didn't want any part of it.

The chores finished, I started to leave the barn, then stopped. The marshal's saddlebags. There might be something in them that identified him.

A man's saddlebags were his and his alone. Any other time, I wouldn't be tempted. But this wasn't like any other time. I looked over my shoulder like somebody might be watching. No one was.

I got the saddlebags and went through one of them. There was a small sack of flour, some bacon, coffee, salt, and baking powder. A handful of dollar coins was in a side pocket. In the other bag, I found a mirror, a straight razor for shaving, a thin bar of soap, a towel, five loose bullets. In the side pocket, there was an envelope. There weren't any markings on it, and it wasn't sealed. I figured it was the warrant for Braden's arrest. I opened it.

There were two sheets of paper. Only one had writing on it. I held it close to the lantern. It was a letter, not a warrant. The handwriting was cramped, and the page was dated *December 27, 1887. Dear Mary,* it began.

I stopped. It was bad enough I was going through a man's saddlebags. Reading that man's letter was even worse. I folded the pages into the envelope and put it in my coat pocket. I'd get rid of it but I wouldn't read the words.

There had to be a warrant. I searched the saddlebags again. I found a narrow inside pocket I'd overlooked before. There was an envelope in it. I opened it.

The handwriting on the single sheet was bold. I picked out some words. Lewis Braden. Kidnapping, unlawful cohabitation, and polygamy. This was the warrant for his arrest.

Two signatures were at the bottom. One was a judge in Nashville, Tennessee. The other was U.S. Marshal Thomas S. Fletcher of Nashville, Tennessee.

This couldn't be right. The warrant should be issued in Utah. That was the only way he could make an arrest here. I held the warrant closer to the lamp. I'd read it right the first time. Tennessee. Not Utah.

There must be another warrant. I looked inside the bags again. Nothing. I went to his saddle. I ran my hands over the worn leather in the seat, then the base of the horn, the skirt, and the leather stirrups. There could be a slit where the warrant was stored but I couldn't find one. I went through the marshal's rolled-up blankets and rolled-up change of clothing. No warrant from Utah.

This didn't make sense. I'd figured Fletcher had been appointed to replace Frank Dyer, Utah's marshal. I figured he had jurisdiction here.

I held the Tennessee warrant in one hand. I had to get rid of it and the letter like I'd gotten rid of the badge. The story about finding a stranger on the bridge had to stand. There couldn't be anything that identified him.

Making sense of the jurisdiction didn't matter. I could think about that after I'd gotten rid of it. I put the warrant in my coat pocket. My fingers brushed the marshal's letter. There might be something in it that I should know.

It was wrong to read another man's mail. I did it anyway. The letter was in parts. The marshal hadn't written it in one sitting.

December 27, 1887

Dear Mary,

We caught wind about a place in the canyons due south and left Salt Lake yesterday. Rest assured. Our

*daughter will come home to you. It is cold here but
our determination burns like a fire. Me and the boys
are keeping well.*

Mary must be Fletcher's wife, I thought. And he wasn't
traveling alone. Others were with him. I read the next part.

December 29, 1887

*The Territory is not all Mormon. Yesterday we came on
a cabin. The man living there is a miner and a Methodist.
He drew us a map of the canyons. Redemption is close
at hand. I'll find our daughter. We will be reunited.
Keep a stout heart.*

January 3, 1888

*This land is nothing like Tennessee. It is sharp-edged
and broken. Trees are hard to come by. The wind is
stiff. When I come home I swear to you I will never
leave again.*

The letter wasn't signed. Likely Fletcher intended to write
more.

These could be his final words. I read it again. There wasn't
anything about Braden or about Fletcher being a marshal. He
was a man looking for his daughter. He never said why. Nothing in the letter said who he was.

His final words to his wife, I thought again. If he died.
Keep a stout heart. His wife would surely need to do that.

I folded the pages and put them back in the envelope. I
should get rid of the letter. *Keep a stout heart.* Fletcher would
want his wife to see his words.

Before I could change my mind, I put the letter back in

the saddlebag. When other lawmen got here, they'd take possession of the marshal's belongings. They'd find the letter. It'd make them think we didn't tamper with things that didn't belong to us. It'd look like we had no reason to be afraid of the man who'd set words to paper.

The warrant in my pocket, I left the barn and walked through the snow to the outhouse. It was behind my cabin set off a ways from my water well. I didn't know what the law said about what happened to a man who destroyed a federal marshal's possessions. It couldn't be good.

The outhouse was a small building made of wood. I went inside. It smelled of the lime I used to keep it from stinking. When I first came to Junction, I'd dug the deep pit, then covered it with a seat that had a round opening.

I tore the warrant into small pieces. I dropped them into the pit.

———

My cabin stank of sour vomit underlined by a faint current of mint. Deborah sat in a chair alongside of the marshal. She held a cloth close to his nose. If the cloth doused in mint helped the marshal, I couldn't tell. His breathing jerked, stopping and starting.

'I dribbled a few drops into his mouth,' Deborah said. 'But I'm afraid to do more. If he should choke, well, I don't want to think about that. It's bad enough as it is.'

And was likely to get worse. I said, 'I regret bringing you into this.'

'None of it was your doing.'

Maybe, maybe not. If Samuel and I hadn't helped the first man who came here four years ago, they would have stopped coming. When we first heard about the family at Floral Ranch and how their place was a hideout, we should have left and found another place to settle. Samuel and I hadn't done either one. We didn't even ponder changing the course of what would become a pattern. When it came down to it, we were more a part of the church than we thought. Helping our own had seeped into our blood.

Deborah said, 'There's food on the table.'

'I appreciate it.' I sat down to the plate of venison and bread she'd put out for me. Sally got under the table and rested her chin on top of my boot. Deborah had warmed the milk and when I drank it, the heaviness in my limbs settled deeper.

Lydia, my wife, was the last woman to put supper out for me in my home. That was nearly six years ago. As bad as things were, it felt good to have Deborah here. But it was peculiar, too. Always before we had Samuel with us.

Just that quick, the image of the rockslide came back to me. When Carson and I were there, I was sure Samuel had been forced to turn around and go north through the Fish Lakes. I was sure he'd find his way through the high pass. I'd told Deborah he'd be home by the second week of January. At the latest. That was this week.

I put my fork down. My mouth had gummed up. Maybe I was wrong. Maybe something bad had happened to Samuel.

Deborah, across the room at the marshal's bedside, said, 'He has a family.'

Samuel bolted from my thoughts. 'What was that?' I said.

'He has a family.'

'Did he say that?'

'He's called out for a woman. Her name's Mary Louise. At least I think that's what he said.'

The daughter's name, I thought. Not the wife's but I

couldn't tell Deborah that. The less she knew, the better off she was.

Deborah said, 'He has a pocket watch. When I moved him to ease the pressure on his head, his watch fell out of his vest pocket. I wound it thinking the sound of it might comfort him.' Her voice shook. 'Inside the casing, there's a photograph. It's of a woman and two children. One's a boy and the other's a little girl. Brother Nels, they're his family. He has a wife and two children.'

'The woman could be a sister. The children might not be his.'

'It doesn't matter. She and the children are family.'

'You don't know that.'

'He has a family. Everyone has one of some sort. No one walks this earth alone.'

Like I was holding it, I felt the weight of the marshal's letter in the palm of my hand. He had a wife. There could be other relations. His mother and father could still be alive. He might have brothers and sisters. And here I sat, wanting a man with a family to die to save the families here.

Deborah said, 'I can't stop thinking about the photograph. He cares about them enough to carry their images. He sees them whenever he looks at the time.' She paused. 'His family's waiting for him.'

'Could be. But anybody related to a man who does what he does, knows it's slippery work.'

'That doesn't make the waiting easier.'

'No, it doesn't.' I understood she was talking about Samuel. Waiting caused a person's mind to play tricks. It was easy to think the worst. Like me thinking Samuel might have trouble getting through the mountains.

Deborah got up. She leaned over the marshal and took

the bunched-up cloth that was against the back of his head. Holding the cloth in her cupped hands, she said, 'It's dripping. I need fresh snow.'

'I'll do it.'

She shook her head. 'I need the fresh air.'

Deborah left the cabin. The marshal's breathing changed. The rasp turned into a watery crackle. It was like he was trying to call Deborah back. The crackling kept on. This was the end. He was breathing his last. I stood up, not knowing what to do.

Deborah came back in.

She clicked her tongue. 'He does that whenever I leave his side.' She put the cloth against the back of his head and sat down beside him. The marshal's breathing stuttered, then went back to a rasp.

Deborah said, 'He's aware of my coming and going. It could be he's aware of what we're saying.'

'I'll pick my words with care.'

She didn't say anything. I ate some of my dinner. Above the marshal's wheeze, branches from the linden outside scraped against the west side of the cabin. After a while, Deborah said, 'You have matters to see to in the morning.'

'I do.'

She lowered her head and I figured she was thinking what I was. While I was taking Braden to Floral Ranch, she'd be on her own with the marshal.

I said, 'I'd put it off if I could. But I can't.'

'I know. But I'm telling you this. I'm not opening my door again. I've had enough.'

'More than enough.'

'That's right. More than enough.'

There might not be a next time. But if we did get out of this scrape, I didn't know how we'd stop the next man from coming. If one came, I couldn't see us turning our backs on him. We wouldn't leave him on his own to wander the cliffs looking for the hideout at Floral Ranch. Neither would we turn him in. That'd be siding with gentiles, people who hated us. The only way out was to leave Utah Territory. All of us in Junction had to leave.

The thought of doing that tore at me. This was home.

Deborah said, her voice low, 'We'll have to get word to his family.'

I understood what she meant. If the marshal died.

She said, 'We have to. I can't bear the thought of a woman waiting for her husband and not knowing what happened. That's the hard part. The not knowing.'

Like how we didn't know where Samuel was. Then I was remembering how Carson Miller had called to me – *Brother Nels* – when he thought he saw something in the ravine. Like it was happening again, I heard the warning in his voice. He thought he saw metal glinting in the light.

Samuel carried wrenches, a measuring traveler, spindle shavers, and a hoop bender in his wagon. He carried axes, hammers, and knives. All were made of iron.

'Brother Nels. Did you hear me? About getting word to his family?'

I looked at her. I did my best to clear my thoughts. I said, 'He likely has friends not far behind. They'll carry the news to his relations.'

She looked down at her hands. She'd bunched the cloth soaked in mint in a tight fist. She said, 'That's right. I wasn't thinking straight. It's not the same.'

Deborah didn't have to tell me what she meant. No one was following behind Samuel. He was on his own.

The marshal's wheezy breathing filled the room, stopping

and starting. It rubbed my nerves. So did the linden's branches scratching against the side of the cabin. Once we got through this, if we did, I'd take an axe to those limbs. If I could, I'd take an axe to Carson's words about thinking he saw glints coming off metal in the ravine.

Deborah said, 'I went to my sister's today like I do every day.'

'Did you?'

'She thinks we've strayed.'

'Strayed?'

'From how others do.' Deborah inclined her head toward the marshal. She was sitting beside him. This was her way of telling me she was picking words that wouldn't mean much to him.

'Maybe we have,' I said.

Deborah nodded. 'My sister doesn't like it that I'm alone every fall.'

'She said that?'

'Not in those words but nearly. And she's not the only one. Especially now, this winter. At church services, people can't seem to find my eyes when they talk to me. The women are uneasy around me. They don't know what to say to me beyond how well I'm bearing up. But I know what's going through their minds. My husband is coming through the Fish Lakes during the winter.'

'He knows what he's doing.'

'You and I know that. But I'm a woman alone, that's how the other women look at me. They're afraid. I see it on their faces. Something like this could happen to their husbands.' Deborah paused, then, 'I believe they're afraid of something else.' Her voice was low. I strained to hear her over the marshal's raspy breathing. 'They're afraid the day might come when someone might think it necessary to claim responsibility for me. But you can be sure I've made it clear that Samuel will come home, and I've made it clear I can take care of myself.'

'Good.' My voice was sharp. I pushed away from the table. The chair legs scraped against the wood floor. I got up, threw open the cookstove door, crouched low, and blew on the embers. God Almighty. The neighbor men were circling around Deborah. Some of them had told me they thought it looked bad for Samuel, him weeks past due home. They said they were concerned for Deborah's welfare. I'd told them Samuel would be home by the second week of January. I'd told them Deborah wasn't alone. Her sister and family were here. And me, I'd thought but held back from saying.

I blew harder on the embers. They glowed, then flared into flames. I hadn't understood what the neighbor men were saying. Only Ollie Cookson had two wives. No one else here practiced plural marriage. It hadn't crossed my mind someone would consider taking Deborah as a second wife. It hadn't crossed my mind their doubts about Samuel getting home were that strong.

She said, 'They're leaving.'

'Who is?' I closed the cookstove door and faced Deborah.

'My sister and her family. They don't like it here. After the baby is born in the spring, they're going back.' She hesitated. 'They want me to go with them.'

I sat down at the table, blood thumping hard in my ears. There was no need for Grace to bring up leaving in the spring. It didn't do any good to talk about something that was months off. She should have waited until the time was closer. Now, Michael and Grace's leaving was one more thing to prey on Deborah's mind.

From the start, I didn't have much use for either Grace or

Michael. Grace expected Deborah to wait on her hand and foot. Michael was a good enough schoolmaster but he didn't know up from down when it came to orchards. He was a big man, tall and sturdy-looking. That didn't do him much good, though. His eyes were weak. He had to wear spectacles. He'd rather have a book in his hands than work the earth.

What got under my skin the most, though, was how he wanted to change Junction. He and Grace moved here early in October. A week later, Michael called a meeting of the men and boys aged sixteen and older. By my count, that was four-teen of us. Fifteen if I counted Samuel, but I didn't. It being October, he was still in southern Utah repairing and making wheels. Eight of us men showed up at the schoolhouse for the meeting.

'Brothers,' Michael had said. He stood at the front by his desk. The rest of us sat corralled in school desks that were too small for us. He said, 'I come to you with a message from our brothers and sisters in western Utah. A message of grave importance.' His thick spectacles had slipped down his nose. He pushed them back into place. 'They're concerned about the people in Junction. Gravely concerned.'

A desk behind me squeaked. Somebody shuffled his feet. Michael said, 'Your brothers and sisters believe you've drifted from the church. I've been called to direct you back to the teachings.'

'Who's saying this about us?' Ollie Cookson said.

'The stake presidents. And some of your families.'

We shot each other looks. Say too much against the church, and we'd be branded apostates. That would bring shame to our relations. They'd be pressed to disclaim us. There'd be no going back home.

Michael said, 'The solution is at hand, Brothers. I propose

we begin by electing a bishop, one who will give freely of his time to organize Junction. He'll appoint counselors and ward clerks. A woman will be appointed to organize a Relief Society.' Michael picked up a sheet of paper from his desk. 'I've sketched out plans for a wardhouse. We can build it here, close to the schoolhouse.'

He handed the paper to Peter Sorenson in the front row. Peter gave it a quick look. Over his shoulder, he handed it to me. My look was just as fast. If we'd wanted a wardhouse, we would have built one. I passed the sketch on.

Michael said, 'As for the matter of a bishop, I propose that those who want to serve, come to the front now. A week from today we'll meet and take a vote.'

Somebody cleared his throat. The sketch of the wardhouse rustled as it made its way around the room. Nobody came forward. Michael studied us, his eyes big behind his spectacles. I figured it would perturb him, a crowd of us not stampeding to the front of the room. Instead, a smile tugged at the corners of his mouth. He fought to hide it. A full beard would have done him some good about now. One trimmed close to the skin didn't do much covering.

He said, 'It's a weighty responsibility, one not to be taken lightly. I understand that. Perhaps you believe you aren't deserving of the honor but as the Prophet Joseph Smith said, we're all equals.' Michael's gaze went from man to man. 'Brothers? Are any of you willing to be considered for the position?'

Did Michael need it spelled out? If we'd wanted a bishop, we would have elected one years back. We came to Junction to get away from being organized into committees. We didn't want to be told what we were supposed to do and how. It wasn't that we didn't hold church services. We did. The same went for how we helped out when a family needed a barn built or a woman was too sick to care for her children. We just didn't want to be made to do it.

Michael stood alone in the front of the room. If Samuel had been there, he would likely have untangled himself from his school desk and gone to stand with Michael. He'd have to reach up, Samuel being shorter than Michael, but he'd reach up and put an arm around his brother-in-law's shoulders. He would get us to give Michael a rousing cheer of appreciation. He'd say how proud he was of Michael for bringing the concerns of the stake presidents to us. Then, somehow, Samuel being Samuel and knowing how to do such things, he would shift the talk so that we looked like far better Saints than Michael had first thought. The idea of electing a bishop would be left to dangle.

It was October, though, and Samuel wasn't due home until the first of December. Michael stood before us, waiting. He pushed his spectacles up into place. 'Brothers,' he said. 'If you'll have me, I'm willing to serve as your bishop.'

I cut a sideways look at Adam Baker sitting in the desk next to me. A fair-minded man, we looked to him to settle our disputes when Samuel wasn't here to do it. He tapped his fingers on the desk. Likely he didn't want a bishop any more than I did. But if word spread that we turned down Michael's offer, the stake presidents could turn us out of the church.

That part didn't bother me. I was a man on my own. That couldn't be said for the men with wives and children. If the church turned against us, the elders would see to it that no Saint would trade with us. In that way, we'd have to leave Utah. We'd have to live with gentiles, people who hated us.

Adam stopped tapping his fingers. He gave me a quick glance, then drew himself up the best he could in the desk.

He said, 'Well now, Brother Michael, this is good of you. Generous, I'd say, you stepping forward like this. And you and Sister Grace new here and hardly settled in. We all appreciate it. But in keeping with church practice, the appointment of a bishop calls for a vote. As you said. Even in a one-man race.'

Somebody laughed.

Adam went on. 'Since not all the men are here tonight, seems we should take a vote when everyone is. I'm thinking about the women and the children, too. They'll want to witness this. I can just hear my wife now. For that matter, all the women. They'll want to bring cakes and pies for a celebration. The election of our first bishop is a momentous occasion.'

'That's right,' Peter Sorenson said. 'A vote at another meeting. As the Prophet Joseph Smith declared all such matters should be handled.'

There was no arguing around the Prophet Smith's word. 'Of course,' Michael said. 'We'll vote a week from today. Next Tuesday.'

The next Tuesday, it rained too hard for everyone to attend the meeting. The Tuesday after that, Ollie Cookson needed a fair number of us to help fix a broken-down fence. After that, the irrigation ditches in the orchards were filled with silt and needed digging out. There were always reasons we couldn't meet. We never did take a vote. Neither did we build a wardhouse.

I was wrong to think Michael would let this ride. He'd been sent to save us. None of us took him up on this offer. Now he'd have to go back to Parowan and report about our downfall. That'd be bad for us. It'd be bad for Michael. He'd been sent to save us, and he'd failed.

Deborah, still sitting by the marshal, said, 'I knew something was wrong when I went to my sister's. She wasn't herself.

I felt sure she somehow knew about this.' Deborah nodded her head toward the marshal. 'But it wasn't this.'

'It's winter talk, this business about leaving, that's all. Don't listen to her.' My words came out too strong. I got myself a lungful of air, then let go of it. 'Folks get restless when they're mostly shut up inside. Their minds fill with peculiar notions. You can't listen to talk brought on by the cold and short days. Your sister and brother-in-law will forget about leaving come spring.'

She didn't say anything to that. I sat at the table, my plate before me empty. We could all be driven away from Junction long before spring. In the lamplight, Deborah's head was bowed. I didn't know what to do if she started crying.

She said, 'You're a good man.'

My hands went still. If she were mine, I'd walk across the room and put my arms around her.

'A good friend,' she said. 'None better.'

I felt a hard pinch in my heart. 'Well,' I said. It was the best I could come up with. I ran my forefinger along the edge of my plate until I found the fair-size chip on one side.

Deborah turned back to Fletcher. I couldn't see her face. We sat, the marshal's breathing stuttering and starting, each of us thinking our own thoughts. After a while, she said to Fletcher, 'You'll be all right, I'll be nearby.'

She got up, carried her chair to the table, and placed it so she'd face away from the bed. She sat down, catty corner to me. I didn't know what to make of any of this. Deborah looked into my eyes. The lamplight was faint and I couldn't see the blue in her hazel eyes. That didn't matter. I felt myself pulled to her.

'Brother Nels,' she said. 'His badge is missing. We have to find it.'

CHAPTER TWELVE

NELS – MOUNTAIN MEADOWS

January 12, 1888

Sitting at my table, Deborah leaned close. 'Did you hear me? His badge is gone.'

Like it was happening all over again, I felt my fingers pick it up from the bed. It must have fallen out of the marshal's pocket. It was warm. He kept it close to his person.

Deborah said, 'What if he lost it near my cabin? In my barn? Or here somewhere in the snow? If it's found, it'll be used against us. It's proof he looked around my place or yours. They'll claim he identified himself to us. They won't believe our story about how you found him.'

I couldn't tell her what I'd done with the badge. When the other lawmen got here, it wouldn't take long for them to figure out it was missing. They'd ask Deborah about the badge. If she knew the truth, she'd have to lie. It'd be one more lie on top of others. Her voice could give way. Panic might show in her eyes. The deputies would see the loose ground in our story.

I said, 'It could be he didn't have a badge. Not all of them do.'

'He had one. He showed it to me.'

'When?'

'When he first got here. Before he searched the barn and my cabin.' She held out her left hand, palm up like the badge might be there. 'We have to find it.'

I had to tell her something. Otherwise, she'd worry herself over something that didn't need worrying about. I said, 'He lost it.'

'But where?'

'It's lost.'

Her forehead puckered. I understood she was deciphering the meaning behind my words.

I said, 'Nobody will find it.'

'You're sure?'

Already I couldn't recall exactly where the crevice was on the trail where I'd hidden the badge. It was before Braden and I got to the pocket. It was one crevice of thousands. The badge was lost even to me. I said, 'It's gone.'

Deborah sat back in the chair. She tilted her head a little like she was looking heavenward. Maybe she was thanking God that the badge had been taken care of. Or she might have been asking God to forgive me for taking something that wasn't mine.

She leaned forward again. 'He's a marshal, not a deputy,' she said. 'Federal marshals don't come after outlaws, their deputies do that. Until now. Doesn't this strike you as peculiar?'

'Some.'

'That's all?'

'It's enough.'

'But you've thought about it?'

'Yes.' Then, 'It's not worth worrying about.'

Doubt showed in Deborah's eyes. She ran the fingertips of her right hand along the edge of the table in front of her. 'Braden,' she mouthed the word, 'told me two or three people were following him. If that's so, where are they?'

'I don't know. I wish I did. Something must have slowed

them down or maybe they split up for some reason. But they'll show up. We have to figure on that.'

'It's January.'

That was all she said but I knew what was under those words. Whatever Braden had done, it must have been bad to bring out a marshal in the winter.

Deborah flicked away some food crumbs from the table. I could tell she had more questions. Any other time, she wouldn't brush crumbs onto the floor. She was trying to make sense of the scrape we were in. I wished she'd stop.

She whispered, 'I thought Frank Dyer was Utah's marshal.'

Deborah was stepping on thin ice. I had to tell more lies. I said, 'I thought so too. Looks like he –' I nodded toward the bed – 'took over the job.'

'He's from Tennessee.'

'He told you that?'

'Yes. When he first got here. Him being from Tennessee made me think of the gentiles that killed Saints at Cane Creek.'

'That was three years ago. What's happening now has nothing to do with that.' Other than Tennesseans did their best to run off Saints. Other than Braden and three other elders went back to preach and managed to convert a marshal's daughter.

Deborah said, 'You think he was at Cane Creek?'

'It's not likely.'

'When he searched my cabin, he brought up Mountain Meadows.'

I bit back a cuss word.

'He said he knew what went on there, that we lied about how those people came to be killed. He said lying comes easy to us. He said it's not his way to hurt women and children. Not like how we did at Mountain Meadows.'

'That's got nothing to do with you.' Anger made my voice rise. I glanced at the marshal. If he'd heard me, it didn't show. His breathing rasped like before. I steadied myself and said, 'He was trying to unsettle you, get you to talk.'

'It went deeper than that. It was how he threw it at me, used it to show I come from bad blood. The way he said it, it was like it happened yesterday. Not thirty years ago.'

'Gentiles have long memories.'

'He might have had family there.'

'Did he say that?'

'No.'

'Then it's best not to speculate.'

'I know. But I can't help but question why he talked about it.'

'He's like most gentiles. It's one more thing against us.' And now his daughter had bound herself to people accused of murdering one hundred and twenty gentiles. It was reason enough for him to track Braden in January. He wanted to get his daughter away from us.

Deborah said, 'I was six when it happened. We lived in Parowan. I remember—'

'Don't.' I inclined my head toward the marshal letting her know nothing about Mountain Meadows should be said out loud.

Deborah bit her lower lip. Then she said, 'Yes. Of course. I'm sorry.'

'It's been a hard day.'

'Tomorrow's apt to be harder.'

The truth of her words weighed heavy. We didn't know

how matters would stand this time tomorrow. If I was arrested, I'd be taken from Junction. I might never see her again.

The thought pierced me. I felt an overpowering need to slide my hand across the table to where Deborah's right hand rested.

Her eyes widened. An odd mix of puzzlement and surprise crossed over her face. She gave her head a small shake, then backed her chair away, and stood up. Not looking at me, she cupped her elbows in her hands. Her gold wedding band glinted in the lamplight. She turned away and went to the marshal.

My face heated with shame. She knew I wanted to touch her.

Deborah stood over the marshal. There, she patted the wrapped pack of snow pressed to the back of his head. She said something to him. Her voice was too low for me to make out the words.

Finally, she turned toward me. I couldn't look at her. Deborah came back to the table. 'Your dishes,' she said, breaking the quiet. She picked up my empty plate with the fork on it. The fork rattled. She drew in some air and said, 'Bad as tomorrow might be, I won't have it said that dirty dishes were left on your table.'

I forced a smile. She hadn't read my thoughts, I told myself. She was thinking about tomorrow and what might happen. She didn't know I'd almost taken her hand. I'd covered such yearnings for years. I was good at it.

Deborah put the dishes in the basin and poured water that had been warming on the cookstove over them. Her back to where I sat, she began to do the washing.

Water sloshed in the basin. She didn't know, I said again to myself. And she never would. Some matters were best kept buried. But that didn't mean they were forgotten. Or that they didn't lay close to the surface.

Like Mountain Meadows. Saints didn't speak about what happened there. People remembered though. The marshal had. Something made him talk about it.

I fastened my thoughts on that instead of on Deborah. I made myself think about how the marshal was from Tennessee and how the people killed at Mountain Meadows were from Arkansas. I conjured up the image of the map of the United States that hung in the schoolhouse and pieced together the states. Tennessee bordered Arkansas.

The marshal might have a tie to the people killed. He didn't look to be much older than me. He'd remember Mountain Meadows and maybe some of the people who had been there.

I was eleven when it happened. Samuel was twelve. At that time, Brigham Young aimed to populate southern Utah with Saints. Our families were new to the Territory. My father had been married to Samuel's mother just a handful of days. Brigham Young directed my father to settle in Cedar City far to the south of Salt Lake City. It pleased my father and our mothers to be called to do Saints' work for the church.

We'd been in Cedar City a few weeks when we got word about a massacre. A wagon party of gentiles camped not too far away from town had been killed by Indians. A hundred and twenty dead, we heard. Seventeen children were spared. They were all six years old or younger. The mysterious ways of God, people said.

The children were taken in by families in Cedar City. Not knowing much about Indians, Samuel and I took up going to the houses where these children were kept. At the first house we went to, we told the woman who lived there we wanted to talk to the two little boys she was looking after.

'How'd they get away from the Indians?' Samuel said to her. She'd cracked open the door just a few inches. I tried to look inside to find the boys but I couldn't see past her. Samuel said, 'That's what me and Nels here want to ask them. How'd they fight off the Indians?'

'So we'll know what to do,' I said. 'If Indians come after us.'

'Boys,' the woman said. Her voice was crisp. 'Go home. Let them be. They've suffered enough.'

'Were they scalped?' Samuel said.

She closed the door. We went to the houses where the other children were. The women didn't let us inside. They told us to go home.

That night Samuel and I got a whipping and a warning from my father. 'Those children aren't your business,' he said. 'We don't know nothing about them. Or what happened. Understand? Nothing.'

The whipping and warning didn't do much good. We were boys, we had good ears. The first Sunday after the massacre, the Cedar City men congregated by the wagons and horses following church services. Samuel and I drifted nearby but not too close. We crouched low and ran our hands over the ground like we were looking for arrowheads.

'They're saying white men, Saints, did the killings,' we heard a man say. 'Not Indians.'

'Who's saying that?' another man said.

Samuel and I edged a little closer. The first man said, 'The survivors. The ones spared.'

'They're children,' another man said. 'They don't know what they saw. I'm telling you it was the Paiutes.'

'Doesn't much matter who did the killing,' someone else

said. 'The men in the wagon party were drunk and vile as the devil. They bragged how they helped kill the Prophet Joseph Smith. An eye for an eye, that's how I see it. They had it coming.'

Samuel and I looked at each other. His eyebrows were shot high.

Weeks passed. After Sunday services and Wednesday-night wardhouse social gatherings, Samuel and I made ourselves small and strained our ears to listen to the men. We heard that in Arkansas, where the wagon party was from, relatives of the dead demanded to know what happened. So did some Saints. Not able to square their consciences with the church's account of the massacre, hundreds of Saints turned traitor and left Utah. They spread the word that seventeen children had survived. Relatives of the wagon party clamored to know who the children were and where they were. Saints who wanted to stay in good standing with the church kept their mouths shut.

The federal government sent the army. They claimed Brigham Young had too much power. Their aim was to invade Salt Lake City. Saints formed their own army. My father didn't join, he wanted nothing to do with killing. 'I have Swedish blood in my veins,' he said. 'Never will I join an army. Not even for Brigham Young.' At night, up in the loft where Samuel and I slept, we plotted. 'Let's you and me go to Salt Lake,' Samuel whispered. 'Watch the fighting.' Before we could, a blizzard slowed the U.S. army. Tempers simmered down.

That wasn't the end of Mountain Meadows. Relatives of the dead wanted the truth. The federal government sent men to investigate. Whenever the men of Cedar City knotted in tight groups, Samuel and I crept close by. Some Saints, we heard, had admitted to investigators they'd been at the massacre. 'To stop the Indians,' they said. 'To help the wagon party, but we were outnumbered by the Paiutes.'

That answer didn't sit well with gentiles. Investigators asked, 'Then how were you able to claim the cattle and trunks of clothes that belonged to the dead?'

'We wrestled them away from the Paiutes.'

'Isn't it true that Brigham Young ordered the massacre?'

'No. He didn't know anything about it.'

'You're lying. None of you in Utah Territory, the Indians too, can take a leak without asking his permission.'

'He didn't know,' witness after witness said.

No one was arrested.

A year and a half after the massacre, the U.S. army rounded up the children and took them back to Arkansas where they'd come from. 'That's the end of it,' my father announced one night at dinner. 'They'll leave us alone now.'

He was wrong. Those children talked once they were back in Arkansas. White men, they said, killed their mothers and fathers, sisters and brothers, aunts, uncles, and cousins.

There were more investigations. Witness accounts criss-crossed. Like before, no one was arrested.

'No more talk about Mountain Meadows,' my father ordered. 'Not in my house.' Figuring it would put the past behind us, when school let out for the day, my father worked Samuel and me hard, teaching us carpentry. Still, the massacre pestered my mind.

I was maybe fourteen and Samuel was fifteen when we were alone in my father's carpentry shed. An old man had died and we were sanding boards for the coffin. Doing that must have stirred up something inside of me. Before I knew it, I was telling Samuel I wanted to believe that Paiutes had done all the killing but couldn't.

'It doesn't stack up,' I said. 'Not when you take it piece by piece.'

'What doesn't?' Samuel kept sanding the board he was working on. I'd stopped.

I said, 'For starters, the dead were left to rot where they'd been killed. They were gentiles but we're supposed to be better than them. We should have given them Christian burials.'

Samuel ran the sandpaper back and forth over a board. The scrape was raw and grinding. The quick look he gave me told me he was listening.

I said, 'And those children, the ones that survived. Remember how they were shut away from the rest of us? Then when their kin wanted them back, the church elders said the Indians had them. The elders said they had to send out search parties to find them. Once they found them, the elders had to work out deals with the Indians to get them back. That's a lie. You and I both know it. Those children were brought here right after the massacre.'

Samuel stopped sanding. He glanced around the shed like somebody might hear.

I said, 'It doesn't stack up.'

'Which part doesn't? The part that maybe some Saints killed women and children? Or that the church is working hard to kick dirt on the truth?'

It took twenty years to pin the blame on someone. John D. Lee, a Saint, was judged and shot dead by a firing squad for killing the wagon party. That didn't add up either. It was Samuel who put words to it. He and I were grown men by that time.

'One man killed a hundred and twenty people?' Samuel had said. 'And some of those people armed with rifles? Lee couldn't be the only one, there were others. There had to be.'

I'd thought the same. Samuel putting words to it made me feel less alone with my thoughts. I said, 'Nothing adds up. John D. Lee was Brigham Young's adopted son. I can't see Lee doing anything without Young knowing about it.'

Samuel nodded his agreement.

Water under the dam, Samuel's mother would claim. That was how she talked about the past. The massacre was a long time ago. She, my mother, and my father made like none of it mattered. It could be that if they thought about it too much, they'd have doubts about Brigham Young. They'd followed him to Utah Territory. They looked to him for guidance. If they thought he had a hand in the massacre, they'd be shook to the bone.

Not talking about it, though, didn't mean it hadn't happened. It didn't mean the relatives of the dead had forgotten. It could make them hate us more than most. Some might still want revenge. The marshal might be one of those.

Deborah finished washing my dinner dishes. She shook the water from her hands and dried them on her apron. In the lamplight, her brown hair glinted with red. She turned and looked at me. 'Brother Nels,' she said.

Something in her tone made me want to get up and go outside. I didn't know what she was about to say. Or what I would.

Deborah sat down at the table. She looked over her shoulder toward the marshal. He was a dark shape in the shadows. His breathing wheezed. She turned back to me and said, 'You're not telling me everything. You know more than you're saying.'

I shook my head.

'It shows on your face. It's in your eyes. I'm pressing you.

I shouldn't, it's not how we do but this time I need to know. There's more to this than polygamy. Isn't there?'

'No. There isn't.'

Her eyebrows lifted. She didn't believe me. She kept studying my face. Silence stretched between us. I'd said all I was going to say.

The marshal coughed. It was watery. He coughed again, harder. He shook from it. 'He wants me by him,' Deborah said.

So did I.

———

It wasn't too long after that when Sally sprang to her feet, barking. There was a commotion outside. It was a man, shouting. Sally, at the door, kept on, her barks deep-throated. Deborah, sitting at the marshal's bedside, stood. Her eyes were wide with alarm. I went to the door telling Sally to quit her barking. She didn't pay me any mind.

More shouting. I glanced at Deborah. I read the look she gave me. The deputies. Then I was thinking it could be Braden. He might have changed his mind. He came back to turn himself in.

'Brother Nels,' a man called through the door. 'Are you there?'

A neighbor. Braden didn't know my name.

In a rush Deborah was beside me. 'It's Michael,' she said, whispering. 'Don't let him in. He can't see the marshal.'

'Brother Nels,' Michael shouted from the other side of the door. 'Sister Deborah's missing.'

'Oh no,' she said. 'Oh no.'

Sally kept barking. Michael kept calling through the

door. I cussed under my breath. Everything that could go wrong, had.

Deborah pulled me away from the door. She said, 'We can't let him in. He can't see the marshal. When the others come, if Michael knows, it'll show on his face. He's not good at covering his thoughts.'

Outside, Michael pounded on the door. The marshal's breathing shuddered, stopping and starting. His right eye was open.

I said, 'I have to talk to him before he wakes all of Junction looking for you.'

'Don't let him in.'

I took hold of Sally's collar. 'Quiet,' I said to her. Then to Deborah, 'I'll talk to him outside.'

CHAPTER THIRTEEN

NELS – THE NEIGHBORS

January 12, 1888

Michael was worked up. He twitched with nerves. We stood with our backs close to the cabin to keep out of the falling snow. 'It's Sister Deborah,' he said. 'Something's wrong, she's not home.' His words came at me in a fast run. 'No lights at the windows, no smoke from the cookstove. I went in. It's cold as a cave. I looked in the barn. The cow hasn't been milked. We have to look for her. Something's happened.'

'She's here,' I said. I had to say it. Otherwise, he'd keep looking for her.

'Here?'

'There's been an accident.' I had to say that, too. I couldn't have him think the worst of her and me. 'I went and got Sister Deborah to help.'

'An accident? What happened? Someone's hurt? Who?'

'It's a stranger. I found him on the bridge. He's bad off.'

'Sister Deborah's here? Inside? Now?'

'She's looking after him. She's all right.'

Michael made a motion to go to the door. 'No,' I said. 'Don't go in.'

'Why not?'

'Commotion of any sort turns his breathing more ragged. Sister Deborah can hardly leave his bedside. When she does, he takes up gasping. If you go in, he could get so riled that he could choke himself to death.'

'Heavenly Father. What happened?'

'His horse showed up here. I went looking for the owner and found him in the snow on the bridge.' My lies came out smooth. 'His breathing isn't right. There's a big knot on the back of his head. It could be his horse threw him and he cracked his skull.'

Saying that made me hear the crack. It made me see the marshal in the snow. His eyes were fixed on me. He was begging for help. Braden was on his knees on the other side of the marshal asking God to forgive him.

Michael said, 'Is he one of us? Is he wearing temple garments?'

I cussed to myself. I should have seen this question coming. An unconscious man, a stranger to Junction. Anybody here would have looked for the garments. But Braden and I hadn't needed to look. Saints who'd been endowed into the church were the only ones who wore them. Gentiles called them long johns but they weren't. We wore the garments every day even when it was hot. Sacred symbols, a V and a backward L, were stitched over each breast. Those symbols were there to remind us of our vows to stay faithful to the church.

I said, 'He's not one of us.'

'A gentile,' Michael said.

'Seems so. Whatever he is, he's bad off.'

'What's he doing here?'

'I don't know. He's too hurt to talk.'

'A gentile,' Michael said again. I couldn't see his face in the dark but I knew he was working to make sense of it. He said, 'When did you find him?'

'Dusk. Around suppertime.'

In the night cold, I felt Michael give me a long look. His hands went to his face. He took off his spectacles and wiped them on one end of his neck scarf.

He put them back on. 'Let me get this right. You found a gentile on the bridge that's near my cabin. He must have gone past our place but he didn't stop. He crossed the creek. Or tried to.' Michael paused. 'He knew where he was going.'

'It's best not to speculate about intentions. He's bad off. Keep it to that.'

'He's looking for somebody. Isn't he?'

Michael was walking this to a place where he wasn't welcome. I figured he'd heard about the men we helped and about the lawmen. Men with plural wives had been hiding in the canyon country for four years. Saints might not talk but they knew how to whisper behind their hands.

Michael said, 'He's after someone.'

The man didn't have any business pressing me for information. It was like we'd voted him bishop and it was his place to know. I didn't appreciate it. I said, 'I don't know the hurt man's intentions and neither do you.'

Michael coughed, then said, 'Who else knows about him?'

'The Bakers. I asked Sister Rebecca how we could help him.'

'They'll never believe you found him unconscious.'

'I don't know what you're talking about.'

'I think you do, but all right. I won't say more, other than this. We need to tell all the neighbors about him.'

'No.'

'Hear me out.'

'Go home, Brother Michael.'

'Listen to me.'

'Go home.'

'He has friends,' he said. 'They'll come looking for him, you know that. But let's say you didn't know. If he were truly a stranger, you'd tell the neighbors about him. There'd be no reason not to. If he were indeed a stranger, you'd call in the women to take turns caring for him. The men would form a posse to see if he's part of a party. There could be others with him in need of help. We have nothing to hide. That's what his friends must think when they arrive. As a town, we have to do all we can for him. He's a stranger found on the bridge. That's all the neighbors need to be told.'

Telling the neighbors wasn't how it worked. It went against the grain. Agreeing with Michael went against the grain, too. Yet his plan had some merit.

I stomped my feet to bring warmth back to them. Michael turned a little away. He tucked his gloved hands under his armpits. He was giving me time to think. If Samuel were here, he'd tell me what he thought of Michael's idea. Maybe he'd disagree with Michael and say how it was best to stick to the plan as usual. But there was nothing usual about this. Samuel might say this was the time to work it the opposite way.

Doing that meant I had to trust Michael. I had to trust he wouldn't say too much to the neighbors. He wouldn't let anything slip out that shouldn't be said. I wasn't sure I could hold him to do that. I didn't know him. The first time I met him was when he moved here in October. When he took up pushing for a bishop and wardhouse, I kept my distance. But him being a pious believer was on my side. He'd do his best to protect Saints.

The neighbors would, too. Nobody had strayed so far that they'd do harm to any Saint. It had to be said, though, they'd been content to let Samuel, Deborah, and me be the only ones to help the men. Nobody stepped forward and said, 'Send the next one to me. I'll guide him to Floral Ranch.' They knew but they looked the other way. For good reason. They had more to risk. They had children. The three of us didn't.

Michael could say too much to the neighbors. Or the truth would show on his face. Deborah said Michael wasn't able to cover his thoughts. Not that the neighbors couldn't figure out the truth. Even some of the older children might guess.

It came down to fooling the deputies. Like Michael said, we had to do like there was no reason to keep the marshal a secret.

I didn't like it. Too many people. Too many chances for mistakes. When the deputies came with their questions, everybody had to say the same thing. They couldn't give anything away.

Samuel, if he were here, would say we were in a corner but even corners had ways out. A man just had to rearrange his thinking and his way of seeing. That didn't mean it came easy. It meant walking in the dark, not sure what was up ahead.

'It's late,' I said to Michael. 'There's no point getting everybody stirred up now.' I paused. Samuel would try this plan. He wouldn't discount it because it came from Michael. If he were here, he probably would have thought of it himself.

I said, 'All right. In the morning tell them about the stranger I found.'

I expected that me giving in to his plan would make Michael gloat. If he was, I couldn't tell. He said, 'He is, isn't he? A stranger. He's not from here.'

'Until today, I've never seen him.'

'A stranger.' Michael said it like he was trying to press the word into his thoughts. He coughed. It sounded like lung burn from the cold. He said, 'There's much in Junction I don't approve of. But what you do for those in need of safe passage, the risks you take, you do for God. God sees all. He knows you take these risks to uphold the revelations and covenants of the church.'

I nearly laughed. God, all-knowing and all-seeing, would tell Michael he was wrong about me. Ask me, and I'd come right out and admit I didn't believe in the revelation that sanctioned plural marriage. Neither did I believe everything church leaders said. The massacre at Mountain Meadows was the beginning of my doubt. Lydia and the baby's deaths deepened it. What Michael didn't know, and what I wasn't about to tell him, was this: I helped the men because I couldn't bring myself to quit the church. Not all the way.

Even with my doubt, I was sealed to it. When I was five days old and still in Sweden, my family and I were baptized Latter-day Saints by missionaries from America. Led by these missionaries, the church carried us from Sweden to Illinois. It pushed us to Missouri, then Nebraska, and finally Utah. I did everything like I should. I was endowed into the church. To this day, I still wore the garments. Lydia and I were married in the temple at St. George. The church was all I knew. Saints were the only people I knew.

I didn't help the men like Braden so I could uphold the covenants and revelations. Those covenants and revelations didn't need me to hold them up. Plenty of others were willing to do that job. I helped the men because I couldn't bring myself to turn against my own.

Michael said, 'I'll speak to the neighbors in the morning.' He pulled off his right glove and put out his bare hand for me to shake.

I got my glove off and took his hand.

He said, 'Look after my sister-in-law.'

'I won't let anything happen to her.'

Michael's grip was firm. So was mine. When our hands dropped, he said, 'God's with us.'

I nodded. I figured Michael might not be so sure about God's stand on this if he knew how the marshal really came to be hurt.

Michael started to walk toward the bridge, then stopped. He turned to face me. 'Tell Sister Deborah I'll milk her cow and feed the chickens first thing in the morning.'

Deborah's animals had slipped my mind. 'She'll appreciate it,' I said. Then I was thinking how Junction had failed Michael. He hadn't been able to bring us back to the church. Now Junction was in a different kind of trouble. This could be a chance for Michael to redeem himself in the eyes of the church leaders. He could report his part in helping us uphold Joseph Smith's holy revelation about plural marriage.

Doing that came with risks. Michael said so himself. He had to know he could lose his home and find himself in jail. He didn't know it could be worse. He didn't know about the kidnapping charge. Or how the marshal came to be hurt.

Whatever Michael's reasons for helping were, he was part of it now. I said, 'A stranger found on the bridge. That's all there is to this.'

'There's no reason to think otherwise.' Michael tipped his hat to me. I tipped mine to him.

'Look after her, Brother Nels.' He left, his footfall crushing the snow.

———

Standing outside of my cabin, I listened as Michael crossed the bridge. He got me to change the plan but he hadn't pressed about who the marshal was hunting. He probably believed I'd gotten the hunted man to Floral Ranch days ago.

I looked up at the cliffs that anchored Junction to the floor of the canyon. I couldn't see the cliffs in the dark but they were there. I wanted to believe the same about Braden. He was keeping his word. He wouldn't go off on his own with the notion of turning himself in. Surely the man understood the trouble that would bring to all of us.

Michael's footfall faded. Nearby, the upper branches of the lindens scratched and creaked in the light wind. It was still snowing. Getting Braden to Floral Ranch in the morning might not go any better than it had today.

Trouble wasn't supposed to find me here. That was what I thought the first time I saw the cliffs and the floor of the canyon. It was the summer Samuel married Deborah. A few days after their wedding, a feeling of restlessness came over me. I put my carpenter tools away and hired on to help move cattle to pastures north of here. When the drive was over, I didn't go home to Cedar City. I went south to do some looking around on my own. I stumbled into the Wastelands. It didn't take long to figure it'd be the death of me with its dusty soil and pillars of rock cliffs. Then I came across what I took to be an Indian trail. I followed it for three days, what there was of it. It came and went, and at times I had to backtrack to find it. I'd just about decided I'd seen enough dust and rock when I heard water off in the distance.

It was the convergence of a creek and river on the floor of a canyon. Years later, I found out they were the Sulphur and the Fremont. The soil was good, there were trees, and the red cliffs held the sun's warmth. I set up camp by the Fremont. I fished, hunted, and didn't see another person. I stayed until the days shortened and something inside of me said it was time to go home. Once I was back in Cedar City, I took up my carpenter tools and did all manner of work to earn my living. Years passed. I married Lydia and believed I would never see this place again. Then she and the baby died. A day after the burial, I closed our cabin, took only what was needed, and made my way to where the creek and the river came together.

Now, I squatted and scooped up a handful of snow. Barehanded, my fingers burned from the cold. I stood and tried to pack the snow into a ball. It was too dry and wouldn't stick. I spread my fingers wide. The snow fell between them.

I looked up. No stars or moon. I was a fool to believe any place sheltered a man from trouble. I was a fool to believe a smart man could always outwit trouble.

Even one as smart as Samuel. He might be buried in a snowdrift high in the Fish Lakes.

I kicked the snow, cursing myself for letting my thoughts dip into a deep pit. I had enough to worry about. The marshal was sick in my cabin. I had to get Braden hidden at Floral Ranch. And right now I had to go inside and explain to Deborah how Michael planned to tell the neighbors about Fletcher.

Praying didn't come easy for me. It'd never done me much good. Tonight, I bowed my head like I was in church.

Heavenly Father. Help us.

CHAPTER FOURTEEN

DEBORAH – THE PROMISE

January 13, 1888

It was still dark outside when I heard Nels stir. I lay on the floor next to the bed with my eyes closed. The blanket that covered me smelled of hay and horse.

Last night, Nels put his bedroll along the door. He was as far from me as he could be. He'd slept in his clothes, and I'd stayed in my dress. Now, his clothes whished as he straightened them.

The marshal's breathing rasped and wheezed. He was alive.

Nels cleared his throat. He pulled on his boots, hopping a little as he did. The floorboards shook. He was getting ready to take Braden to Floral Ranch. More whishing, then the clink of tinned cans. He was putting supplies in a knapsack. Sally's toenails clicked on the floor. She sniffed my hair. I stayed still as though I were asleep. It was better that way. I was a woman who'd slept in the home of a man who wasn't my husband or a relative.

Last night, Nels and I hadn't talked about it but we both knew I needed to stay. He had to get an early start in the morning. It wouldn't be right to leave the marshal alone.

The marshal's teeth rattled. The cabin was cold. The cook-stove door squeaked opened. Nels put wood in and blew long puffs of air to stoke the fire. Last night, speaking in a whisper, he'd told me what he and Michael had decided about telling the neighbors.

'I wasn't for it,' Nels had said. 'Not at first. But then I came to see the sense of it. We have to look like we have nothing to hide.' The way he said this made me think he expected me to put up an argument. Instead, I let the idea settle on me. It was what Samuel would do. I didn't like the thought of Grace and the boys being part of this but Samuel would tell me to set my concerns to the side. Think about this from all angles, he'd tell me. Study it before making a judgement. I did that and after a while, I had said, 'Michael's right.'

Flames in the stove crackled, catching hold. The wood popped. Nels closed the cookstove door and walked a few steps. His coat whooshed as he put it on. Next were his scarf, hat, and gloves. I didn't want him to go. I didn't want to be alone with the marshal.

Nels, now dressed for the cold, seemed to hesitate. I thought he might say something, and all at once I wanted to tell him to take care of himself, be safe, don't disappear, I was waiting for his return, and above all else, he was dear to Samuel and to me.

I held back the words. They were too tender.

The door opened. Sharp air blew in. The door clicked closed. Nels was gone.

'Godspeed,' I said as though he could hear me.

———

Nels gone, I got up. The marshal reeked of urine. A shudder crawled down my spine. I should do something about that.

I held a lamp over him. Yesterday, I had tucked some of Nels' spare clothes against the marshal's chest to keep him on his left side. During the night he had rolled onto the clothes so that now he was partway on his stomach.

Sally poked her nose into the marshal's blankets. 'No, girl,' I said. 'Get away from there.'

The marshal's breathing turned shallow and quick. He was afraid, I thought. An image of Samuel hurt and helpless flashed through my thoughts. 'You're not alone,' I said to the marshal. 'I'm here.'

His breathing eased some. I said, 'I have to go outside but I'll be back. You have my word.'

I put on my coat and went outside into the dark. Sally came with me. I breathed in the crisp air and held up the lantern I carried. It had stopped snowing. A drift against the cabin looked to be knee high. A trail of deep footsteps led away from the cabin. These were Nels' from a few minutes ago.

Sally and I followed the path Nels had broken. It'd be slow-going for him and Braden. Getting to and from Floral Ranch could take most of the day. At least the snow had quit. Nels wouldn't get turned around like he had yesterday.

I used the outhouse, then started the walk back to the cabin. Dread sat on my shoulders. The marshal could die today. Or get better. But I wouldn't be alone. The neighbors, or some of them, would be here.

My cheeks burned from the cold. I didn't know where Nels had taken Braden last night. Wherever it was, the man must be half-frozen. His three wives must be worried sick. They might cluster together, their children with them. They waited to hear word of their husband's welfare. They waited to hear if he'd been caught.

I stopped a few yards from Nels' cabin. As early as it was, a light showed on the other side of the bridge. Grace and Michael were up. She might be cooking Michael's breakfast before he left to milk my cow and feed the chickens. After that, Michael would tell the neighbors about the stranger Nels had found. From there, matters would take a direction I couldn't predict.

Unless the marshal got better. I knew what would happen then.

———

The stench inside the cabin was a fist to my stomach. I backed outside into the fresh air, leaned against the closed door, and gulped in the cold.

The marshal's bowels had emptied. It was a harbinger of his near death. Women who cared for the dying talked about this in whispers. When the bowels loosened, the end was soon, they said. The body was cleansing itself before meeting God.

He might have an hour. Maybe a little longer. He might be dead when I went back inside.

Cold as it was, I began to sweat. I wanted a man's death. It could save us. Not that I would say that out loud. But God knew.

The deputies would know, too, if they found the marshal dead and laying in his own filth.

I had to clean him.

Yesterday, I'd bargained with God that I'd take care of the marshal. In turn, someone – a woman, I hoped – would take Samuel in if he were in need of help. I hadn't let myself think that tending the marshal meant more than washing dirt from his face and boiling mint leaves.

I didn't have to wash him now. I could wait until he died. I could wait until some of the neighbors were here to help.

That could be hours from now. The deputies could get here first.

The marshal was still alive. He was one of God's children.

Whatsoever ye would that men should do to you, do ye even so to them.

Then I was hearing my mother's lesson. *If ye do not remember to be charitable, ye are as dross, which the refiners cast out.*

God was testing me. It was wrong to let the marshal lay in his own filth.

I went back inside. I wrapped my scarf around my mouth and nose to keep out some of the stench, then took off my coat. Sally paced, unsettled. I warmed water on the cookstove and laid out the rags I'd washed last night. I found scissors in a canning jar where Nels kept needles and thread.

'Are you awake?' I said to the marshal, standing over him. He was still partway on his stomach but his left eye showed. I asked him again. His eye opened partway. He shuddered. I understood I was a peculiar sight with the scarf over the lower half of my face.

'This won't be easy for either of us,' I said. 'But I've got to tidy you up.' I hesitated, picking my words. 'Your trousers.'

His eye closed. His face bunched, deepening the lines on his forehead. 'I'll try not to move you any more than I have to,' I said. 'I know it hurts your head.'

His lips moved. I thought he'd formed the word yes.

'I'll wind your watch,' I said. 'It will give us something to listen to.' Fumbling, I found his vest pocket and wound the stem. The ticking matched the beat of my heart. I clicked open the casing and didn't let myself look at the photograph.

I set the hour and minute hands to half past five. That wasn't the right time but was a guess. Right or wrong, it would measure the passage of time. I put the watch back into his vest pocket, then pulled the blankets down to the foot of the bed. For Samuel, I thought.

I got the warming stones I'd kept by his feet and put them on the floor. I cleared the bed of the clothing that I'd used to keep him propped on his left side. I laid out one of the horse blankets I'd slept on last night. I took hold of the marshal's shoulder. I drew in some air and then rolled him onto his back and the horse blanket. He cried out, then fainted.

My hands shook. The top button on his trousers was stuck. Sister Rebecca, who did our nursing, would know how to do this. She would take charge and manage this with ease. I wanted her here but the baby she expected was due soon.

Maybe one of the neighbor women was on her way now. It didn't matter who, just someone who could help me.

I fumbled with the button. It was too soon for Michael to have told the neighbors about the marshal. It was too soon for a woman to get here. The snow was deep, and some, like Sister Rebecca, were in no condition to manage the trip. No one might come.

Finally, the button slipped through the hole. The other four were easier to unfasten.

I tugged on his trousers. I lowered them inch by inch. Under them, he wore long johns. My stomach churned from the stink. For Samuel, I told myself.

I worked at getting the trousers off. Tears ran from the marshal's closed eyes. I blinked away my own tears. Heavenly Father, I prayed. Ease his pain. Help me. Help us both.

I pulled harder on the trousers, jostling the marshal. He moaned. I could almost feel the sharp jabs of pain pierce his head.

Two more tugs and the trousers came off.

Next were the long johns. They were one piece and I didn't have it in me to wrestle the marshal out of his vest and shirt. Using the scissors, I cut the long johns at his waist, moving and turning him to do this. Finally I was able to pull them off. My stomach heaved from the smell and from the sight of a man who was not my husband.

I couldn't bear the stink. I bunched up the long johns and trousers, took them outside, and dropped them in the snow.

Back inside, I got the basin of warm water and rags. 'Are you awake?' I said to the marshal. The only response was his watery breathing. I began to wash him. My stomach heaved, I swallowed the bile. *Heavenly Father, do you see what I'm doing for this man? And for the woman who mended his stocking, for the woman and children in the photograph, for the woman the marshal called out for. Mary Louise. Do you see how I'm holding up my end of the bargain? Send Samuel home. Send Samuel home.*

The marshal's eyes were still closed. His raspy breathing was quick. I heard myself say, 'My husband's a wheelwright.' I didn't know where these words came from or why I said them other than I needed to think about something that was different from what my hands were doing. 'He should be home but a rockslide blocked the trail and he's had to find another way to get here. He'll be home any time now.'

Using a cloth, I wiped up the filth that spattered the marshal's privates. 'My husband knows the back country, he's not one for getting lost. He's a man sure of his way. He always has been.' I washed the marshal's legs, moving him from side to side, hearing his groans but trying not to. 'I was eighteen when I met him, and we courted for a month. Some might say that wasn't enough time. But I knew and so did he. We married on my nineteenth birthday. Our wedding . . .' My voice broke.

The marshal's eyelids twitched. Keep talking, I imagined him thinking. To ease his humiliation. And mine.

I said, 'We danced, my husband and I, at the wardhouse after the wedding. My brothers and sisters were there, and their families. Neighbors, too. So many children. All of us danced, my mother and father together, my husband's family, waltzing. Those are my favorites. The fiddler wouldn't let us rest but kept us on our feet, all of us circling around the room, some of us bumping into the others. My husband has many fine qualities but keeping time isn't one. I don't think he noticed. He and I, we danced. "The Dew-Drop Waltz". "The Minnesota Waltz". And round dances from Sweden for my father-in-law and his wife. My father asked the fiddler to play a tune for a longways dance. That was what my mother grew up dancing in England. The fiddler didn't know any so he made do with a Virginia reel. "Turkey in the Straw".'

Tears burned the backs of my eyes. Today was January the thirteenth. By Nels' calculation, Samuel would get home this week.

It was only Friday. Samuel was close. He'd be home any time.

The marshal's breathing stopped. I waited, listening hard. It started again.

My hands shaking, I wiped the last of the filth from him. Then I blotted the linens, trying to clean them, doing what I could to keep my end of the bargain. For Samuel.

Finished, I propped the marshal on his left side and covered him with the blankets.

His mouth moved. 'What is it?' I said.

His lips twitched. His right eye was open, looking at me, pleading. I strained to hear him. The muscles on the right side of his face quivered and bunched as he tried to speak.

The other half of his face was flat. There was something he had to say. I believed it had nothing to do with knowing Braden had been in my barn. It was greater than that. It might be a message to his family, a prayer to God, a plea for forgiveness for having done a wrong. He might be forgiving a wrong done to him.

'What?' I said. 'What?' These could be his dying words. I waited. He didn't try again.

————

His breathing was shallow. I heated water on the stove, then washed my hands over and over again in the dish basin to get rid of any filth on me. I scrubbed my nails, my palms, the backs, between each finger, and my wrists. I was sick with shame. The marshal's silence could save us. The only reason I was here was to make us look good in the eyes of the deputies. I took care of him for Samuel and for the bargain I'd made. I'd washed him so God and the deputies would think better of me. I hadn't done it for the marshal.

He was our enemy. That was how I thought of him. Until he tried to speak. Or I thought he was trying. I might have imagined it but that didn't matter. The notion that death silenced everything that needed to be said made my heart hurt. I hurt for Thomas Fletcher, the person. I hurt for all the words he wanted to say to his wife and children but couldn't. I hurt for all he'd left undone and would never finish.

All I knew about him was the work he did. I didn't know what made him laugh or what caused him sorrow. Surely being a lawman was just one side of him. Maybe he whistled tunes or played the fiddle. Or he sang with a clear voice. He might have a knack for predicting the weather. His heart might go soft when he held a baby. He might like to study the night stars. He might draw pictures.

Nels drew. Some of his pictures were tacked on the cabin walls. Only one was framed but he'd done all of them with pencil on sheets of white paper the size of a book page.

One was a peach that hung from the end of a drooping branch with four leaves. The peach was shaded in such a way to show it was ripe and ready to be picked. Another drawing was of three carpenter tools – a flat plane, a spirit level, and a ruler – on a workbench. The one tacked near the door showed two boys on their stomachs on flat dusty ground. Their shirts were wrinkled and one boy had a tear near the hem of his pant leg. Their heads were close together as they watched a trail of what looked to be ants. Their faces couldn't be seen but the cowlick in the one boy's hair and the lankiness of the other boy told me they were Samuel and Nels.

A framed portrait of Lydia, Nels' wife, hung on the back wall over the foot of the bed. It was from her shoulders up and if my memory was true, Nels had drawn her wearing her wedding dress. Her starched lace collar stood up about an inch. The bow at the base of her throat was crisp and the ends of the ribbon hung even. Her dark hair was parted in the center. Her head was turned just enough to show that she had woven her thick hair into a braided knot at the back of her head.

Lydia was beautiful. I had forgotten just how much until seeing the drawing. Her eyes were dark and long-lashed. Her nose was straight and the corners of her lips were turned up in a soft smile.

They had married seven years ago. Nels was thirty-three and she was nine years younger. Samuel and I lived in Parowan then, and Nels lived in Cedar City. Samuel and I traveled to St. George where they were married in the temple. It was the first time we'd met Lydia. She was so shy she couldn't look either of us in the eye. Lydia didn't seem to know what to say to us or to any of the guests. She stayed by Nels' side letting him speak for her. Nels wasn't a wordy man, and Samuel and I marveled that they had managed a courtship.

She died fourteen months later during childbirth.

A few days after Lydia and the baby's deaths, Nels gathered his carpentry tools, left their home in Cedar City, and came to the floor of a canyon where Sulphur Creek flowed into the Fremont River. Samuel worried about Nels being on his own. Two months later, we carried our possessions in a wagon and came here. A few other families heard about us and after a while, they made their way to the place we came to call Junction. We built our cabins along the Sulphur. Others settled on the Fremont. None of us platted our homes in a square as Brigham Young said we should. Nobody said anything about building a wardhouse or voting for a bishop. All of us, I believed, were in search of a new start. None of us wanted to be judged by the church. We needed distance from whispers and knowing looks.

Because of Lydia's death, Nels and the rest of us came to the canyon country. She changed the direction of our lives. Yet, I knew only two things about her. She was pretty, and she was uneasy around people. Surely there was more to her. There always was. The same was true for the marshal. Thomas Fletcher.

Off in the distance, the school bell rang. I stopped scrubbing my hands. The bell rang again. Usually Michael shook the handheld ringer fast and sharp to summon his pupils. This morning, each ring was slow and measured. The sound ricocheted off the cliffs, muffled some by the snow. It rang again. Then again. My skin crawled. This was our call to the neighbors to gather at the schoolhouse. Trouble, the bell said. Michael was going to tell them about the man Nels had found on the bridge.

I dried my hands. Everything was about to change. The neighbors would come. They would make decisions. The marshal was a stranger to them. He didn't have a name. This might be the last time I would be alone with him.

I sat down by the marshal. 'Mr Fletcher,' I said. I hadn't called him by his name before. 'Can you hear me?'

The only movement was the slight rise and fall of his chest. 'I know your name,' I said. 'The others don't. They can't. To them, you're a stranger. But to me, you're Thomas . . .' I stopped. Something marked the pillow close to the marshal's right cheek. I got a lamp. A stain. A red stain.

I felt myself sway. Blood. It came from his ear.

The lamp in my hand rattled. I put it down on the kitchen table. I went lightheaded. My skin turned clammy. I got myself outside. The cold air slapped. I breathed it in. My lungs stinging, I blew out the air.

It was my fault. I'd jostled him when I undressed him and when I moved him onto his back, then onto his side. I'd made him worse. I could have been gentler; maybe I'd moved him more than I had to. I had hastened his death.

The wind tangled my skirt around my ankles. Strands of my hair lifted and blew into my eyes. I shook and wrapped my arms around myself. I wanted the marshal's death. Now God was showing just what that meant.

Something bumped against my leg. I swatted at my hair, getting it out of my eyes. It was Sally. She pushed against me with her nose. She looked up at me, trust showing in her brown eyes. All at once, a feeling of calmness came over me.

My motives didn't matter. I had done my best for the

marshal. His injury was not my doing. None of this was. Leaving him to die alone, though, would be my doing.

Sally with me, I went back inside. My knees felt unhinged. The red stain on the pillow was bigger.

I got a clean cloth, raised the marshal's head, and put the cloth under his ear. I sat down by him. Gathering my courage, I said, 'Mr Fletcher. This is a sorrowful thing, you being so far from home and your family. You don't know me. But I want you to understand that you aren't alone.'

There was no sign that he heard me. He was dying. The inside of his head was bleeding. It wouldn't be much longer.

'You asked for Mary Louise. It would comfort you if she were here, but there's only me.' Tears were on my cheeks. I brushed them away. 'Mr Fletcher, I promise I'll do my best to find your wife. When I do, I'll tell her she was uppermost in your mind.' I paused. 'Mary Louise Fletcher. That's her name, isn't it? Your wife.'

I said that like I expected him to answer but there was nothing. I said, 'I'll do my best to return your pocket watch and your other things to her. You have my word.' I didn't know how I'd do that but I would sort that out later.

I leaned back in the chair and waited. Sally laid beside me with her head between her front paws. My voice low, I sang a hymn for the marshal. I sang it for me and I sang it for Samuel.

> A *mighty fortress is our God,*
> A *tower of strength ne'er failing.*
> A *helper mighty is our God,*
> O'er *ills of life prevailing.*

Thomas Fletcher stopped breathing.

—-—

CHAPTER FIFTEEN

DEBORAH – THE DECISION

January 13, 1888

I said a prayer for Thomas Fletcher. I wasn't sure what to say since he wasn't a Saint. Praying the only way I knew, I asked the Heavenly Father to take Thomas Fletcher's hand and deliver him to the realm in Heaven where family waited for him. I asked that he find peace and that all his worldly woes be lifted from him.

After the prayer, I took the watch from his vest pocket and opened it. The woman in the photograph had to be the marshal's wife. Mary Louise. Now she was a widow. The children – the boy and girl – were fatherless.

They didn't know. It could be days, maybe weeks, before they found out. At this moment, for them, he was alive.

That might be true for me, too. Samuel could be dead.

No, I thought. No. I couldn't think that way. I'd kept my end of the bargain and did my best for the marshal. In turn, Samuel would come home. He was alive. He had to be.

The watch vibrated in my hand as it ticked. Samuel was all right.

Mary Louise Fletcher might be telling herself the same thing about her husband. She didn't know that a handful of minutes ago, he was alive. Now his face was beginning to take on a waxy color. His mouth had dropped open.

The watch showed it was sixteen minutes after eight. I had

guessed the time when I'd set it earlier so this wasn't right but it was close enough.

I closed the watch and pulled up the stem. The ticking stopped. I put the watch back into the marshal's vest pocket and placed the blanket up over his face.

———

The marshal's walk on earth was over but I had more to face. I left him in Nels' cabin and made my way to the schoolhouse. The sky was gray but wasn't as heavy as it had been yesterday. A faint pink glow showed in the east. For the first time in days, the sun might break through.

Each step into the deep snow made me winded. Sally, following behind, panted as she leaped to the places where I'd crushed the snow. I held up my coat and skirt with one hand. With only one arm to steady me, my balance was shaky. I was tired. My mind was tired. I yearned to go home and sleep but I couldn't. There was much more to do.

Off to the right, tracks marked the surface of the snow. Some were long and thin. A running rabbit. Other tracks were paw prints with claws. Not Sally's. They were too small. A fox.

Everything around me felt fragile. I had been afraid of the marshal. He had crowded my cabin. He had been so angry about the sixteen-year-old girl. Now he was dead.

Across the creek and to the west, the light in Grace's window drew me. I wanted to go there and not to the schoolhouse. I wanted to put my arms around Grace and feel the baby she carried. I wanted to see my nephews – Jacob, Zeb, and Hyrum – who were noisy with life. I longed for the comfort of family. I longed for Samuel.

I crossed the bridge, slipping on the ice under the snow.

A life had ended. I hurt for Mary Louise, who didn't know

what had happened or where her husband was. Yet, as tired as I was, I felt lighter. A burden had been lifted. His suffering was over. I knew, though, that wasn't the only reason I was relieved. His death could save us.

Now on the other side of the bridge, I stopped. A path of deep holes broke the snow. It came from Grace's and led toward the schoolhouse that was farther down the creek. Michael's footprints, I thought. He was at the school with Junction's men.

The light in Grace's window pulled me. It meant family and warmth. It meant the comfort of being with people who knew me and knew where I came from.

Not yet, I told myself. I turned away from the lamplight and took the snow-broken path to the schoolhouse.

———

The neighbor men's voices were loud. I heard them just as I put my hand on the school door handle. They were arguing. I couldn't make out their words but I knew. Trouble. It had come to Junction and they didn't know what to do about it.

I opened the door. The cold air I let in rushed to the front of the room. The raised voices sputtered and quit. The men, squeezed into the desks, turned around. Michael stood by his desk. They stared at me.

The men were all there. Len Hall was with his two oldest sons, Ben and John, gangly boys of sixteen and fifteen. Carson Miller, who had gone with Nels in December to look for Samuel, was there with his father Orson Miller. Adam Baker, Ollie Cookson, and Pete Sorenson were there. And Michael. Everyone but Samuel and Nels.

I stepped inside and closed the door behind me. That brought the men back to their senses. They came at me with questions: 'Where's Brother Nels?' 'What's happened?' 'Is the gentile talking?' 'Has he said who he is?' 'Said what he's doing here?'

Their voices floated around me. The men's beards bobbed up and down as they talked.

'Sister Deborah,' Michael said. Without my realizing it, he had left the front of the room and was now standing close to me. 'You don't look well.' He took my arm and steered me past the rows of desks to his schoolmaster chair. He had me sit down. The men had gotten themselves out of their desks and were standing. They came closer and circled around me. They smelled of wet wool and sweat. For a moment, I thought I might be sick.

Len said, 'Where's Brother Nels?'

I looked up at him. He was a long-faced man with a white scar off to the side of his nose. Sweat beaded his forehead. He kept blinking his eyes. I looked at the other men. Their nerves showed, too. Orson Miller's hand tapped the side of his leg. Adam Baker shifted from one foot to the other. A muscle twitched under one of Pete Sorenson's eyes. Ollie Cookson kept swallowing hard like something was stuck in his throat. Carson Miller picked at a scab on his hand. Michael's eyes looked bigger than usual behind his spectacles.

'Sister Deborah,' Len said. 'Where's Brother Nels?'

'I don't know. He left before dawn.'

The men gave each other quick looks. I was all at once sweating. Not meaning to, I had just told them I'd stayed the night at Nels'.

'He's by himself?' Ollie said.

Adam Baker sucked in some air. The men gave Ollie hard looks. Where I was last night didn't matter. It was Ollie's question they didn't like. It was dangerous to know too much. Nels leaving me with a hurt man could mean only one thing. He had to get somebody to Floral Ranch.

I said, 'The stranger died.'

Someone let out a whistle. The men drew closer around me. I felt small sitting in the chair with them looking down at me. 'He started bleeding from his ear . . .' I stopped. I didn't know what made me say this.

'He's dead?' Len Hall said. 'You're sure?'

'Yes.'

Len said, 'They'll pin it on us.' His sons, Ben and John, edged closer to him.

'We had nothing to do with his death,' Michael said. 'Sister Deborah and Brother Nels were taking care of him. We'll explain that.'

'That won't matter to them. He's dead. A gentile here on some kind of gentile business.'

Gentile business, I understood, meant lawman business.

Michael said, 'We'll make them see reason.'

Pete Sorenson said, 'Reason? They don't care a lick about that. A gentile died in a Mormon town. They'll see to it that somebody hangs. Or goes before the firing squad.'

'God help us,' Adam said. 'Our families, our children.'

The plea for God's help echoed, the men repeating it, their faces etched with distress. Len Hall's two boys were wide-eyed.

'They'll come after me,' Ollie Cookson said. He had two wives, the only one in Junction who did.

'Or they'll come after Brother Nels,' Len said. 'He found him. And maybe even . . .' He looked at me.

My heart lurched.

'No,' Michael said. 'That won't happen. We won't let it.'

That was echoed, too, the men saying no, no, none of us

here should take the blame, we had nothing to do with it, we knew nothing about the gentile, wasn't that so?

Ollie said to me, 'Brother Nels left just this morning? And the dead man was already here?'

Sweat dampened my forehead. There were so many eyes looking at me. I understood what Ollie was thinking, what they all were thinking. Usually, the hunted men got here first. Then Nels guided them to Floral Ranch. A few days later, the deputies arrived. But this was different. It was out of order. The story Nels and I told made it look like the lawman was here before the hunted man.

I felt myself waver. The weight of telling lies and shading the truth since Lewis Braden's arrival bore down. It would be a relief to tell the men about him and how I let him sleep in my barn. It would feel good to tell them Nels and Braden hadn't been able to find the cut to Floral Ranch, and that the man who died was Thomas Fletcher, a marshal. I'd like to tell them that this morning Nels was trying again to get Braden to the ranch.

It was all there on the tip of my tongue. A burden shared by many was easier to bear than when carried by just two.

What you don't know, you can't tell.

Samuel's words. Nels was abiding by them now. He hadn't told me everything. He was protecting me. Like I had to do for the neighbors.

Ollie said, 'Sister Deborah. Brother Nels left this morning? Is that what you said?'

I nodded, then found my voice. 'Yes. This morning. Early.'

Len said, 'Was the gentile traveling with a party?'

'Brother Nels found him alone on the bridge.'

'Brother Michael told us that.' Len's words were clipped with impatience. 'But do you know if there are others somewhere?'

My coat collar was tight. I unfastened the top buttons. Michael stood with his hand on the back of my chair. He was directly beside me so I couldn't read his face.

'Sister Deborah,' Len said. 'Did you hear me? Are there others?'

'I don't know.' This was another lie. Lewis Braden told me two or three men were after him.

'Likely there are more,' Pete Sorenson said. 'They travel in packs.'

A few of the men voiced their agreement. Pete said there was no time to waste. It had stopped snowing. The dead man's friends could be here any time.

Ollie put his hand up, palm out, as if to hold back the men's impatience. He said to me, 'Is he carrying anything that shows who he is?'

'He has a silver watch with a chain.' As if I needed to explain how I knew this, I said, 'It fell out of his vest pocket.'

The men hovered over me, waiting. I said, 'There's a photograph of a woman and two children inside the casing.'

'Any inscriptions?' Adam said.

I shook my head.

Ollie said, 'Is there anything else? Other than the watch.'

There'd been a badge. A badge that Nels took and then lost. I said, 'There's nothing else on his person.'

'Letters? Papers of any kind?'

'No.'

Ollie said, 'You're saying there's nothing on him that tells who he is? Nothing that shows his reason for being here?'

'There's only the watch.'

'With no markings,' Len Hall said.

'A loner,' Orson Miller said.

Ollie looked at each of the men. I went cold. They were deciding what to do with the marshal's body.

They could make Thomas Fletcher disappear. They'd do that for the sake of their wives and children. I read that on their faces, how they eyed each other without saying a word. This trouble came to us uninvited but that wouldn't spare us. Lawmen wouldn't want to believe the marshal's death was an accident. They'd been trying to catch us helping men with plural wives. Now a lawman was dead. They'd come after us with the full might of the federal government.

Beside me, Michael clasped his hands as if in prayer.

They could take the marshal's body into the canyons where it would never be found. They'd take his horse with them and see to it that it disappeared also. The deputies wouldn't be able to prove the marshal was ever here. He could have gotten lost in the Wastelands. He must have fallen into a deep ravine.

It would be like none of this had happened.

His family would never know what became of him. They wouldn't know that someone was with him when he died. They wouldn't know that he died in a bed. Their wait for his return would be endless.

'He has a family,' I said.

Ollie ducked his head but not before I saw the misery in his eyes. I looked at each of the men. No one could meet my eyes.

'Sister Deborah,' Len said. His voice was soft. 'We have families too.'

And you don't, I imagined him thinking about me. Not the same way that Len did. Not like all of them did.

I stood and turned to Michael beside me. He was pale and through his spectacles, his eyes were dark with anguish.

He was a good man. They all were. But we came from people who had been driven from New York to Ohio to Missouri to Illinois and finally to Utah Territory. Our Prophet and his brother were murdered by a mob. Saints in Tennessee were burned out of their homes. Some were killed. The governor of Missouri issued an extermination order against us. We knew what could happen.

God was testing us. We could make the marshal disappear. But God would know. We all would. The burden of carrying that secret would ruin us.

I'd bargained with God. I'd cleaned the marshal, tried to ease his suffering, and promised I would do my best to return the watch to his wife. I thought that would be all. It wasn't.

I said, 'We have to be better than them. We have to be able to live with ourselves.'

The men were quiet. I said, 'I want him kept in my barn.' I didn't know where these words came from but as soon as I said them, I believed them to be true. 'When his people come looking for him, they can decide what to do. If they want to take him home, they can. If they want him buried here, we'll do that when the ground thaws. Either way, I want them to know that a woman took care of him. If they accuse us of killing him, I'll say that might be so. I'll tell them I didn't know what to do for him, I couldn't make him better. I stayed with him, though, and did what I could. He wasn't alone when he breathed his last.'

Ollie said, 'They'll say we killed him.'

'But we didn't, did we?'

'It's not that simple. They don't listen to reason. The man's dead. What happens now doesn't matter to him.'

'It matters to his family,' I said. 'It matters to God.'

No one could look at me.

I said, 'Who will help me carry him to my barn?'

Their gazes skipped from one man to the next. My children, I imagined each one thinking. What will happen to them if their father is accused of murder?

I looked at the boys, Ben and John. They were stirred up. Their eyes were bright with excitement. This was bigger than farm chores and school lessons. They were part of something dangerous. They were watching their father and the other men make decisions that could change the course of their lives.

The boys were sixteen and fifteen. That was close to the ages Samuel and Nels had been when they saw the gap between what was preached and what was practiced. Like Samuel and Nels, I grew up in the shadow of Mountain Meadows. I'd clamped my hands over my ears to keep out the whispers. I told myself that Saints wouldn't leave gentiles to rot where they'd been killed. My father would not allow such a thing. Neither would the other elders in Parowan. But they had.

Now, thirty years later, a gentile who meant us harm was dead on our soil. Ben and John were witnesses to what we would do about that.

I said, '*Ye shall remember your children. How ye grieved their hearts because of the example ye have set before them.*'

Len looked at his sons. As if directed to do so, all the men looked at the boys. Ben and John were long-limbed like their father. Their Adam's apples slid up and down their throats. Ben, the older one, looked to be trying to grow a beard. John's nose and cheeks were flecked with freckles. As the men studied them, John flushed and looked down at the floor. Ben, his eyebrows pulled together, looked at his father.

The fear that gripped the room shifted to shame.

Ollie said, 'We'll store him in Brother Nels' barn.'

Where he might disappear, I thought. He could disappear from my barn but I had to be able to tell myself I'd done my best to stop that. Caring for the marshal was mine to see through until the end. That was part of my bargain for Samuel's return home.

I said, 'Brother Nels has shouldered enough. I want the man in my barn. I took care of him, and I need to do this last thing.'

Pete Sorenson shook his head. He didn't understand my reasoning but that didn't matter. I said, 'He's going to my barn even if I have to carry him myself.'

'No, Sister Deborah,' Michael said. 'There's no need for that.' He paused just long enough to bow his head as if in prayer. Then, looking at me, he said, 'I'll help you.'

Someone cleared his throat. A floorboard squeaked. Carson Miller stepped forward. 'I'll help.'

'And me,' Adam said.

Orson said, 'There's need for a coffin. I've got spare lumber.'

One by one, the others – Len, Pete, and Ollie – agreed to help. The boys, Ben and John, did too. God was watching. So were Junction's children.

CHAPTER SIXTEEN

DEBORAH – THE UNSPOKEN

January 13, 1888

Two o'clock in the afternoon. My parlor clock ticked the seconds. I waited for Nels' return from Floral Ranch. I waited for the lawmen. I waited for Samuel.

The marshal's body was in my barn. He was wrapped in blankets to keep out varmints. Ben and John Hall brought four sawhorses from Nels' barn and the men laid the marshal on top of them. That had to do while Orson Miller made the coffin.

The clock's second hand jerked each time it moved. I waited in the kitchen for Nels. I waited by the parlor window looking for lawmen. Sally watched me from where she lay on her side under the table. I'd brought her home with me when the men carried the marshal's body to my barn. I didn't want to be alone.

Three o'clock. I stared at the calendar, then at the map that showed Samuel's route home. He could get here before the lawmen came.

I carried in more wood and stoked the cookstove fire. I tried not to think about how the marshal had suffered. Instead, my thoughts dwelled on how it would be when Nels got to his cabin and found the marshal and me gone. He wouldn't know what to make of that. Surely he'd come here to look for me.

I waited by the kitchen window, then the parlor window. The sun never broke through. It snowed but it was half-hearted, stopping and starting. I thought about what Michael might have told Grace about the gentile who died at Nels'. I thought about what he might not want her to know and how his story probably had holes. All our stories did.

Weariness pulled my arms and legs. I sat down at the kitchen table. I let sleep take me and then I jerked awake sure that I heard men's voices.

Four o'clock. I put lit lanterns in the two windows. I held Samuel's black-and-white rock in the palm of my hand. I got the record book I kept for my glovemaking. I touched the scraps of leather and the thread I'd pasted on each page. I read the measurements for Samuel's hands, then for my mother's and my father's. Grace and Michael's hands were here. I touched the leather I used for my brothers and my sister Sarah, and for their families. My fingers skimmed over the deerskin I'd used for Nels' gloves. I thought of that Christmas when the three of us were together.

Five o'clock. I made myself eat. The venison and slices of bread were like grit in my mouth. Sally gulped down the venison I gave her. I filled the dish basin with hot water and scrubbed my dishes. Dusk deepened. Something had happened to Nels. He wasn't back from Floral Ranch. Or maybe he came across a neighbor who told him what happened to the marshal. Maybe Nels knew I was home and felt there wasn't a reason to come here.

The dinner dishes washed, I carried a lantern and warm water to the chicken coop. Sally came with me and I was glad for her company. She'd hear Nels or the deputies long before I did. At the coop, I changed the water and let down the flaps on the sides to keep out the cold. In the barn, I milked

Buttercup and allowed my forehead to rest against her warm
flank. Using the toboggan, I carried the milk home. I strained
to hear horses or men's voices. Nothing.

At the cabin and my chores finished, I sat down at the
table. My eyelids were heavy.

All at once, Sally bounded to the door, startling me awake.
Her tail swung from side to side. Whining, she scratched at
the door, then looked at me.

Nels.

———

'You're here,' Nels said when I opened the door. 'Thank God.'

'You're safe,' I said, the relief of seeing him making my
eyes water.

He came inside. Sally circled around him, her tail swinging. 'I went to my cabin,' Nels said. He put his right hand out
toward me, and I thought he might touch my arm. He didn't.
His hand dropped to his side. Nels said, 'You weren't there.
The marshal was gone. I thought his deputies got here and
they'd arrested you.'

I blinked back the tears. 'I was worried about you.'

He didn't say anything but swallowed hard. Then, 'What
happened? Where's the marshal?'

'He died this morning.'

'Where is he?'

'His body's in my barn. Brother Orson and some of the
others are making a coffin.'

'How much do they know?'

'They know it's trouble. And you? What happened?'

'The landmarks were easier to read.'

Nels had gotten Braden to Floral Ranch. My knees went

loose. I sat down at the kitchen table and fought back tears. Braden was gone. That part was over.

'You did good,' I said, looking up at Nels.

'I don't know about that, it doesn't seem so.'

'You did.'

He looked away from me, shaking his head a little. I believed he was thinking of how much had gone wrong. After a moment, still wearing his coat, Nels sat down across from me. The skin around his eyes was dark with weariness. He took off his gloves, the ones I'd given him two Christmases ago, and put them on the table. He said, 'Was it bad at the end?'

I knew he was talking about the marshal. I said, 'It was a mercy when he died.'

Nels didn't say anything. He and I had wanted the marshal's death. We hadn't said it in words but we both believed it could save us. Now, no one but Nels and I knew Braden had been here.

I said, 'The marshal said a woman's name. Mary Louise.'

Alarm swept across Nels' face. 'What else did he say?'

'Nothing. He called for her two times. She must be his wife.'

'Put all of that out of your mind.'

'The more I tell myself to forget, the more it sticks.'

'The mind's a stubborn cuss.'

I smiled.

'That's a fine sight,' he said.

'What is?'

Something inside of Nels seemed to turn inward. He fixed his gaze on the flame in the table lamp. 'Nothing,' he said.

The corners of the cabin were deep pockets of dark. A kind of hush had all of a sudden descended on the room. Now

Nels was looking at me. I felt myself lean toward him. His gaze held me. In his eyes, I saw a kind of wanting.

We were alone. It was nighttime. This wasn't like before when the marshal's presence filled the room. This was different.

It took everything I had to look away from Nels. My gaze darted to the parlor chairs, the clock, the cookstove, anywhere but at Nels. An uneasy silence stretched between us. Samuel should be here. It should be the three of us.

Nels began to tap the floor with his foot. I picked up one of his gloves. The leather was soft from use but the stitches still held. I put it back down.

He backed his chair away from the table. 'It's been a long day.' He stood up. The silence between us cracked loose but nothing was like it had been before. I had seen something deep in Nels' eyes.

He said, 'Might be best for you to stay at your sister's. I'll take you.'

I couldn't look at him.

'Sister Deborah?'

'No.' The word came out sharp. Nels stepped away from the table. I got up. 'This is my home. I belong here.'

'The marshal's men could show up.'

'I'm staying here.' My tone was still sharp. It had to be. Nels had come to care for me in a way that shouldn't be. I saw it in his eyes. I had allowed it to happen. I depended on him too much.

It had to stop.

He said, 'I'll come by in the morning to make sure you're all right.'

'No. Don't.'

He flinched.

'Coming by will look peculiar. Like you're expecting the deputies.' I had to harden myself against Nels. I had to put distance between us. Yesterday, for a moment, I thought I'd seen how he felt about me. It had so taken me by surprise that I convinced myself I'd imagined it. Now I knew I hadn't. I nodded toward the door and said, 'It's late. You're tired, I've kept you here long enough.'

He looked away but not before I saw the hurt flash across his features. It wounded me to do this to him but I had to. He went to the door and opened it. Turning toward me but not meeting my eyes, he said, 'In the morning, I'll find a reason for coming by.'

Before I could argue against that, he left, Sally going with him. A crush of aloneness swept through me.

CHAPTER SEVENTEEN

DEBORAH – THE BARN

January 14, 1888

Two men came the next day. Wrapped in my shawl, I watched them from the parlor window. They each carried a rifle. Leading their horses, they pushed through the snow along the creek. Every step brought them closer to my cabin. I knew who they were. Thomas Fletcher's men.

One of the horses limped. This must have been what kept them from coming with the marshal. Everything would be different if the horse hadn't gone lame and the three men had stayed together.

They passed out of my sight. I wanted Sally with me. I should have asked Nels to leave her.

It had stopped snowing during the night. The sky was a piercing blue and the sun made the snowfall glitter like crystals. Long, pointed icicles hung from the roof at the front of my cabin. Waiting, I held Samuel's black-and-white rock in my hand.

The knock on my door was loud. The room tilted sideways. Stay with the plan, I told myself. I had to make like I didn't know anything about the dead man other than he got hurt and I did my best to help him. These were his friends, they were looking for him.

A second knock. I gathered myself, slipped the rock into my apron pocket, and opened the door partway. The men's neck scarves were high. They wore their hats pulled low. There were only their eyes. The men held the rifles down at their sides. They stared at me. I willed my knees not to crumple.

One of them pushed his scarf down to his chin. 'This here Junction?' he said.

The words were thick and stretched long. A Southerner.

'Yes,' I said. 'Who're you?'

'Name's MacGregor.' He nodded toward the man standing beside him. 'Henry Fletcher.'

Fletcher. The marshal's name.

MacGregor said, 'You got a husband?'

'Yes.'

'We want to talk to him.'

I swallowed down my nerves and tried not to look at their rifles. 'He isn't here.'

'Where is he?'

'He's working. Fixing wheels.'

MacGregor gave me a squinty look. He glanced at Henry Fletcher, then over his shoulder like he thought something was behind him. All I could see were their horses. Turning his attention back to me, he said, 'Where's the rest of this town?'

'On down the creek.'

'How many people?'

'There are eight families.'

'Who else is here? With you?'

'I have family on the other side of the orchard.'

'I'm talking about here. On your property.'

'Just me.'

'Where are the other wives?'

'What?'

'Your husband's other wives. Where are they?'

'I'm his only wife.'

'That so?'

'Yes.'

MacGregor pushed his hat back like that would help him get a better look at me. It took everything I had to hold his gaze. He said, 'We're on government business.'

I took that to mean they were lawmen. I expected them to show me their badges. They didn't. I said, 'Are you here looking for somebody?'

MacGregor's eyebrows shot up.

I said, 'We found a stranger. He was in a bad way.'

'Where is he?' This came from Henry Fletcher. He spoke like a Southerner, too.

Treat these men like I had nothing to be afraid of, I told myself. Their friend was dead. Show charity, not fear. I said, 'It's cold. Come in.'

Henry shook that off. 'Where is he?'

'In the barn.' Both men's attention was fixed on me. 'He died yesterday.'

'How?' Henry said.

My teeth chattered. I was standing in the open doorway but it was mostly nerves that made me shake. I wrapped my arms around myself. I said, 'A neighbor found him on the bridge.' My words were choppy from the chattering. I clamped my jaw and spoke through closed teeth. 'The bridge was icy. His horse might have thrown him. He had a knot on the back of his head. His breathing was bad, uneven.'

The men looked at each other, then at me. I couldn't keep my teeth from clattering. The men were cold, too. MacGregor's eyes were red-rimmed and the end of his nose was red. Henry's lips had a blue cast. MacGregor said, 'You sure about being here alone?'

I nodded.

He looked toward the creek. Henry studied my orchard. They were twitchy with nerves. Outnumbered in Mormon country, I could almost hear them thinking. Nothing had gone as planned.

The men turned back to me. For a moment, I saw weariness in MacGregor's eyes. That made him like all the other men who came to my cabin. He said, 'It's cold. Like you said. Your offer to let us in still hold?'

It was a question with only one answer. I opened the door wider for them.

MacGregor came in first. He went to the bedroom and looked in. 'She's alone,' he called out to Henry who then stepped inside.

The men made the cabin feel small and narrow like how the marshal had. I stood close to the table. MacGregor was about my age. He was stocky and his nose was off center as if it had been broken. Henry, his scarf now pushed down, was young, maybe twenty. He was a tall, narrow man and the stubble on his face was patchy.

MacGregor said, 'What's the dead man's name?'

'I don't know. He was bad off and couldn't talk.'

'You see Marshal Tom Fletcher?'

'Who?'

Henry said, 'The dead man got a thick dark beard? He around thirty?'

I shook my head. 'No beard, and he was older than that. By maybe twenty years.'

Henry sucked in some air. He and MacGregor looked at each other, talking without saying a word.

MacGregor said, 'When'd you find him?'

Think, I told myself. The past days were a smear of time.

I couldn't confuse Braden's arrival with the marshal's. 'The day before yesterday. Around dusk. That's when we found him. He died yesterday morning.'

MacGregor gave Henry a sideways look. 'No,' Henry said to me. 'You're lying.' Looking at MacGregor, he said, 'She's aiming to trick us. It's not him. He wouldn't let nothing like that happen to himself. He wouldn't let his horse throw him. She's lying.' To me he said, 'What bridge? We didn't see a bridge.'

'It's three-quarters of a mile farther down the creek.'

'He have a marshal's badge on him?'

Not now, I thought. 'No.'

'It's not him,' Henry said. 'It's somebody else. It's not Pa.'

Pa. This young man was the marshal's son. The resemblance was before me. It was his eyes. They were wide set like the marshal's. Henry could be the boy in the photograph. Grown, and a lawman like his father. He was a son who might want revenge when he saw his father's body in my barn.

'You're playing us for fools,' MacGregor said. 'Nobody's dead. You're fixing to trap us.'

I shook my head.

MacGregor said, 'Your husband the one that took Braden to Floral Ranch?'

'Who?'

'Braden. We're tracking him. Your husband take him to Floral Ranch?'

'No.'

'Where is he then?'

'Braden?'

'Him and your husband. Where are they?'

'My husband's working. In a town south of here.'

'That's mighty convenient.'

'It's true.'

Henry said, 'Where's Braden?'

'Is that the dead man's name?'

'It's a trap,' MacGregor said. 'You're trying to lure us into your barn.' His hand gripped the rifle.

My heart was high in my chest. I said, 'I have no reason to trap you.'

'You're a Mormon. It's what you people do.'

I put my hand on the table behind me to steady myself.

Henry said, 'You saw my pa, we know you did. You described him. Where is he? When'd you last see him?'

'He died yesterday morning.'

Henry said, 'If anybody's dead, it's Braden. I'm going to the barn to see for myself.'

Desperation underlined his words. He didn't want to believe his father was dead. An unexpected rise of pity came over me. Henry going to the barn convinced about one thing and finding another could punch the air out of him. Be charitable, I told myself. Be kind to this young man. Prepare him for hard news. Even if he was my enemy.

I said, 'The man who died has a watch. It's silver with a chain. It was in his vest pocket. It still is.'

Henry pulled in some air.

'Hell,' MacGregor said. 'That's Tom's.'

Henry said, 'Braden, the bastard. He stole it off of Pa. I'd wring his neck myself if he weren't already dead.' His face twisted with anger. 'I want to see him for myself.' He jerked the door open.

'Wait,' I said.

'Like hell.'

'The man in the barn. You have his eyes.'

Henry's mouth opened in surprise, then all at once his face collapsed.

'It's a trap,' MacGregor said.

Looking at Henry, I said, 'I'll take you to him.'

———

Last night, Orson Miller and some of the other men nailed together a rough-hewn coffin for the marshal. They got his spare trousers that were rolled inside his bedroll and put them on him. After that, we wrapped the body in a blanket and laid him in the coffin. Orson put heavy rocks on top of the closed lid to keep varmints away.

The coffin was off to the side of barn door and away from Buttercup's stall. The flame in the lantern that I held wavered. MacGregor might have thought it was a trap but he came with us. He and Henry moved the rocks and opened the lid. MacGregor pushed aside the blankets so the marshal's face and chest showed.

Henry's breathing hitched.

'Hell,' MacGregor said.

'No, Pa,' Henry said. 'No.' He touched his father's forehead, then pulled his hand away. He buckled. MacGregor reached out to steady him. Gulping in air, Henry bent over with the palms of his hands flat on his knees.

'Why?' Henry said. 'Why?'

I ducked my head not wanting to witness his pain. MacGregor put his hand on Henry's back. Henry shuddered, drawing in air. Finally he pulled himself upright. Looking at his father, he said, 'Pa. How'd you let this happen? What am I going to tell Mama?'

I winced, recalling the image of the woman in the photo-

graph and hearing again the marshal call for his wife. Mary
Louise.

'Henry,' MacGregor said. 'Get yourself some air.'

'I'm not leaving him.' To me, Henry said, 'Who did this to
him?'

'We found him on the bridge.'

'Who's we?'

'A neighbor. He found him. He came and got me to take
care of him.'

'Pa broke horses. He wouldn't fall off his own horse. Not
a good one like Cinch.'

'The bridge was icy.'

'That's what you say.'

My pulse rushed.

'Where's this neighbor of yours? Is he the one? He killed
my pa?'

'He found him. He carried him to his cabin to take care
of him.'

'Your husband do it? Is that why he ran off?'

'No, no. He's been gone since September.'

'Somebody killed him and you know it. He wouldn't fall
off his horse.'

I shook my head. My breathing was ragged.

MacGregor said, 'Where's his horse?'

'At the neighbor's.'

MacGregor didn't say anything. The corners of the barn
were dark. I was alone with these two. They didn't believe
anything I said.

MacGregor bent over the marshal's body and moved the
blankets.

'What are you doing?' Henry said. 'Leave him alone.'

The watch chain clinked as MacGregor pulled it from

the vest pocket. He handed it to Henry, saying, 'Get yourself some air.'

Henry didn't seem to see the watch. He said, 'What are you doing to him?'

'Making sure her story holds up.' MacGregor's voice had softened. 'It'll be easier if you aren't here.'

'I'm not leaving him.'

MacGregor gave him a long look. 'All right,' he finally said. Putting the watch in his pocket, he turned back to the marshal. With one hand, he lifted the marshal's head. He felt the back of it with his other hand. 'Damn,' he said. 'Somebody hit him hard.'

My knees went loose. He didn't believe the story about the marshal falling off his horse.

MacGregor eased the marshal's head back down and pulled the blanket down to the dead man's knees. He was looking for other wounds, I realized. He studied the body and then said to me, 'Where's Braden?'

'I told you. I don't know who you're talking about.'

'He was headed this way.'

'I didn't see anyone.' I inclined my head toward the marshal. 'Only him. Braden, whoever he is, must have gotten lost in the Wastelands.'

'Where's Tom's badge?'

'I don't know. I didn't see it.'

'You're lying.'

I was but I couldn't let him see that. I shook my head.

Henry said, 'You all Mormons here?'

'Yes.'

'They charm you into joining?'

I looked at him, bewildered.

'Were you charmed into being Mormon?'

'No. I was born a Saint.'

'Saint?'

'That's what we call ourselves.'

MacGregor said, 'Saint? Good God. You call yourself a Saint? When you're lying for a killer and a kidnapper?'

'Kidnapper?'

Henry said, 'My sister's with Braden. He used that book of yours to charm her.'

I felt myself staring at Henry, trying to make sense of his words. His sister was with Braden.

Brother and sister. I went lightheaded. Their father was the marshal. The little girl in the photograph. Now sixteen years old. Braden's third wife was the marshal's daughter. This was what Nels had kept from me. And the claim of kidnapping.

'God damn it,' Henry said. Whirling around, he walked off and slammed his fist into the side wall. The wood cracked, breaking. 'Damn it to Hell,' he said. 'Pa's dead.'

I froze.

'Damn the Mormons. Damn every last one of you.' His face was twisted with rage. 'Braden killed him.' He came close to me. 'Pa didn't fall off Cinch. Braden killed him. He charmed my sister and did this. You know it and so does that neighbor of yours.'

I couldn't move. Henry stood over me, his fists clenched.

MacGregor said, 'What's his name?'

I understood he meant Nels. I told him.

'How many people live with him?'

I stepped back a little from Henry. It was hard to think with him bearing down on me. I said, 'He lives alone.'

'Where are his wives?'

'There was only one. She died. Years ago.'

'He doesn't have others?'

Think, I told myself. Find a way to ease their anger. I had to make them believe we weren't their enemy. I said, 'We're not like that here.'

'Not like what?'

'We don't practice plural marriage.' That was a lie. One family did but they had come to question it. I said, 'It's why we live here. We don't agree with everything the church says.'

'Is that so?' MacGregor said.

'Yes.'

MacGregor said, 'They drive you off?'

'We left on our own.'

His eyes narrowed. I felt him deciding how much of my story was a lie. Henry's attention had shifted. He was staring at his father. Think, I told myself. Say something to make them both believe me. I said, 'Mr Fletcher.'

Henry didn't move. He might think I was speaking to the marshal. I said, 'I don't know anything about your sister. But we did all we could for your father. I tried to get the swelling down. Mint leaves helped his pain.' Henry was looking at me now. I said, 'I stayed by your father's side. He died in a bed. He wasn't alone.' I paused. 'That's something you can tell your mother.'

Henry squeezed his eyes shut. MacGregor ducked his head. Henry opened his eyes, blinking them wide like he was afraid he might cry. 'Hell,' MacGregor said. He put his hand on the marshal's shoulder and leaned closed to the body. 'Damn it, Cousin,' he said.

Cousin, I thought. The three men were family.

'I shouldn't have let you go off on your own,' MacGregor was saying. 'I could have pushed my horse to keep up, gimpy leg and all. If I'd been with you, this wouldn't have happened.'

His apology was heavy with regret. I heard guilt, too. Like Braden's apology to the marshal had been. Both men blamed themselves for what happened to him.

MacGregor cleared his throat and straightened. He said, 'Henry, you done looking at your pa?'

Henry nodded. MacGregor covered the marshal's body and face with the blanket, then closed the coffin lid. He patted the lid twice before turning to me. He said, 'Where's this neighbor you keep talking about?' The apology was gone from his voice. It had turned harsh with accusation.

'He lives about a mile down the creek.'

'Who all's between here and there?'

I couldn't lie. I had to say it. 'My sister and her family.'

'How many of them are there?'

'Five. She and her husband. Three little boys. The oldest is seven.'

MacGregor looked at Henry. Henry's attention was fixed on his father's covered body. MacGregor said to me, 'You're taking us to your neighbor. I've got questions to put to him.'

—·—

CHAPTER EIGHTEEN

NELS – CONVERGENCE

January 14, 1888

Sally's bark broke the quiet. I came out of my barn. Deborah was on the bridge with two strangers. Sally ran to me, then bounded through the snow toward the creek. I followed her, hurrying, trying to run, the deep snow slowing me, everything inside me pounding. The marshal's men. Deborah with them. Something had gone wrong.

My heart about to bust out of my chest, I shouted at Sally to get back and quit barking.

'Hold up,' one of the men called out. He aimed his rifle at me. So did the other man. Deborah was between them on the middle of the bridge. I came to a stop. 'Control your dog,' the first man said.

Growling, Sally's fur bristled on her back. I grabbed hold of her collar with one hand and held up the other to show I wasn't armed.

'Brother Nels,' Deborah said, her voice raised. 'This is the man's family. His son and cousin.'

'You the one who says he found Tom Fletcher?' This came from the older of the two. The cousin, I thought.

I said, 'That's the man who's dead?'

'That's him.'

'I found him.' I was sweating. Both rifles were fixed on me. The son said, 'Where's Braden?'

I couldn't let myself look at Deborah. I couldn't show my worry for her. Or that we knew more than we were saying. I said, 'Who?'

'Lewis Braden. Where is he?'

'I don't know what you're talking about. Your father was alone.'

'You're lying. We were on Braden's trail. You or somebody from here took him to Floral Ranch. He ambushed my pa. Killed him.'

'Nobody was killed. He fell.'

The cousin said, 'You see it happen?'

'No.' I cussed myself for my carelessness. It was hard to think clear with two rifles pointed at me. I said, 'Just put together what likely happened.'

'Where's her husband?' The cousin waved his rifle toward Deborah.

I didn't know what Deborah had told him about Samuel. I took a chance and said, 'He's been fixing wheels. He's making his way home.'

'You sure he didn't run off to Floral Ranch? After helping Braden kill Tom Fletcher?'

'I don't know what you're talking about.'

All at once, Sally started barking, lurching to break free from my hold. Movement on the other side of the bridge caught my eye. Deborah and the two men turned to look behind them. It was Michael.

He hurried toward us slipping some in the snow. He was bareheaded. His coat was unfastened and flapped around his legs. I put my hand over Sally's muzzle to make her quit barking. My insides roiled. Michael would make things worse.

'What's going on here?' he called out.

The son aimed his rifle at Michael. Michael came to a stop. The cousin's rifle was still pointed at me.

Michael put his hands out, palms facing us. 'I'm not armed.'

'Who're you?' the cousin said.

'She's my sister-in-law.' Michael nodded toward Deborah. 'What's going on here?'

The son said, 'My pa's dead in her barn.'

'That's your father?'

'Braden killed him.'

'What's this? Sister Deborah, Brother Nels. Who's this Braden person?'

Michael talked like there wasn't a rifle aimed at his heart. If he and I hadn't shuffled around the truth the night the marshal was dying, I would have said Michael didn't know what this was about.

Deborah said, 'I don't know. Neither of us do.'

Michael kept his hands up. His spectacles had slipped down his nose. 'Brothers. There's no need for rifles.'

'We aren't your brothers,' the cousin said.

'We're all brothers in the eyes of the Lord.'

'Don't give us any of your Mormon talk.'

Michael swallowed hard, then, 'Gentlemen. Let's sort this out. He was found on the bridge. It was icy. We believe he fell.'

'You're in on this too,' the cousin said. 'You're hiding a murderer. And a kidnapper. He stole Tom Fletcher's daughter.'

Michael's face went wooden.

Sally started barking again, this time a series of shrill yaps. She strained to get away from my hold on her. Michael's two oldest boys, Jacob and Joe, were crouched by a bush off to the side of the bridge.

I clamped my hand over Sally's muzzle. Everyone was looking at the little boys. The bottoms of their gray coats bunched around them and the brims of their hats were pushed back. Their eyes were wide and unblinking.

'Boys,' Michael said. 'Go home. Now.'

The boys didn't move. It was like they were stuck. Their gazes were fastened on the tall man's rifle that was aimed at their father.

The cousin said, 'Mind your pa. Go home.'

Joe made a squeaking sound.

Michael said, 'It's all right. Do like he says.'

'I'm scared, Papa.' This came from Jacob, the older one.

'They have rifles.' Joe, hunched low, had an arm around his brother's back. He was crying.

'Jacob,' Michael said. 'Joe. Go home. Now.'

'Papa,' Jacob said. 'I'm scared.' His voice was high-pitched. A seven-year-old boy's voice. 'Why are they doing this?'

The air went still. The marshal's son, his rifle aimed at Michael, worked his hands, gripping it tighter.

Michael, his hands still up, looked from his boys to the two men. He blinked hard, squinting, his spectacles too low on his nose to do any good.

'Boys. It's hard to understand.' It was Deborah. Her back was to me and I couldn't see her face. She said, 'These men have had sad news. Someone has died.' Her voice broke. She gave herself a small shake and went on. 'And someone else moved far from home. It makes their hearts hurt with sadness. That's why they're doing this. Their hearts hurt.'

The boys stared at her. They didn't say anything. Deborah turned to the marshal's son beside her. His rifle was still aimed at Michael. 'Please,' she said. 'Don't hurt these boys in any way.'

Her words hung over us. No one moved. The air felt so brittle it could crack. All at once, Henry shuddered and with that, I sensed a shift, a kind of loosening. He tilted his head back and looked up at the cliffs.

'Henry,' the cousin said. 'You see something up there?'

Henry looked at him, then at Jacob and Joe. The color had drained from Jacob's face. His lips quivered. Joe began to blubber again, crying. Henry's gaze went back and forth from the boys to their father. Then he turned a little toward the direction of Deborah's cabin and barn.

'What're you doing?' the cousin said.

Henry lowered his rifle.

'What's wrong with you?'

'I'm taking Pa home.'

'What? We're tracking Braden.'

'I'm not leaving Pa in Mormon country.'

'What about Braden? Your sister?'

Henry shook his head.

'These people here know where Braden is. He killed your pa.'

Henry looked off again toward Deborah's place and then back to the cousin. He said, 'You wrestle it out of them, then. I don't want Pa kept in a barn. I'm not leaving him with Mormons. I don't want him buried here.'

'Braden's got your sister.'

'That's Pa talking. That's his account. That's what he wanted to believe.'

MacGregor said, 'What's gotten into you? Braden charmed her with that book of theirs. You said so yourself.'

'Maybe I did. But he didn't steal her. I never believed that, not all the way. That was Pa's talk, not mine. Mary ran off. She was hell-bent on being a Mormon. She said so in that note of hers she left. Her mind was made up.'

His rifle still on me, the cousin said, 'Me and you agreed to help catch Braden.'

'I know it. Because no daughter of Pa's was going to take up with Mormons. And now he's dead. I'm taking him home. Catching Braden can wait. You can go after him but I'm taking Pa home.'

The cousin shifted from foot to foot, still holding his rifle on me. He squinted at me. My heart walloped against my ribcage. He was a man with a debate raging in his mind. He was outnumbered in Mormon country. He didn't stand much of a chance catching Braden on his own. Yet he'd likely given his word to the marshal that he'd help run down Braden.

'Damn it,' the cousin said. He spat into the snow. 'Your pa would have my hide if I let you go off on your own.' He lowered his rifle.

I heard myself blow air out. A great weakness came over me. I felt the urge to sit down. Like it was happening from a far distance, I saw Deborah walk to the little boys. They ran to her, sliding on the icy snow. They wrapped their arms around her legs. She bent over them, her hands pressing them close to her.

Pushing his spectacles up into place, Michael started to go to them. He stopped. Sunlight glinted off the glass in his spectacles, making it so his eyes couldn't be seen. He coughed and turned to Henry. He said, 'We'll help you get your father ready for the trip home.'

CHAPTER NINETEEN

NELS – THE WARNING

January 15, 1888

Dawn was breaking when Michael, Carson Miller, and I rode through the snow to Deborah's place. Henry and MacGregor had bed down in her barn for the night. Michael had offered his barn but Henry, the marshal's son, wouldn't have anything to do with that. He said he wanted to be where he could keep an eye on his pa. I took that to mean he didn't trust us.

We didn't trust them either. Last night, the men of Junction decided that Carson would travel through the Wastelands with the marshal's relations. It was uneven country. In places, the coffin would have to be carried by hand. An extra man would make a hard job some easier. That was what Michael planned to tell the marshal's family this morning. He'd keep it to himself that this was a way to make us look like good people with nothing to hide. He wouldn't tell them we wanted to make sure they really did leave Junction.

Michael, Carson, and I wove our way through the orchard toward Deborah's. The dawn's light was a glimmer of orange on the peaks of the higher cliffs that surrounded Junction. Looking up at those cliffs that edged Junction made me feel the weight of our obligations. Michael was keeping his promise to help get the marshal's body ready for the trip home. Carson had the job of guiding gentiles who had meant us harm. My obligation was to Samuel. He'd expect me to see for myself that Deborah was all right.

It worked on me, the men sleeping in Deborah's barn. Michael hadn't liked it either. Not wanting Deborah to be alone in her cabin with the men on her property, he'd asked her to stay the night with him and Grace. Deborah shook her head against that. What she did do was ask me if she could borrow Sally for the night. I'd agreed. I wasn't any good at telling her no.

We halted our horses when we got close to the edge of the orchard. Up ahead, lantern lights moved and flickered near Deborah's barn. Men's voices carried. Metal clinked. It sounded like Henry and MacGregor were hitching their horses.

My voice low, I said to Michael, 'We'll wait here.'

'God willing, there won't be any trouble.'

'God willing,' Carson said.

I felt Michael waiting for me to say the same. When I didn't, he clicked his tongue and his horse began to walk toward the last row of plum trees.

Me and Carson staying behind was the plan the three of us had worked out earlier. Believing Henry and MacGregor were likely to be twitchy with nerves, we figured it would be best for Michael to approach them by himself. They trusted him as much as they could trust any Saint. He'd tell them about Carson coming with them to help get the marshal through the Wastelands. Once they were agreeable to that, Michael would signal to Carson to come on in. As for me, I'd stay in the orchard to keep watch.

This worked on me, too, staying behind. I wanted to speak to Deborah. I wanted to hear for myself that Henry and MacGregor hadn't done her any harm.

The thinking side of me, though, told me to stay away from those two. Seeing me could set them off. It could make them come at me with more questions about how I'd found the marshal.

I had to settle for Michael looking after Deborah. He'd do a fair job of it. I never thought to say this, but I'd come to see that he was steady in the face of trouble.

Michael had cleared the orchard now and was in the open. He called to Henry and MacGregor, said who he was. They didn't answer. Carson and I waited, our breaths clouds of white in the cold.

'All right,' one of the men finally called. 'Come on in.'

Michael and his horse, dark shapes in the dawn light, moved forward.

Carson and I watched. He leaned forward in his saddle. I felt his unease. If things went as planned, he'd be alone in the Wastelands with two gentiles. I gave him a sideways glance. Everything about him was tight.

Michael was close to Deborah's place. Talk went back and forth. Carson and I were too far off to make out the words. The light was still dim but I was able to see the shapes of the men and the horses.

Carson said, 'Looks like the coffin's strapped to a toboggan.' His eyes were better than mine. He said, 'Must be Sister Deborah's, she'll miss it sorely. They got the toboggan behind a horse, probably hitched to it.'

I nodded to that but I was thinking about Deborah. Find her, I willed Michael. Go to her cabin. Make sure she's all right.

Michael got off his horse. The three men knotted together by the toboggan.

Carson said, 'Why isn't he signaling for me? What's taking so long?'

I shook my head.

One of the men left the horses and walked to the cabin. 'It's Brother Michael,' Carson said. A voice called out. Michael's. More voices and this time one was a woman's. 'It's Sister Deborah,' Carson said. 'She's with your dog.'

'My eyes aren't that bad,' I said, the words clipped. I strained, looking, the dawn light brightening some. Her steps high in the snow, Deborah went back to the barnyard with Michael.

'She looks all right,' I said.

'Seems so.'

They got to the barnyard. There was more talk. Beside me, the leather in Carson's saddle creaked as he kept shifting. I figured that thinking about riding with the gentiles was working on his nerves. The eight miles through the Wastelands would feel like eighty. After getting the men and coffin through, Carson would turn back and Henry and MacGregor would go on to Thurber. It was another seventeen miles and the town had a telegraph office. Once they got to Thurber, I believed they'd make a straight line to the telegraph office and notify Marshal Frank Dyer up in Salt Lake about Fletcher's death. When word got out the federal marshal from Tennessee was dead, Dyer's people would likely descend on us with a vengeance.

Anybody not from here would say we should all leave Junction before Dyer's people showed up. But it was January. Some of the women were expecting. There were young children, babies. On the trail, wagons were drafty and canvas coverings didn't do much good against the cold. Snowstorms could blow up from nowhere. Narrow mountain trails were hard going even in the summer.

We were better off keeping with the story about finding a stranger on the bridge.

At Deborah's place, one of the men went inside the barn. Beside me, Carson kept shifting in his saddle. 'You all right?' I said.

'Yes.' He cleared his throat and leaned over the far side of his horse and spat. He cleared his throat again, then said, 'Brother Nels. I've got to tell you something, something that's been weighing on me. I've got to say it while I can. Before I go off with the gentiles. It's about the rockslide.'

A bad feeling came over me; I didn't like Carson's tone. 'What about it?' I said.

'I keep thinking about what I saw in the ravine.' He was whispering but his words were loud in my ears. 'The glints, the shape of an arc. I told you it was rocks with crystals. But since then I keep picturing it for what it really was. Not an arc but almost a full circle. One made of metal.' Carson paused. 'A wheel.'

'A wheel? Is that what you said?' My words were a hiss. 'A wheel? God Almighty. Why didn't you tell me?'

'I didn't want it to be. And when you didn't see it, I thought I was wrong. But the truth of it won't leave me alone.'

I pulled in some air, breathing hard. A wheel.

Carson said, 'We'll go back to the ravine, we'll get all the men. Once this is over. I'll go down and look.'

'No.' The word was sharp with anger. My anger was against Carson for not telling me sooner. It was against what rode under his words. Without him saying so, the wheel might have come off Samuel's wagon.

'I'm willing,' Carson said.

'Don't be a fool.'

Carson winced. I didn't care. I said, 'There's not a rope long enough to send you down. If we tied some together, they could break. There'd be no getting you out. You'd live out your days trapped. All for something that might or might not be a wheel. All for something that has nothing to do with Samuel.'

'But—' His words broke off. A shout came from the barnyard. It was Michael calling for Carson.

'Go on,' I said, the words hard.

'I'm sorry, Brother Nels. I should have told you.'

'Go.' The nod I gave him was sharp. He reared back in his saddle, then gave me a nod as sharp as mine had been. Without another word, he flicked the reins and set off toward Deborah's.

Carson's image blurred. A wheel. The two words crowded my thoughts. I pushed against them. I had to pay attention to what was playing out before me. There wasn't room in my mind for anything else. The marshal's body was in Junction. His son and cousin were at Deborah's.

I rubbed my eyes. My vision cleared. Carson had reached the barnyard. There, two of the men got on their horses. It took some doing to get themselves arranged but finally the three horsemen began to move. They rode single file. The riderless horse that pulled the coffin was followed by one of the horsemen. Deborah, and who I figured was Michael, stayed where they were in the yard. From where I was, Carson, Henry and MacGregor were nothing but dark shapes against the snow as they headed toward the Wastelands. It didn't take long for them to fade from my sight.

After a while, Deborah and Michael walked back to the cabin. Midway, they stopped. Facing my direction, Michael raised his hand to me.

He wasn't beckoning me to join them. It was a gesture meant to say that everything was all right. I was glad for that. But I wanted to be waved in, told that I was wanted.

I wasn't.

I raised my hand in return. Then I turned Bob around and headed toward home, Carson's words – a wheel – bearing down heavy in my mind.

———

When the sun was well up, I put the blankets used by the marshal into my wash basin and poured warm water over them. I got my soiled mattress, hauled it outside, and set it on fire. Orange flames shot up and ate the dry straw ticking in the mattress. Gray smoke pillared upward. The gray cloth blackened and curled. The snow under and around the fire sizzled and shrank into streams of water.

I watched the flames do their work. I'd make a new mattress when I was able to buy cloth. Until then, I'd sleep on the floor. Doing that seemed like a kind of justice. Not only because I'd lied about what had happened to the marshal and got rid of his badge and the warrant. Today was January fifteenth. I'd believed Samuel would be home by now. At the latest. I believed it so much that I made Deborah believe it too.

A wheel in the ravine.

I stirred the fire with a long poker. Red sparks shot up. I tried to shut out Carson's words.

My hands shook. I dropped the poker and jammed my hands in my coat pockets. My gloves, the ones Deborah made for me, were inside them. I'd forgotten they were there. I put them on to steady my hands.

Just because Carson thought he saw a wheel didn't mean

it had anything to do with Samuel. It could have been there for years.

As for Samuel getting home by now, I could have mis-figured the time. He might know of a longer but easier trail other than through the Fish Lakes. Or he could be holed up in a miner's cabin waiting out the weather. People were known to disappear in the canyon country. They were given up for dead. Months later, they turned up. A broken leg, a crushed foot, or maybe a long-lasting sickness had caused their delay.

A wheel.

Maybe I should tell Deborah what Carson thought he saw. She was the kind of woman who would want to know.

A funnel of black ashes rose from my mattress. The sooty smoke caused a rawness in my throat. I coughed; my eyes watered from the fire.

Telling Deborah would hit her hard. It would tear her up bad.

I couldn't do it, wouldn't do it. Carson was wrong. His imagination had gone off-track. I hadn't seen any glints of light in the ravine. Good as his eyes were, he couldn't know for sure it was a wheel. The floor was in shadows.

Samuel was all right. The wheel was someone else's. If there really was one. It was me. I'd figured the time wrong. Maybe I'd figured the route wrong. Nothing was certain in the canyon country. I'd had no business pinning Samuel's getting-home time to a fixed week.

That was what I had to tell Deborah. She had pushed me away but I had to ease her worry. Today.

———

The fire was burning itself out when all at once, Sally came leaping through the snow toward me. She'd been at Deborah's.

She circled around me, then ran back to the bridge. Deborah, wearing her coat and hat, stood on my side of the creek. It was like she knew I had something important to tell her.

I raised my hand to Deborah and walked toward her. She was fixed on the fire. Her gloved fingertips skimmed the top of Sally's neck.

Before I could reach her, Deborah shook her head. I stopped. Her gaze pierced me. I felt her anger. She said, 'You told me Samuel would be home by now.'

'I was wrong. The snow, the weather, the trail, I misfigured the time.'

'Something bad happened. Didn't it?'

'No. It's the weather.'

A wheel.

I shook my head against that and said, 'The trail through the Fish Lakes is high, there's more snow than here. I didn't figure it right. I was wrong.'

She gave me a long look. Finally she said, 'Don't ever do that to me again. Don't you ever give me something to hold onto, not unless you know for sure.'

'I won't. I'm sorry.'

'I am, too.' From the distance, Deborah's anger bore into me. She turned and walked over the bridge away from me. Sally went with her. A hand seemed to reach inside my chest and squeeze my windpipe.

I watched Deborah walk farther from me. My windpipe squeezed tighter. I'd hurt her. I deserved her anger.

On the other side of the bridge, Deborah came to a stop. Sally ran on ahead of her. Deborah faced east toward the schoolhouse. Today was Sunday. There'd be services. A federal marshal had died in our town. More trouble was bound to come to Junction. And Samuel wasn't back.

Deborah turned away from the schoolhouse. 'Go home,' I heard her call out to Sally. 'Where you belong.' Sally's tail drooped. 'Go home,' Deborah said again. This time, Sally obeyed and came back to the bridge.

Deborah walked toward her cabin. Hers and Samuel's. Where she belonged and where I didn't. Her anger, I understood, wasn't only about me being wrong about Samuel. She knew how I felt about her. I had given it away when the two of us were alone. I had betrayed Samuel, and Deborah had come to warn me to stay away.

My face heated with shame.

———

It was full dark when Carson got back to Junction. He came by and told me how Henry and MacGregor didn't give him any trouble. 'Every gully we came to,' he said, 'took the three of us to get the coffin out of it.'

He said this standing inside my cabin with his back close to the door. He didn't unfasten his coat buttons. He didn't intend to linger, and I didn't ask him to. The way we had left matters this morning put unease between us.

Carson said, 'The nails in the coffin lid came loose a few times. From all the jostling. Me and MacGregor used rocks to hammer them back into place. Henry couldn't take it. All that pounding and his pa's body under it. He had to walk away each time.'

'That's the boy in him,' I said. 'Even grown men have the boy in them when their fathers die.'

Carson ran a hand over the stubble of his beard. He studied me, taking in my words. I took them in, too. It wasn't just the loss of a father that could turn a man into a child.

I cleared my throat. Carson said, 'When we got through

the Wastelands, the trail west to Thurber was clear enough. There was no call for me to stay with them. I turned around like I was coming directly home. But I held up for a while by a butte and watched them head west until I couldn't see them anymore.'

'You did good,' I said and meant it. Our disagreement about what he thought he'd seen in the ravine had nothing to do with this.

He shrugged. It was how he accepted praise. Then he ran his hand over his face. I tensed. There was something more he intended to say.

'Went to the mail tree,' Carson said. 'After Henry and MacGregor were gone.'

The mail tree was on the far side of the Wastelands. We kept a bag nailed to it so people passing by could leave mail should there be any. Most usually this time of year there wasn't any.

'There were three letters,' Carson was saying. 'I took them to Sister Deborah before coming here. She lit up when she saw them. It was Brother Samuel's handwriting.'

'Letters? From Samuel? Is that what you said? God Almighty, that's good. Good. I knew he was all right. When were they written?'

'I don't know. She didn't open them. Not with me there.'

I laughed, something I hadn't done in a long time. I said, 'That's right, she wouldn't. Don't know what I was thinking. We'll probably have to wait until morning to hear.'

Nodding, Carson said, 'Probably so. Letters like that are between a man and his wife.'

'That's so.' The tightness I'd been carrying in my shoulders loosened. Word from Samuel. News about where he'd been and where he was headed.

Carson said, 'I couldn't help noticing how two of the envelopes were ragged and dirty. It was like they'd traveled a long way. The other one wasn't near as worn.'

I felt myself grinning. Word from Samuel. I said, 'If I were a betting man, I'd wager my last nickel that Samuel, in that last letter, the one not so worn, I bet he wrote how something came up, a change in plans, that he'll be longer than he figured on.'

'You think so?'

'I know it. He's been delayed. He missed the rockslide by weeks, months even.' My words came out fast, each one stepping on top of the other. 'He still had to turn around when he came across it, still had to come another way. But the slide happened before he got to it. That last letter will prove it so. You'll see.'

'It'll be welcome news.'

Word from Samuel. I wasn't the only one grinning. Carson was too.

He said, 'All right. That's it, then.' He tugged his hat into place. 'Best be getting on home, Ma being the kind to worry.'

'You did good work for Junction today,' I said. He shrugged off the praise like he always did. Him doing that made me grin all the wider. Carson turned toward the door, started to open it, then stopped. He looked at me. His face had clouded. His grin was gone.

'About the ravine,' he said. 'I pray I'm wrong.' Then he left, cold air blowing in and taking his place.

—·—

CHAPTER TWENTY

DEBORAH – OUT-OF-
THE-WAY PLACES

January 15, 1888

Three letters from my husband. I was airy with relief. I sat at
the kitchen table with them laid out in front of me. Samuel's
letters.

When Carson Miller gave them to me, I turned woozy and
light at the same time. The worry I'd carried, lifted. News
from Samuel. He was all right.

I had opened the letters as soon as Brother Carson left.
Samuel had penciled the words and in places the letters were
smudged. It was his handwriting, though. I would know it
anywhere. His penmanship lacked flourishes and slanted
hard to the left. I read the letters in a rush, my heart rattling
against my breastbone. The words floated in front of my eyes.
The second time I read them, the words took on meaning and
it was almost as if Samuel were in the cabin with me. I
laughed at the notion of a man so in need of wheels that he
waited for Samuel by the privy. I laughed to think of Samuel
jumping to touch the stars. The third time I read the letters I
was sure I heard the mules wheezing and bellowing their
complaints.

Now the letters were spread flat on the table with the
envelopes beside them. I had the wall calendar and Nels' map
also on the table. I picked up the first letter and angled it

toward the slivers of light from the two lamps on the table. I willed myself to read slowly and to think about each part.

September 29, 1887

I studied the calendar, counting as I turned the pages back. Three months and sixteen days between today and September the twenty-ninth. It wasn't all that long ago. Yet I didn't have any memory of what I had been doing on the day Samuel sat under his wagon and wrote to me.

Kindling is so heavy with Water the notion came to Me it would be handy to have your Wringer.

It hurt me to think of him in the rain. Yet, it was his way to make light of the weather. He didn't want me to worry.

I left Escalante 2 Days back and am going South to Henrieville.

I didn't know for sure where either Escalante or Henrieville was. They weren't on the map Nels had drawn for me but I believed that Escalante was nearly due south. Samuel traveled there most every fall and had told me it sat in a valley with high mountains on all sides. 'It's named after a missionary,' Samuel once told me. 'Catholics claimed the place before Brigham Young was even born.'

Escalante has more Houses and Streets than it did last Year. Do not let that disturb You. I did not get lost.

I traced the last sentence with my forefinger. Samuel had not gotten lost in Escalante, and he would not get lost coming through the Fish Lakes.

If You were here We would listen to drops of Rain fall from the Trees. With you beside me it would be a cheersome Sound.

My breathing went ragged. I put the letter down, picked up Samuel's black-and-white rock that I kept on the table, and held it to my cheek. When I finally gathered myself, I put the rock down and read the second letter.

October 15, 1887

He had been in Johnson, a new outpost with two families and a child buried in a cemetery.

The Creek is down to a trickle.

Fear gripped my heart. I understood what this meant. Like the families in Johnson, Samuel was suffering, parched dry.

Do not worry about me. My bones got so wet from the Rain up by Escalante that I will be a long Time drying out.

Come home, Samuel. For all your words of reassurance, that's the only way you can ease my worry.

In the Morning I go North and some West to Mt. Carmel. It will not take long to get there.

This was the turning point. From that time on, he'd be making his way north toward home.

The last letter was dated November 3, 1887. Two months and twelve days ago. I skimmed over the beginning and read the end.

I am lonesome for You. But not for long. Look for Me by December 1. You will know Me by the Grin on my Face.

Every part of me ached; I couldn't read more. I needed air. I got up and opened the door. The cold swept in, scattering the papers and sending them swirling. I slammed the door closed and chased the letters and envelopes that drifted along the floor. I scooped each one up, not wanting anything to happen to them.

One of the pages had torn at a top corner. I held it near the lamplight. It was the last letter, the one that had pierced my heart and caused me to need air.

This Outpost is so fresh new the Familys have not come up with a Name for it. It is 5 miles South of Mt. Carmel.

I read these sentences again. Something didn't fit right.

Samuel had written in his second letter, the one dated October fifteenth, that he was going to Mt. Carmel. *It will not take long to get there.* Yet in the third letter, written on November third, he was five miles south. For some reason, it had taken longer than he'd expected.

Samuel traveled to Mt. Carmel every fall. He knew the wagon trails and was a good judge of distance. Maybe he meant to write that the new outpost was five miles north of the town.

That didn't feel right. It wasn't like him to make that kind of mistake. I searched Nels' map. Mt. Carmel wasn't on it.

Maybe Samuel had already been there. Maybe he backtracked south to the place that didn't have a name. The families there needed three wheels fixed. There might have been more families in other out-of-the-way places in desperate need of wheels. Samuel was tender-hearted. Once he heard someone needed help, he'd find it hard to refuse them.

Maybe it wasn't just the rockslide that slowed him. Maybe Samuel took on more work than usual. Maybe he got a late start getting home.

Yes, I thought. First a late start, then the trail blocked by the slide. This explained why he wasn't home yet.

Holding the letter, I walked from the kitchen to the parlor to the bedroom and back to the kitchen. It would worry Samuel that I didn't know he was delayed. The November third letter said he would be home by the first of December. He might have written a fourth letter, one that hadn't arrived, to let me know he'd be home later than expected. Then he came across the rockslide and was forced to come through the mountains, slowing him all the more.

That was what happened. It was too soon to expect Samuel.

Too soon. The words turned me lightheaded. My hands shook. I circled around the table, then went to the parlor window that faced the Wastelands. There was nothing to see but the dark.

Too soon. It could be a few more weeks.

I picked up the calendar from the table. It took two tries to get it on the wall nail.

Samuel was all right. The last letter made it so. If he turned back for one family, he had done it again. I was sure of it.

I ran my palms along the sides of my skirt. My hands still jittered but I managed to fold the letters and put them back in the envelopes. Two of the envelopes were worn with dark smears. Dirt, I thought. I laughed. That was so like Samuel. He was a man who admired rocks. He was a man who saw things in the soil that no one else did.

In the bedroom, I put the letters under one of Samuel's rocks on the dresser. From there, I hurried to the front door and got my coat. Then I was out the door and plunging through the snow.

Too soon. Too soon. The words bubbled in my mind. I had to tell Nels.

In my hurry, I'd forgotten a lantern. It didn't matter, I knew the way. Holding my skirt up out of the snow, I stumbled my way toward the creek. The center, the part not frozen, rushed and glinted in the starlight.

Close to the bank, I turned east. The icy snow crackled as I broke through it. Because of Braden, the marshal came to Junction. Because the marshal died, his family had to take him home. Because they needed help getting through the Wastelands, Carson Miller went with them. If those things had not happened, it could have been weeks before anyone found Samuel's letters at the mail tree.

Those would have been weeks of more worry, weeks that would tear at me.

I passed Grace's cabin. It was dark, they were asleep. I'd tell them about Samuel's delay first thing in the morning. I hurried, the chant – *too soon* – driving me on toward the bridge. Nels would be so relieved. I could picture his smile as if he were with me now.

Midway across the bridge, I slipped, then caught myself. Out of breath, I held onto the rail and gathered myself.

Up ahead, Nels' cabin was dark. He might be asleep.

The thought drew me up hard. I shouldn't go there. Not at this time of night. Even with good news, the kind that would lift our spirits and make us lighthearted, I couldn't. I'd seen how he felt about me.

I leaned against the bridge rail, my disappointment sharp. I wanted to tell Nels the good news; I wanted to relieve his mind. Yet it was late. He was sleeping. I thought how it would seem if I woke him, the two of us alone. I had to keep my distance.

Carson Miller, I recalled, had said something about intending to go by Nels' place after he left me. My thoughts had been too scattered about the letters to pay him much mind. Now it came back to me. He said he would let Nels know he had gotten the marshal's family through the Wastelands. Carson, I felt sure, would also tell him about the letters. That had to be enough for now. Nels would hear the news about Samuel's delay in the morning.

All at once spent, I turned around. Holding onto the rail, I went back to my side of the creek. Dawn wasn't more than a handful of hours away. At first light, I'd go to Grace's and ask Michael to tell the neighbors. And Nels.

CHAPTER TWENTY-ONE

NELS – THE LEAVE-TAKING

January 16–February 8, 1888

Deborah's letters from Samuel were a mighty easement. What she said about Samuel stopping at out-of-the-way places fit with what I thought had happened. Even Carson Miller said it could be so.

It was Michael who told me what was in the letters. He hadn't read them. They were Deborah's, but from what she reported to him, it could be close to February before Samuel got home.

After telling me, Michael went to the Miller place to let them know that Samuel had been delayed. From there, it didn't take long before everyone in Junction knew.

The good news made me smile from ear to ear. The good news made me want to see Deborah. I wanted to see the worry gone from her features. I wanted to tell her I regretted saying Samuel should have been home by the second week in January. I wanted her to know I was sorry for adding to her worry.

But Deborah had sent Michael to tell me about the letters. The silent warning she gave me on the bridge still stood. She wanted me to stay away from her. I had been careless, she'd seen how I felt about her. If I could change that, I would.

Samuel's letters didn't change anything about Utah's Marshal Dyer or his deputies. I was sure that once Dyer got word about Marshal Fletcher's death, he would come after us. He was bound to want someone to pay. Nobody in Junction put this in words but I believed everyone was thinking it. During the first week after the marshal's relations left with the body, some of us patched Pete Sorenson's barn roof. It had given way in three places from the weight of the snow. While we cut boards to size and nailed them to the roof's beams, Orson Miller kept looking off toward the Wastelands, the direction the deputies would come from. Ollie Cookson was so jumpy he kept dropping nails. Pete Sorenson had acquired a twitchy muscle under his right eye. Adam Baker seemed to lean in the direction of his homestead like he expected trouble to first show its face there.

The days passed. Pete Sorenson's barn roof was fixed. Nights, I didn't sleep. Instead, I walked the orchards with Sally, cold as it was. I waited for Dyer's deputies. I waited for Samuel.

Carson's claim about seeing a wheel in the ravine stuck in my mind. He was so sure. If he was right, that wheel belonged to somebody. Thinking that made me want to go and have another look.

I decided against it. I had to be here when the deputies came with their hard questions. They'd start with Deborah. She'd been with the marshal when he died. His death happened in my cabin. They'd have questions for me. It would go against me if I weren't here when the deputies showed up.

January twenty-ninth. Sunday. It was two weeks to the day that the marshal's relations left. There were still no signs of lawmen. Or of Samuel.

It wasn't like me but I felt the urge to attend church services at the schoolhouse. It was a way to make sure Deborah was all right. Good news could carry a person only so far. The wait for both Samuel and the deputies had to be wearing on her. It was wearing on me. Even if she wasn't at church services, I could find a way to inquire about her. I hadn't seen Deborah since she'd come to the bridge to warn me off. From that time on, she stayed on her side of the creek. I stayed on mine.

Deborah was at services. She sat in a desk close to the front. It was where the other women and younger children were. Her sister Grace sat at the desk to Deborah's right. Not having enough desks, I stood in the back with some of the other men. Boys mostly over the age of ten stood along the walls. Prayers were said for Samuel's safe passage home. Grace held Deborah's hand. Some of the men said prayers asking God to look after us during turbulent and uncertain times. Readings from the Bible referred to the righteous. I took that to mean us. A passage from the Book of Mormon reminded us to keep the commandments so God would strengthen us and *provide means for us while we sojourn in the wilderness*.

When the last hymn was sung, Ollie Cookson called out and asked everyone to stay. He left the back of the room and went to the front. 'Brothers and Sisters,' he said. 'There's something that wants saying.' He swallowed hard, then ran his hand over his dark beard. His gaze darted to his two wives and to his children. There were eight of them.

'Spit it out,' Pete Sorenson said.

Some of the children laughed. Their mothers glared at

them. Ollie said, 'It's a hard notion, the orchards coming along like they are and all. But we're leaving Junction. Tomorrow.'

That set off a wave of questions. 'Where will you go?' 'What will you do?' No one asked why. We knew. Ollie Cookson had two wives and didn't want to come to the attention of deputies.

Adam Baker went to the front of the room. 'Rebecca and I are leaving, too,' he said. 'Not tomorrow but as soon as it warms up.'

'Where will you go?' The question, clipped with panic, traveled around the room again.

'To Nevada,' Ollie said.

'Idaho,' Adam said.

'It's not safe here,' someone said, and that made its way around the room. Ruth Hall's baby let out a shrill squawk. Ruth, Cecilia Miller, and Mary Sorenson left their seats in the front and went to their husbands. Their little children, unsteady on their feet, clung to the women's skirts. Standing by her husband, Ruth rocked from side to side to calm her baby. Her hand was quick as she patted the baby's back. Cecilia's face was flushed red. Mary's eyes were wide with alarm.

Two families leaving, I could see them thinking. Sister Rebecca won't be here to do our doctoring. Only six families left. That's if you count Sister Deborah and Brother Nels as two of the families. The stranger who died will bring us trouble. Lawmen will come any day. More Saints – men with plural wives – in need of our help will start coming in the spring. We have to leave.

'Brothers and Sisters,' Michael said. He stood at the front of the room. Everyone went quiet. The crying baby settled to a whimper. 'Grace and I have also made the decision to leave.' Michael's eyes were big behind his spectacles. He said, 'I've prayed about it. We both have. We beseeched God for guidance and He spoke to me. "It's time to go home, Brother Michael," God told me. "Your work here in Junction is finished. You are needed elsewhere." When God sees fit to send us a long warm stretch, we'll go.'

That set off more talk. 'The schoolmaster's leaving.' 'What will we do?' 'What should we do?'

I moved so I could see Deborah better. Her back to me, it was like she was cut from stone. Beside her on the other side of the aisle, Grace was looking at her. Deborah didn't turn her head, she didn't move.

'Leaving.' The voices around me were loud in my ears. Most of us came here to have air between us and the church. We thought we'd be left alone. We were fools to believe that.

Three families leaving. That left the Sorensons, the Millers, the Halls, Deborah, and me. Others would leave, too. I felt sure of it. Fear did that. It was a disease easily caught, especially when there were children to think of.

A pain shot through me. Deborah might want to leave once Samuel got home.

The women had clumped together. They talked. Their voices overlapped. Deborah was with them but at the same time, was apart from them. She stood looking at her hand and twisting her wedding band.

I wanted to go to her and bundle her close to me.

Not yours, a voice said in my head. Stay away.

Deborah looked up from her wedding band. Her gaze skipped around the room and landed on me. For a moment, it was only the two of us. I read despair in her eyes. I saw her need to be comforted.

I took a step toward her. As I did, Grace's youngest, Hyrum, went to Deborah and took her hand. Startled,

Deborah looked away from me and at Hyrum. He said something. I couldn't hear what it was over all the commotion and chatter. Deborah bent and took both of his hands. She must have said something because Hyrum smiled. She did, too.

She gave me a quick glance before turning her back to me. I made my way to the door. Even without Samuel, Deborah wasn't alone. She had family. She didn't need me.

Outside, the crisp air caused my eyes to water as I went home.

February sixth. Still no sign of Dyer's men. Still no sign of Samuel.

Since the church services, it snowed off and on but not all that much. It was cold but it'd been colder than this. I still couldn't sleep. My mind played tricks. Once I thought I heard a posse of horses ride into Junction. Another time I was sure I saw Samuel walking across the bridge toward my place.

Since that day at the church, I'd kept to myself. I didn't want to hear if other families had declared themselves wanting to leave once spring broke. I didn't want to think what Michael and Grace's leaving was doing to Deborah. Or how it was for her as she waited for Samuel. She had shaken me off. She wanted me to stay away.

I busied myself with repairs to the cabin and barn. I oiled my carpenter tools and sharpened knives. I worked saddle soap into my saddle and rubbed it until the leather shone. I did the same with the gloves that Deborah made for me. My hands busy, I listened, waiting for lawmen and hoping for Samuel.

February eighth. Two months and seven days after Samuel expected he'd get home. Twenty-four days since the marshal's relations left with the body. I sat at the kitchen table. It was evening, and the wind had picked up. My fingers itched to draw, something I hadn't done in weeks. If my pencil wasn't down to a nub, I'd draw a picture of the shoulder-high snow-drift that was along the north side of the barn. It arched like a great wave of water. Or maybe it was more like the pocket in the side of the cliff where I'd hidden Braden the night I couldn't get him to Floral Ranch.

The thought of the pocket was hardly in my head when I found myself getting my coat. The suddenness of this startled Sally who'd been sleeping under the table. I went outside. Sally followed me, yawning and stretching herself awake. I looked up at the cliffs behind my barn. The trail Braden and I took that night blended into the jagged cuts. Even in the daytime, it was hard to pick out. A man had to be on the trail to see it.

The night sky was clear and lit up from the Milky Way and the moon that was still nearly full. Hell-bent deputies coming from Salt Lake could have gotten here by now.

A notion sprang to me from out of nowhere. Marshal Thomas Fletcher had taken the law into his own hands.

My pulse quickened. I looked up at the night sky, turning the notion over in my mind. Him working outside of the law could explain why we'd been left alone. I began to walk toward my orchards thinking it through.

Fletcher's daughter had run off with four men who were Latter-day Saints. She married one of them. Fletcher had to save her from a life of perversion. He got an arrest warrant issued in Tennessee. By that time she and Braden were in another state.

Once that happened, Braden's arrest was out of Fletcher's hands. He'd have to turn the search over to the marshal who had jurisdiction. That wouldn't sit well with him. Nobody cared about his daughter like he did. Only he could handle this matter. His son and cousin were backup. Maybe he'd deputized them back in Tennessee, maybe not. Either way, Thomas Fletcher was in charge.

Speculation. But the pieces fit. Maybe, when Henry and MacGregor got to Thurber, they hadn't notified Dyer up in Salt Lake. Maybe they came to believe that the marshal's daughter didn't want to leave Utah, that she'd made her choice and there was no changing her mind. The shame of the girl joining the Saints might be something best left alone. The shame of the marshal working outside of his jurisdiction could be something his family didn't want known. Maybe they wanted to bundle this up and put it someplace where it could be forgotten.

People did such things. Covering up was what folks had a tendency to do when the truth didn't make them look good. We Saints weren't any different. We all had something we didn't want known.

Dyer, Utah's marshal, might not know the particulars about Thomas Fletcher's death. Utah deputies might not be coming for us.

Speculation, I thought again. I was fooling myself. I had to stay on guard. It was winter. Travel was slow and hard even for men on horseback. But that wouldn't keep them from trying. A federal marshal had died in a Latter-day Saint town. Dyer's men would come for us.

Unless they didn't know.

CHAPTER TWENTY-TWO

NELS – THE TRUTH

February 12, 1888

Four more days went by. On Sunday morning, I saddled Bob and rode up the trail behind my barn. It was the one Lewis Braden and I took the night I had to hide him when I couldn't get him to Floral Ranch. Sally came with me. I hadn't been on it since that night. Now I felt the need to rise above Junction. I couldn't explain my thinking other than to say I wanted to see something more than the floor of the canyon.

The tracks Braden and I had made were long gone. The wind and rounds of melting snow and fresh snowfall made it look like we'd never been here.

At the crest of the cliff, I got off Bob. I looked east toward Floral Ranch, then west toward the Wastelands. Rows of snow-covered cliffs and craggy buttes circled from all directions. If anybody was coming to Junction, I couldn't see them.

From where I was, the rooftops of cabins and barns showed. They were Samuel and Deborah's, Michael and Grace's, and mine. The roofs were covered with snow making them look low to the ground. Even though I wasn't able to see it, I picked out the place where the schoolhouse should be. Some of the neighbors were likely there, this being Sunday. Deborah was probably there. More of them might be announcing their intentions to leave Junction when winter lost its hold.

I shifted my attention away from the schoolhouse. I found the place where the Sulphur and the Fremont converged and flowed south to Arizona Territory. Looking up, I studied the sky. It was clear. No sign of snow clouds. I looked back down at the convergence of the creek and the Fremont. The water churned where the two joined together.

Almost a full circle. Carson Miller's words about what he saw in the ravine. I heard him like he was standing here beside me. *One made of metal. A wheel.*

It came off of Samuel's wagon.

The realization ricocheted against my heart. The rockslide had caught Samuel's wagon. He might have tried to jump off. But Samuel was in the ravine. Samuel was dead.

I didn't want it to be. But like it was happening again, I was back at the ravine and Carson was calling to me. There was a warning in his voice. He'd seen something.

My chest squeezed up. My eyes weren't working right. They kept watering. I couldn't make them stop.

Samuel. He hadn't been overly delayed by unexpected work. He wasn't coming the long way home. He was dead.

Winded, I bent over with my hands on my knees. Maybe I had known it all along. I just hadn't wanted to face it.

Samuel. My stepbrother and most of all, my friend. He'd been that since the day he and I took up together. Our families were on the trail from Missouri to Utah. I was eleven and Samuel was a year older. A stubborn cowlick sprouted from his brown hair and he carried a far-off look in his green eyes. Samuel was always wandering away from the wagon party. I was the one bringing him back. While on the trail to Utah, he'd see a creek or a boulder or any such thing, and off he'd go to have a look. It worried his mother. There were only the two of them. She'd come to my mother and father, say how she'd lost Samuel again, and they'd send me to look for him. Tracking came easy for me even then. Once I found him flat on the ground watching a trail of ants. He made me get down with him to admire them. He appreciated how they could carry loads bigger than themselves.

Until then, I didn't care a whit for ants. They were something to step on and get rid of. But not for Samuel. He said they lived in colonies. That meant they weren't all that different from us. Just because they were smaller didn't mean ants couldn't have opinions about the ways of the world. He shamed me into not stepping on an ant again if I could help it.

By the time the wagon party got to Salt Lake, my mother and Samuel's were as close as sisters. My mother was the one who had a revelation. An angel told her my father should marry Samuel's mother. It would keep us together. We were far from home and our mothers were lonesome for the families they'd left behind. The marriage made Samuel and me brothers.

Samuel and I looked after each other. I kept him from wandering off. He kept me from seeing only the hard side of living. We didn't talk of it, but I figured that was one of the reasons why he and Deborah followed me to Junction after Lydia and the baby died. He didn't want me falling into a pit of hard thoughts.

Samuel was dead.

Something bumped into my leg. Sally. She looked up into my eyes. It was like she knew. I got down on my knees in the snow. Holding onto Sally, I let myself bawl like a baby.

———

When I'd cried myself dry to the bone, I rubbed my face with snow. I got to my feet and looked down at Samuel and Deborah's cabin. Gray smoke rose from the cookstove chimney pipe. Deborah was there, waiting. She had warned me to stay away. But Samuel would want me to tell her about the wheel. He'd want her to be free to leave with her sister's family.

I bent over again, out of air.

I'd cared about Deborah since the first time I saw her. It was their wedding day. After the ceremony, there was a dance at the wardhouse. She wasn't the prettiest woman, her cheekbones were too high for that. It was Deborah's eyes. They were rings of hazel with flecks of blue. Each ring was lighter and clearer than the other. When she smiled or laughed, her eyes gave off a shine. It was hard to look away. I danced with her once. A waltz. Her hand was small in mine and I couldn't think of a thing to say. She didn't seem to mind. She hummed as we danced. This filled the gap between us, strangers bound together because of Samuel.

He'd want me to tell her. He'd expect that of me.

'All right,' I said. 'All right.' I got on Bob and rode down the trail to the floor of the canyon, Sally leading the way.

***

At Deborah and Samuel's cabin, I called through the door saying it was me. Deborah opened the door. 'There's something I have to tell you,' I said.

If she didn't like it that I was on her doorstep, it didn't show. Neither did she look surprised. A kind of flatness had come over her features. She said, 'Is this about the marshal?'

'No.'

I stood on the threshold. Sally brushed past me and went inside. Deborah's cheeks had hollowed. She was thinner than she'd been when I saw her two weeks ago. I couldn't meet her eyes.

'What is it?' she said.

My thoughts jammed up. I didn't know what to say.

'This is about Samuel. Isn't it?'

I nodded.

'Something's happened,' she said.

'I believe so. A while back at that rockslide.'

Alarm flared in her eyes.

I said, 'Can I come in?'

Deborah stepped away from the door. I went inside. 'What's happened?' she said.

Sweat ran down my sides. I looked past her and toward the parlor. Sunlight coming through the window lit up one of the black horsehair chairs. An image of Samuel sitting there with his legs stretched out in front of him, his ankles crossed, darted through my thoughts. He'd expect me to tell Deborah.

I said, 'Brother Carson, when him and I were at the rockslide, he saw something in the ravine below. I didn't see anything but Brother Carson thought he did.'

Deborah wobbled. I caught her arm and steered her to the table in the kitchen. I got her to sit down. I sat across from her. A black rock with white in it was on the table. I figured it was one of Samuel's. She put her hand on top of it.

I said, 'What he saw were glints of light coming off a circle of iron. In the bottom of the ravine.'

The fire in the cookstove popped, startling me. Deborah didn't seem to notice. She sat without moving with her hand on the rock.

I said, 'I think it's a wheel.'

'A wheel.' Her voice was flat. Her eyes were blank.

'Yes.' My voice had taken an odd turn. It felt like it might crumble into pieces. The muscles in my face felt the same.

Deborah said, 'Why are you telling me this?'

'It grieves me bad. I don't want to believe it. But I think the wheel came off a wagon. Samuel's.'

Her breathing turned shallow and quick. The little color she'd had in her cheeks was gone. She lowered her head and covered her face with her hands. I expected her to cry. I wanted to press her hurt into me.

Deborah kept her face covered with her hands. She didn't move. She didn't make a sound. I didn't know what to say or do. After a long while, Deborah lowered her hands. The flecks of blue in her hazel eyes were dark. She said, 'Are you telling me Samuel's in the ravine? That he's dead?'

Her flat tone bored into me. 'Yes. That's what I'm saying.'

She picked up the rock that was on the table. Her fingers curled around it. Her knuckles were white.

Her grip on the rock loosened. A kind of dull curiosity showed in her eyes. 'You knew,' she said. 'All this time. You knew.'

'I didn't. Brother Carson wasn't sure what he'd seen. Not at first.'

She shook her head like she was trying to make sense of this. 'But now he says it's a wheel. He changed his mind. Somehow. For some reason.'

'It's not so much that he changed his mind. He wouldn't let himself think it was a wheel. Didn't want it to be. But after a while, he couldn't talk himself out of it. That's what he told me. It was a wheel even though he didn't want it to be. Then when Samuel's letters came saying how he was delayed, going to out-of-the-way places . . .' My voice trailed off.

She pressed her lips together, then gave her head a small

shake. She said, 'Samuel didn't say that, not in those words. It was me wanting—' She stopped.

I stared at her, not knowing what to say to this. Other than she was like me, seeing only what she needed to see.

Deborah said, 'When did Brother Carson tell you he was sure it was a wheel?'

'Last month. The morning he helped get the marshal out of Junction.'

'That was weeks ago.' Her hollow tone unnerved me. 'You should have told me. You both should have. Even if you weren't sure.'

'Yes. I should have.'

'What you told me about Samuel turning around at the rockslide. What you said about him coming through the Fish Lakes. I believed you.'

'I believed it, too.'

'I've been waiting. All this time. Day after day. Hour by hour.' Her voice had a far-off sound. It was like she was talking about something that didn't matter to her. I wanted her to raise her voice, yell at me. Anything would be better than her empty tone.

She said, 'Every time I thought about Samuel being hurt or lost out in this weather, I told myself he'd been forced to take a longer route. Like you told me.'

'I was wrong.'

She closed her eyes and pressed her lips. I understood she was doing her best not to give way to tears. I said, 'I'm sorry, Sister Deborah. I'm sorry.'

She didn't seem to hear. She held herself still. All at once, a shudder ran through her. Her face crumpled, her pain plain to see. She was imagining Samuel dead, I thought. She was thinking how he'd never come home.

I stood up. 'I'll get your sister.'

'No.' The word was sharp. Deborah looked up at me. Her eyes had all at once acquired a strange glitter. It was like a quick fever had come over her. She said, 'You didn't go down and look.' Her words came fast, the flatness in her tone now gone. 'You saw it from a distance. Isn't that so?'

I understood she meant the wheel. I said, 'Yes.'

'It could have come off someone else's wagon. It could have happened years ago.'

Standing across from her at the table, I shook my head. Her mind, like mine, wouldn't let her think the worst.

I sat back down. My voice low, I said, 'I believe it's Samuel's.' I paused to think through what needed to be said next. When I found words, I said, 'He should be home by now. Even if he did extra work. Even if he had to come through the mountains. Samuel should be home.'

Deborah stood up, went to the cookstove, and opened the oven door. It slipped from her hand, banging shut. She flinched. Then she turned toward me. Her cheeks were flushed. She said, 'I want to see the ravine. I want to go now. Before the next storm sets in.'

'It's a three-day journey. It's February.'

'I want to see for myself. I'll know if it's a wheel. I'll know if it's from Samuel's wagon.'

'It's too risky this time of year.'

'Then I'll go on my own. I have the map you drew me.'

'That map's rough.'

'I have to see for myself.'

'You might not be able to see much. Not with the snow and all.'

'I'll know if it's Samuel's. I'll feel it.'

'I'll take you in the spring.'

'And keep waiting, not knowing for sure? I can't bear it. Do you hear me? I can't bear it another day longer.' She stopped herself. It was like she'd heard something frightening in her voice and needed to tamp it down. She put her hand on her breastbone and pushed against it. She said, 'You lost Lydia. You know the hurt. But think how it would be if you didn't know where she and the baby were.'

The image of the cemetery in Cedar City took shape in my mind. The soil was newly dug and heaped high on one side of the open grave. At the other side, a coffin that held Lydia and the baby waited to be lowered. Nearly everyone in town was there. No one knew what to say to me. I said nothing to them. The day was hot but I was frozen.

Deborah said, 'I have to see the ravine. I have to see it now. Samuel, if that's where he is, he won't be able to rest. He has to know that I'm not worried sick about him, that I'm not looking for him every moment of every day. Once I go, if he's there, we can both rest.'

I looked at the rock on the table. Likely Samuel had a story about it that I didn't know anything about. Probably it meant something to him and Deborah. I looked over at the parlor chair. It was like Samuel was there, watching and waiting for my answer.

'All right,' I said. 'I'll take you.'

SAMUEL

Seventy-nine days ago

November 25, 1887
Utah Territory

Dear Wife Deborah,

I am Home nearly. Just a few Days away. Snort and Wally know it. They gave up their Complaining and are in a hurry. I will give You this Letter myself. The notion of Me writing a Letter so close to Home will surely make You laugh. But last Night I saw a Wonder in the Sky. I have to tell You about it while the Sight is strong in my Mind.

It was a Waterfall of Shooting Stars. So many I could not count Them. The Stars glowed. They were on Fire. They curved toward Earth. A Waterfall of Them. That is the only way I know how to say what the Stars did. They fell from Heaven. Before my Eyes They fell. Before I could blink the Fire faded out of Them. They went Dark. That quick the Stars were gone.

It was a Wonder. The Kind that causes a Man to think he dreamed it. I did not. I saw It.

It will be a Wonder to be Home with You.

> *Your Husband,*
> *Samuel Tyler*

CHAPTER TWENTY-THREE

DEBORAH – HOME

February 13–15, 1888

Nels and Carson Miller came for me at dawn the next day. The sky was clear. The last of the stars were dimming but the half-moon still showed. We rode single file into the Wastelands with Nels in front and Carson behind me. Our bedrolls were tied to the backs of our saddles. I rode one of Adam Baker's horses. I wore Samuel's Sunday trousers belted tight and the cuffs rolled up a few inches.

The recent days of sun and spells of warmer afternoons had melted the snow so that it was only calf deep. As day broke, we rode past and around rock formations shaped like cathedrals. Massive pillared walls of rock streaked orange and white sat on top of buttes. Nels steered us away from deep cracks in the earth that appeared without warning. Above us, hawks rode on drafts of air with their wings stretched wide. From time to time, Nels put his right hand up, signaling us to stop. He sat listening, his gaze taking in the land. He was looking, I believed, for lawmen.

Other times we stopped so Nels and Carson could study the landmarks to get their bearings.

This discussion of landmarks was the only talk they did. I had nothing to say. We were going to the place where Samuel might be. It was all I could think about. Even the notion of encountering lawmen didn't matter much to me.

Yesterday, Nels made me agree we wouldn't start out if there were any signs of snow. 'And once we're on the trail, if it clouds up or the air smells like snow, we're turning back,' he said. 'You have to promise me you won't dispute me on that.'

'You have my word.'

He gave me a long look like he was trying to seal me to my promise. I said, 'We'll turn back if the weather looks threatening. Junction doesn't need any more trouble.'

'All right then. I'll talk to Brother Carson about coming with us. I'll see about getting you a horse.'

Late afternoon yesterday, I went to Grace and Michael's to tell them Nels was taking me to the rockslide. Nels wanted to go with me to Grace's but I'd told him no. The word came out as a snap and settled matters. I couldn't tell him I wanted to walk through the orchard Samuel and I had planted years back. I couldn't tell him I wanted the cold to freeze the pain that threatened to crush me.

When I got to Grace's and she saw I had something of importance to say, she sent the boys outside. She, Michael, and I sat at the kitchen table. They felt far away from me. I gripped the edge of the table to keep myself steady. I told them what Nels had said about Samuel and the ravine. My words were far-off and dull in my ears.

Michael said, 'We've feared the worst with each passing day.'

Grace got up and put her arms around me. She cried some but my eyes ached with dryness. Then I told them that Nels and Carson Miller were taking me to the ravine.

I expected them to put up an argument. I was a married woman traveling with men who weren't family. The weather could turn. The journey would be rough going and dangerous in places.

Grace said, 'You need to go. If it were me,' she glanced at Michael, 'I'd have to.'

He said, 'If the wheel is Samuel's, and I pray it's not but if it is, it will free your mind.'

'You'll come home to Parowan with us,' Grace said. 'Samuel would want that.'

My throat had narrowed. I couldn't talk. Grace kept her arms around me. Her lips were near my ear. She said, 'Samuel was always good to me. When you courted and it plagued me that you had more time for him than me, he'd have me come and sit on the love seat between you. He'd ask me what I'd learned in school. I'd tell him and he'd rear back, amazed, and say that a smart little girl like me was bound to grow up and be a schoolteacher. After you married and I was homesick for you, Samuel fixed a room off your kitchen for me. He put in a cot for me. He made me feel like I still had you.'

Grace's memories made my chest burn with an ache. When I left their cabin, Jacob, Joe, and Hyrum were waiting for me outside. They were dressed for the cold and snow but they hadn't rolled snowballs or made a fort. They just stood, peeking glances at me, then at each other. 'You look sad, Aunt Deborah,' five-year-old Joe said.

I smiled for them. I thought my face might break from the effort but it didn't. Then all at once, the boys were bunched around me, their arms reaching up. I leaned down to hold them close to me. My family, I thought. I wasn't alone.

On the trail, Nels, Carson, and I snaked our way through the Wastelands. The rock formations thinned out and the land rolled in soft waves. We came to a grove of trees where we cut toward the south. When the sun was directly overhead, we stopped for a cold meal of ham, biscuits, and canned peaches. We stood in the snow while we ate, stomping our feet from time to time to keep the blood moving. Carson shot me quick glances. He tugged at his hat and his square jaw was clenched. He was uneasy around me. Nels asked two times if I was all right.

'Yes,' I said both times. 'I want to do this.'

Back on our horses, we rode due south toward Boulder Mountain. The snow was deeper as we climbed and the horses worked harder. I felt Samuel with me. This was the route he took each time he left Junction and went south. This was the route he took when he came back home.

Grace and Michael wanted me to go back with them to Parowan. Doing that meant leaving the cabin, the orchards, and the irrigation ditches. Samuel and I had built the cabin together. We'd planted the trees together. We'd dug the ditches together. Leaving them would give me nothing to touch that proved we'd been in this world together. They were the landmarks of our marriage.

Grace and Michael probably expected me to live with my mother. She was fifty-seven and her hands were crippled from years of hard use. She'd welcome my help and my company. My father, who spent most of his time with Caroline, his other wife, would approve. My mother wouldn't be alone.

In Parowan, the church would tell me how to spend my time. There would be Sunday services, Family Night prayer time on Wednesdays, and weekly Relief Society meetings. No one would know what to make of me. I was a woman without children. I made gloves to earn my keep. I was a woman whose husband didn't have a marked grave.

The marshal's wife was spared that. She'd have her husband back to bury even if he wasn't home yet. Much depended on when his son and cousin got his body to the train station in Salt Lake. I felt sure Henry would telegraph his mother ahead of time. She would know to expect her husband. She'd know he died in a bed and he wasn't alone.

Nels and Carson could be wrong about Samuel. There wasn't a wheel in the ravine. If there was, it wasn't Samuel's. But if it wasn't his, where was he?

———

We camped the first night on the floor of a three-wall lean-to made by the Indians years back. It was cold and I was glad for that. It slowed my thinking. It dulled my worry about what we'd see in the ravine. Nels laid my bedroll so that I was between him and Carson. 'It's warmer this way,' he said. I didn't argue.

I listened to the night breathing of the two men, neither of them my husband or blood relative. Since the marshal's death, a crevice split the ground between Nels and me. The evening he came and told me he'd gotten Braden to Floral Ranch, he and I were alone. The marshal's body was in my barn. We sat at the kitchen table and I saw something in Nels' eyes. He cared for me. Not as a friend did but as a man did for a woman.

Since then, I'd kept away from Nels. I belonged to Samuel. I wanted to belong to him. I yearned for him to come home. Yet keeping away from Nels made me miss him in ways I hadn't expected. He was a man whose presence was a comfort.

Never had that been truer than now. Earlier, when we stopped at the lean-to for the night, Nels told me Samuel probably used this lean-to when he traveled. I needed this to be so. He'd looked up through the chinks in the roof and seen swatches of the Milky Way. He'd listened to the coyotes, yapping and howling. He'd heard an owl's long hoots.

His campfire, just outside of the lean-to, had brightened the dark.

Samuel would feel at home in a lean-to. It was a shelter yet it wasn't all-the-way enclosed. Maybe he thought of it as an in-between place.

———

The weather held the second day. Nels didn't seem to listen to the land as hard as he had yesterday. Lawmen would come from the north, not the south, the direction we were heading.

On the trail, I studied the crevices in the cliffs and the shapes of the snow-covered rocks. I wanted to see them as Samuel did.

We camped the second night in a pocket of rock carved out of the side of a mountain. It made me think of Braden who had done the same in a pocket close to Junction. I hoped his wives knew he was safe. Then I told myself to stop thinking about him.

The third morning we rode in the quiet under a blue sky. Like before, we traveled single file. The cliffs were higher and the snow deeper. The horses blew clouds of steam as we climbed the switchbacks. The trail was just wide enough for a narrow wagon. Samuel would have been careful when he came this way. It'd be easy for a wheel to slip off the edge.

Nels' horse moved slow and at times, Carson fell a good ways behind us. The trail was steep but it wasn't just that. I felt the men's dread. I understood they didn't know what I might do once we got to the rockslide. I didn't know, either.

It was midday when Nels had us stop. 'We'll walk from here,' he said. My blood seemed to drop. We were there.

'You all right?' Nels said.

I nodded.

He studied me for a moment. I nodded again. He looked at Carson and they staked the horses. When they were finished, Nels looked at me. 'You ready?'

'Yes.'

'I'll stay here with the horses,' Carson said.

'No,' Nels said, the word coming quick. He was uncertain about me, I thought. He wanted Carson with him to help keep me steady.

The three of us began to walk. The snow was eight inches deep or so. The narrow trail was cut into the side of a rock cliff. I stayed on the inside close to the wall. Nels was beside me on the ravine side. Carson was behind us. Samuel would walk his mules on this stretch, I thought. He'd take them through slow. He'd tell them they'd traveled this before and they could do it again.

We rounded a bend. I came to a standstill. The rockslide.

'You all right?' Nels said to me.

'Stop asking me that.'

A boulder bigger than my cabin had taken out the trail. It'd come to a stop just below where the path had once been. The boulder was at a slant so that one end gouged the cliff. The other end hung in midair. A spillage of rock slabs and broken trees flowed into the ravine.

I took a step forward. I stumbled. Nels took my arm. Carson was on the other side of me. I said, 'Show me where.'

Nels must have given Carson a signal of some sort. Carson walked to the edge. Nels kept me back. His hold on me was firm. Carson looked down into the ravine, then walked along the edge. He stopped and got on his hands and knees in the snow. He leaned forward. He was quiet as he studied the ravine.

Samuel, I thought. Samuel.

Carson stood up and walked to us. His voice low, he said, 'The light's stronger today. More direct.' He paused. He couldn't look at me. His gaze was fixed on Nels.

'Stay with her.' Nels let go of my arm and then it was Carson holding me up. Nels went to the place Carson had been. He got down on his hands and knees. Finally he backed away from the edge and stood up. When he turned around, I knew. Nels' eyes carried a stricken look.

'I have to see,' I said.

The men walked me to the edge. We got down in the snow.

The ravine was a straight plunge. There was nothing to break a fall. There was nothing for a man to hold onto. The side was sheer rock.

'Where?' I said.

Nels pointed.

The bottom was strewn with rocks and deep drifts of snow. Stunted trees and low brush grew where the sun reached. I strained to pick out the particulars. My vision blurred. I blinked, then saw it. A wheel. It showed in a shaft of light.

There were boards, too. It was the back end of a wagon. The rest of the wagon, if it hadn't broken apart, was lost under a dense tangle of snow-covered brush.

Samuel had painted his name on a right-hand sideboard near the front. I couldn't see it. I wasn't able to see anything that proved it was Samuel's. But I knew it was. There was something about it that was deeply familiar.

A great choking pain welled up in my chest.

'Sister Deborah,' Nels said.

The air was thin, my ears rang. 'Steady,' he said. 'Breathe.' I did as he said. My hearing cleared.

I looked again into the ravine. The snow-covered branches of the brush that shrouded the wagon glimmered in the narrow sunlight.

'Samuel's there, isn't he?' I said to Nels.

'I believe so.'

I turned to Carson. He said, 'Yes. Most likely.'

I'd missed Samuel from the moment he left on the first day of September. That was five and a half months ago. Since the beginning of December, I'd looked for him. I kept expecting to hear him call out to me, telling me he was home. Seventy-six days. It wasn't all that long. Unless a person was waiting each minute of those days. Unless a person didn't know where someone was.

A sense of calmness, something I didn't expect to ever feel, came over me. Samuel wasn't hurt and afraid. He wasn't at the mercy of strangers. Samuel was here.

I looked at Nels. 'Do you think he suffered?'

'No. It would have been quick.' His voice broke. He cleared his throat. 'Samuel wasn't the suffering kind.'

I felt myself smile. Then I thought of Thomas Fletcher and how it pained him to move even a little. I heard again the wheeze and rasp of his breathing.

It wasn't that way for Samuel. Maybe there was only a moment of fear. Maybe there wasn't any pain.

Carson said, 'We'll go back to Junction and get the men. We can try to get Brother Samuel out.'

'No,' I said. 'He wouldn't want you to risk it.'

'We can try.'

An image of my husband, his body broken, being hauled up the cliff by rope flashed through my mind. Then I thought of my bargain with God. I'd take care of the marshal and God would send Samuel home. In His way, God had done that. I knew where he was. Samuel was with his rocks.

I said, 'There are all kinds of graveyards. I want Samuel left here.'

Carson glanced at Nels. Nels gave him a quick nod. I said, 'I'd like to put a marker here for Samuel.'

Nels said, 'We can do that.'

'I'd like a drawing of Samuel. If you're willing, Brother Nels.'

'I am.'

'I'd like him to be holding one of his rocks. I want him smiling.'

'That won't be hard to do.'

'You're a good friend.'

Nels ducked his head. He turned away from me but not before I saw that his eyes were heavy with sadness.

Carson said something about wanting to get back to the horses. 'If nobody minds.'

'Go on,' Nels said. 'Likely we won't be long.'

Carson left, rounding the bend.

Nels said, 'You want to stay here by yourself for a spell?'

'No. Not by myself. I'd like you here.'

'All right.'

We stood near the edge of the trail. Nels took off his hat and put it over his heart. The sky was a crisp blue. The sun lit the cliff on the other side of the ravine. The snow that clung to its ridges glittered like flecks of clear crystals. The ravine was my husband's cemetery. The cliffs were his marker.

I said, 'I'm not leaving Samuel.'

Nels' eyebrow shot up.

'I'm not going back to Parowan. There's nothing of Samuel there.'

'It might not be safe in Junction. The law won't forget about Braden.'

'We did nothing wrong.'

A strange look darted across Nels' face. Something had happened to the marshal that I didn't know about. I wanted it left that way. After a moment, he said, 'We helped a felon, that's how they'll see it. Even if they leave us alone, and I'm not sure they will, but if they do, more hunted men are bound to come through.'

'I'm not leaving.' I looked down at my hands. The leather in my gloves had deepened in color. The yellow had gone a mild shade of brown. 'I can't leave Samuel. I can't leave the trees we planted together or the cabin we built.'

'Your sister's going. The Bakers are too. Others are apt to clear out once spring comes.'

It hurt to think of being parted from Grace and the boys, from Michael, too. I'd miss them more than I could put words to. It could be that there would come a day when I'd change my mind and go back to Parowan. If that day came, I'd do that. But not now.

'Samuel's here,' I said. Then I was thinking of his hands. They were scarred and nicked from years of making wheels. His palms were ridged with callouses. For all that, his touch was always tender.

I'd never see his hands again. I'd never feel his fingertips caress my cheek.

Pain wrapped itself around me and tightened.

'Sister Deborah,' Nels said. He was holding me up. My knees had gone weak. 'You've seen enough. We're going back.'

I gathered up some air and steadied myself. 'Not yet.' I walked to the edge of the trail. Nels held onto my arm. I got down on my hands and knees. He did, too. I looked into the ravine.

The wagon covered Samuel, I told myself. He'd been wearing gloves I'd made for him when the slide happened. They were on his hands now. He had something of me with him when he died.

Images of Samuel – the first time he had dinner with my family, the two of us dancing after our wedding, the stones he found in the creek, and his goodbye when he left last September – flashed through my mind. My heart hurt. I believed it always would.

Samuel wasn't suffering. He wasn't frightened. This comforted me.

Nearby, a bird rustled in the underbrush. Another bird called a two-note trill. The wind was a low whistle. These would keep Samuel company.

I turned to Nels. Like mine, his eyes watered. I said, 'Are you leaving Junction in the spring?'

'I'm never leaving. Unless I'm run off.' He looked up at the cliff on the other side of the ravine. 'Junction's home.'

Samuel was gone. But Nels was here. I wasn't ready to think past that. It was enough to have the comfort of Nels' steady presence. It was enough to know that I always would. Unless he was run off by lawmen.

There was nothing I could do about that. What I could do was stop waiting for what might happen.

'Nels,' I said. 'I'm ready to go home. If you are.'

Today, orchards planted by early settlers thrive in what is now Capitol Reef National Park. These settlers named their town Junction and were members of The Church of Jesus Christ of Latter-day Saints (LDS). Yet, unlike most LDS communities, the Junction families didn't build a wardhouse. Nor did Junction have its own bishop. The families didn't conform to the typical LDS pattern of building their homes close to one another. Historical evidence also indicates the families were not called by the church to settle this remote part of Utah Territory. It appears they came on their own, one or two families at a time. It seems they had their own reasons for settling in this isolated part of Utah.

Floral Ranch did exist, and historical evidence indicates it was a place of safety for LDS men hiding from federal deputies. Located about eleven miles south of Junction, it was difficult to find. Although documentation is limited, it seems likely that LDS men charged with polygamy came through Junction on their way to Floral Ranch. A trail known as Cohab Canyon overlooks the Junction orchards. It is believed that 'cohab' is short for 'cohabitation' and that men hid there until they were able to travel safely to Floral Ranch.

The population of Junction during the 1880s was about eight families. Only one family practiced plural marriage.

The Massacre at Mountain Meadows began on September 7, 1857, and ended on September 11, 1857.

Junction's name was eventually changed to Fruita. Under the care of the United States National Park Service, the orchards flourish and visitors are welcome to pick the fruit. The original irrigation ditches are still visible. Visitors can hike the Cohab

Canyon Trail, and old cabins and barns stand at Floral Ranch. Indian pictographs reveal the presence of the first inhabitants. The convergence of Sulphur Creek and Fremont River can be seen from vantage points high on the red rock cliffs.

The Glovemaker is a work of fiction, but I did my best to keep the historical details as accurate as possible. I have been fascinated by Junction's early LDS settlers since my first visit to Capitol Reef National Park years ago. The area is remote and the landscape is daunting. Yet a handful of settlers called it home. *The Glovemaker* is my attempt to remember the brave and hardy people who lived in the rugged canyon country during difficult times.

For further reading:

Red Rock Eden: The Story of Fruita by George Davidson (Capitol Reef Natural History Association, 1986).

Echoes from the Cliffs of Capitol Reef National Park by Max E. Robinson and Clay M. Robinson (Ol' Gran'pa Stories, 2004).

I Walked to Zion by Susan Arrington Madsen (Deseret Books, 1994).

Mormonism: A Very Short Introduction by Richard Lyman Bushman (Oxford University Press, 2008).

The United States Marshals in Utah Territory to 1896 by Vernal A. Brown (Graduate Thesis, Utah State University, 1970).

The Mormon Menace by Patrick Q. Mason (Oxford University Press, 2011).

Blood of the Prophets by Will Bagley (University of Oklahoma Press, 2002).

ACKNOWLEDGMENTS

Once again, I'm forever indebted to my husband, Rob, for believing not only that I could write this story but that I must; and to Judithe Little, Julie Kemper, Lois Stark, Rachel Gillett, and Bryan Jamison whose input shaped every scene and whose encouragement sustained me when the blank page loomed large.

I owe an immeasurable debt to my editors Josie Humber and Maria Rejt at Mantle for seeing possibilities that I didn't and for pushing and pulling me to make the book the best it could be. My thanks go to everyone at Pan Macmillan for their commitment to the written word including Jon Mitchell, rights director, for his problem-solving ability; Anna Alexander, senior rights manager, for casting a wide net; Kate Tolley, editorial manager, for guiding *The Glovemaker* through the perilous pipeline; and to Anna Bond and Stuart Dwyer, sales directors, for delivering the book into the hands of readers.

My gratitude goes to Mary Chamberlain, copy-editor, for her extraordinary talent and for making the process fun; and to my agent, Margaret Halton, who understands when a phone call is needed and then knows what to say.

My appreciation goes to Ellen Feldman for her friendship and wisdom; and to Sharron Vaughn, Al Kazmir, and Shelia Armstrong for their spirited and funny pep talks.

Lastly, my thanks go to the staff at Utah's Bicknell Public Library for opening the library early so I could do research; and to the entire staff at Capitol Reef National Park in Utah for allowing me to read oral histories in the park's archives and for being guardians of the orchards that were planted by the first white settlers in the 1880s.